Moonlit
Massacre
BY JAMES COOPER

Published by Literati Press
3022 Paseo Oklahoma City, OK 73103
Find us online at literatipressok.com & @literatipress

ISBN: 978-1-943988-43-3

Cover illustrations by Garrett Young
Book design by David Woods

Printed in the United States of America

This is a work of fiction. Any similarity to actual persons, living or dead, business establishments,events, or places is entirely coincidental.

First Edition 10 9 8 7 6 5 4 3 2

To Mom, Marion, my students,
OKC's Ward 2, Wes Craven

PART ONE

A History of Bad Men

CHAPTER ONE

Hills stretch into mountains out west. South, too. Prairie to the east gives way to prairie and cloudless sky. Same to the north.

Through this land runs a highway, four paved lanes from rising to setting sun. On this road travels a pickup truck heading east. A lone metal traveler—beat-up, steel, and blue.

Dry air blows against the '67 Chevy and through a rolled-down window on the pickup's passenger side.

Out this window, he stares. Hears nothingness gust across scorched land. Sun upon his pale, freckled face. He feels warm wind move in fits through each lock of his auburn, curly hair. And he searches deep into a southern horizon for a distant, unknowable place where land and sky must surely meet. The boy, barely ten years on this earth.

His gray eyes follow fences of barbed wire at sixty miles per hour, handmade wood signposts with words like "ranch" and "angus" and "land for sale." He turns to his mom as she drives. Her hands at ten and two on the wheel. She never returns his stare, and he wonders why. But, her eyes remain fixed on the road and the task ahead of them.

The boy scratches his nose. His denim overalls cotton and tailored. His hand moves from the window frame to his hip pocket retrieving perforated paper no bigger than a ten-dollar bill. "Milk" in pencil above the first red line, each letter the same size, "Bread" on the next. He looks at a dusty windshield. He takes a handkerchief from a pocket on his overalls, wipes sweat from his forehead, leans back in the pickup's bench cloth seat. The town, he realizes, is just ahead of them beyond vast flatness, home nestled where prairie rolls into wooded green hills.

Engine stops, and the boy clicks off his seatbelt, drops his grocery list on his lap. He grabs a crank on the passenger door, rolls up his window, his mother doing the same to her driver side.

On a sidewalk, they walk east down a paved hill.

Her favorite summer dress. Breezy and cotton. Lemon and vibrant. Worn. Sleeveless. Round about her neck, front and back. At her thin waist, a canary yellow matching tie belt. Around her wrist, a beige bracelet of beads marking a precise place where her long dark brown hair, straight as a line, finally ends from flowing along her face. Beside them, his mother's reflection, beautiful in large glass windowpanes that allow him to see through shops and offices.

On each tan or maroon brick building, words like "real estate," "lumber," and "law."

Sidewalk ends at the bottom of the paved hill. On the street's south side, a blacktop parking lot, mostly empty, in front of a grocery store. The boy walks across asphalt to the smell of hot tar. He stares at a tall signpost, Sooner Foods and Since 1954 in white cursive on crimson.

"Hey, mom."

"Hey, Ben," she says, playful, direct.

He looks from the signpost to his mother, who is walking slightly ahead of him. "May I walk over to The Music Store?"

She stops, turns to him. "Whatever happened to earlier this morning's 'Sure, mom, happy to drive into town, help with groceries?'"

Ben's hands drop into his pockets. He's thoughtful enough to recognize annoyance in his mother's tone, but he can't tell if she's faking anger to teach a promise-keeping lesson, or if she's genuinely upset.

He decides to plead his case. "If ya let me walk to The Music Store, I'd rent us movies. For when Nathan and Marc stay tonight." Each word falls from his mouth as if he's many years older, a charming Southern lawyer.

"To be fair, you never let me do any actual helping. I just end up reading car magazines or comics for an hour at the checkout while you do all our shopping."

In a brief silence before his mother can respond, Ben recalls what seems an eternity of memories. His reading, standing propped against wooden shelves, sitting cross-legged on tile floors, musty old books, American muscle cars on colorful covers. She with her encyclopedic knowledge of nutrition, her selectiveness and careful examination of oranges and watermelons, ingredients and expiration dates.

"I don't know, Ben." She sighs. "Mr. Hanson won't want to look after you while he's running a business." She squints, her hand at her sweaty forehead, blocking afternoon sun from her eyes. "On the condition you promise to unload all bags as soon as we get home? I'd like to start dinner before your dad's off work."

He smiles his father's sincere salesman smile. "I'll even throw in a round of doing dishes after dinner."

"You play a good game, boy."

"That's a *yes*, isn't it?"

She folds her arms over her yellow dress. "Nowhere else, Benjamin Bullock." She's stern in this demand.

"Nowhere else. Scout's honor."

"Nowhere else." She unfolds her arms, closing the space between them, placing her left hand on his shoulder.

He notices the beige beads hanging around her wrist. "Stay on sidewalks," she says, "Directly to The Music Store. Tell Mr. Hanson I'll pick you up as soon as I'm done."

"Affirmative," he says, his entire body stiffening, his right hand to his forehead with a solemn soldier's salute.

At an intersection in front of the store, the boy stands, stares at heat rising from pavement. A gravelly, older man's voice behind him to his mother, "Afternoon, Stella."

"Afternoon, Sheriff."

"How's this ninety-seven-degree weather treating ya?" Ben hears the sheriff ask.

"Ah, you know. About three degrees from Hell." Stella's voice is pleasant, but biting.

Ben smirks. He crosses the street at the intersection, walks east on a sidewalk, the sheriff and his mother's voices fading into the humming wind. Sweat on his forehead, his town's public school beside him. He looks across the street to the grocery store, can barely see his mother, a distant blurred haze of yellow cloth and dark brown hair, her hand again at her forehead to shield her eyes from the summer sun as she talks with the sheriff.

Concrete sidewalk becomes rust red brick. Each brick the same size as his tattered black Converses. A darker row with 1910 etched into the center brick. On surrounding bricks, names of students who graduated that year. A few steps more, 1911, another row 1912, and more names and more years. His father's name, John, beside his mom's, 1968.

Ben imagines climbing oak trees in his parents' backyard. An evening sun setting, a cool breeze. Plucking single strings on Teddy Bunn's acoustic guitar. Sidney Bechet's soprano saxophone, "Summertime" playing from a turntable in an A-frame tool shed Ben's father is busy building. Ben's dad comfortable in a lawn chair, explaining to Nathan and Marc how Hank, Sr. is the best country musician, why the sax is the world's most soulful instrument, and how without Hank Sr., there's no JJ Cale in Tulsa.

Ben's no longer on the brick path. He's at the top of a steep paved hill, stares at a church's stained-glass windows. He walks up stone steps to an arched wooden door, studies two gold lanterns on either side of the church entrance. He grabs the door's handle, locked.

He walks east on the town's Main Street, Muskogee. On a sidewalk, he strolls past vacant brick buildings and shuttered storefronts. He sees in glass window-panes his reflection and deserted boxes, plastic paint buckets and damaged drywall.

A white brick building advertises haircuts for five dollars, one of the few businesses left on this lonely, paved two-lane street. Another is a store selling saddles and harnesses.

On the north side of the street, next-door to a two-story brick bakery, a shuttered movie theater, a pink building made of brick and stone, a sign spelling Carousel in capitalized circus letters.

Ben walks up to the movie theater's abandoned ticket booth, his black shoes crunching broken glass, and he tastes red dirt in the air. All that remains of the theater are chunks of discolored concrete, brick, and stone abandoned after the previous owners ripped the last movie poster from the building.

Beside the pink movie theater, a chestnut red brick building once upon a time home to an auto repair store. Groovy, hand-painted letters spell The Music Store on an aluminum glass garage door next to a neon Open sign. Another sign, We Sell Guitars, a different sign, Hi-Fi, Antiques. Next to it, a single hand strumming a guitar on a black-and-white poster of Eric Clapton's *Slowhand*.

Ben's walking past a poster on the glass garage door of Miles Davis' *Kind of Blue* album cover, and he mimics into the air Davis blowing his trumpet. Beside the garage, on a glass door entrance, a *Jaws* film poster, nearly as wide as the boy is tall, an image of a great white shark moving through deep blue sea toward a woman swimming at water's surface.

Metal wind chimes clank, and the glass door pushes open from inside, an attractive young woman with tawny brown skin in front of him. Blaring onto the street, Van Halen's "Running with the Devil" with its relentless opening bass guitar and drums.

She looks at him, smiles, a shopping bag in her hands. With her back, she holds open the glass door, and a tall man rushes in, nearly knocks Ben to the sidewalk.

Her smile's gone, and she looks into the store for the tall man. But, he's gone. Her brown eyes meet Ben's. She tucks a dangling strand of her wavy black hair behind her ear, leans down, kisses the boy on his pale, freckled forehead.

"Thank you," he says with his earnest southern twang, looks up, returns her smile.

"Be good," she tells him, holds the door as he enters the store.

At the doorway, Ben watches through the closing glass door as the girl hops into the driver side of her red Jeep, talks with an older teenage boy sitting beside her, shows him the album she's bought. Then, her red Jeep drives west on Muskogee. A turntable spinning Van Halen catches his attention. "Running with the Devil" playing its second verse.

Paul Hanson at the back of the store behind a wood paneled checkout counter, thumbing through receipt paper while also rubbing a red apple on his baseball shirt's navy-blue sleeve, his messy black hair across his forehead.

"Gimme a sec," Paul says, bites into his apple. He walks from behind the counter. Above him, exposed metal piping runs alongside steel beams strung with white Christmas lights. Paul walks between two rows of wooden shelves stretching parallel to the front of the store, each wood structure five feet tall, shelves stocked with new and used vinyl records.

The turntable sits on a shelf attached to a strip of red brick wall between Ben and the glass garage door.

"Thought that was you out there," Paul says.

"Hey, man, how's it going?'"

"Oh, you know." Paul sighs. He adjusts a volume knob on a stereo receiver. "Watching over the store for Pops, waiting for Annie to return with lunch." Music in the store lowers, and Paul glances out the glass garage door, white sunlight through windows across Paul's plump, bearded face. He bites into his apple. "Whatcha got going?"

"Nothing much. Looking to rent movies."

"Ah, lucky day, little dude." Paul nods his apple in approval toward Ben, then points to a red brick wall lining the store's west side. He walks a few steps to a doorless entrance leading into an adjoining room. "New videos arrived yesterday. Pops had me put 'em on the shelves this morning." Paul stops at the doorway, glares at Ben. "Knowing you, though, you likely already have a movie in mind?" But, Ben is no longer looking at Paul.

"Whoa!" Ben laughs, points behind Paul. "Where'd that come from?"

Eddie Van Halen's first guitar solo intensifying, Ben runs past Paul.

"Oh, you mean Justus D. Barnes?" Paul calls out over the music.

Ben's mouth is open, his eyes wide. He stares at a life-size cardboard poster on the red brick wall, an image from the chest up, on what looks like grainy black-and-white and sepia film stock, of a mustached man with a tuft of hair sticking out from his cowboy hat, the man's brows furrowed, eyes squinting, leering at Ben, a bandana around his neck, his revolver pointed at Ben as if firing into the store.

"Dude!"

"I know."

Ben shakes his head. "Leader of the Outlaw Band, Justus D. Barnes."

The Great Train Robbery.

"1903." Ben's astonished. "Where'd you find this thing?"

"Shoulda known you'd lose your fucking mind when you saw it."

"Swear words," Ben says, his accent growing thicker, "will not distract from my question."

"The city." Paul stands at Ben's side, the two staring at the cardboard cowboy cutout as if at an altar in worship. "One of the old movie theaters downtown had it and, on account of them closing …" Paul bites again into his apple, then tilts the half-eaten fruit to the front of the store. "Also where I got that sweet *Jaws* poster I put up on the door this morning. What kind of player you need, by the way? Betamax or VHS?"

Ben grins at Paul, "Beta."

"Ah, a Beta Man." Paul, impressed, has a closed-mouth smile on his face. "Nice choice, little dude. That's officially three weekends in a row renting a Beta player. Pretty badass, huh?"

"You have any in?"

"Sure do." Paul takes a final bite from his apple, now at its core.

He walks behind the checkout counter, a guitar solo at the start of Van Halen's "Eruption" playing across the store. "Oh, and I know you're a horror fan so try not to shit yourself when you see the *Night of the Living Dead* Beta that came in the mail yesterday."

Paul tosses the apple core, thuds into a metal trashcan. "Other than that, man, it's still mostly Twentieth Century-Fox. Only big studio putting anything on home video." He looks to Ben, the boy kneeling, tying his shoelaces under the Justus D. Barnes cutout.

Paul's hands in his brown corduroy's back pockets. He hears David Lee Roth swooning, "Girl … you really got me now." Paul calls out to Ben, "I'll have Annie grab you one of our Beta players when she gets back." He stares at the countertop, confused, says quietly to no one, "Think Annie's got my storage keys."

The metal wind chimes jangle above the door, catching Paul's attention. "Speak of the devil." Ben bolts up from the floor, remembers the cute girl with pretty brown skin who kissed his forehead earlier, then the bullish tall man who nearly knocked him to the ground, realizes he has not seen him

in the store.

A young woman in a light blue tank top and long white bell-bottoms stands on the outside sidewalk, holds open the door for Annie.

"Found a pretty person loitering at the diner," Annie proclaims, mockingly, as if announcing royalty, wearing big, round, dark sunglasses, nods back to Darla.

Ben watches Annie stride down the center of the store carrying two grease-stained paper sacks. Barely visible behind the bags is her white t-shirt, Rolling Stones beside a lone image of a giant red tongue sticking out through large, luscious red lips. A plaid flannel shirt wrapped around her waist and over cut-off black denim shorts. Her thick curly black hair bouncing up and down as she makes her way to the back of the store.

"Ah ... " Paul walks from behind the counter. "She arrives." He kisses Annie with a light peck on her soft, rosy cheek. "Thank you, thank you." His eyes follow Annie's porcelain white hands as she places the bags on the countertop. "Not a moment too soon. Just telling Ben here I was *this* close to eating my own arm."

Annie holds two of her fingers close to Paul's face. "This close, huh?" she echoes, taking off her sunglasses. "My boyfriend, the Walking Hyperbole. Good to see you, Ben."

Paul looks to Ben, motions the boy toward the front of the store. "Go get you some movies, man. I think *Night of the Living Dead*'s on one of the bottom shelves."

"*Night of the Living Dead*, Paul?" Darla scoffs, glares at Paul half-seriously. "You're going to frighten the poor kid half to death."

"That little horror fiend?" Paul laughs dismissively, reaches into the greasy bags. "Yeah, right." He leans against the countertop, eats a french-fry. "Go on, ask our little junior film and music critic his favorite death scene in *Black Christmas*."

Annie nods to a rectangular, tan thirteen-inch television on the counter next to Paul. "I see Van Halen officially replaced *Gilligan's Island*."

"Nothing lasts forever, Annie. Not even this album." Paul tosses a fry into the air, and it falls in his mouth. "It's all a rerun anyway."

"And, he says the sweetest things, too." Annie smiles playfully at Paul, re-wraps her flannel shirt around her waist. She reaches past him, turns on the television, mutes the volume as *Gillian's Island* appears in black-and-white across the glass screen.

Ben walks toward the front of the store, glances back at Annie and Paul emptying paper bags of their remaining contents. The room smells now of grease, grilled onions, and salty french-fries. In the aisle between the two rows of wooden shelves, Darla stands at a distance from Annie and Paul, twirls her long blonde hair without a care in the world as she flips through vinyl records.

Then, Ben sees him. The tall man stands transfixed a few feet from Darla, mesmerized and still, staring at three guitars hanging on the east brick wall. From the doorless entrance, Ben can see only the tall man's back over the top of the wooden shelf. He hears Paul call out from the counter to the tall man, "Hey, man. Let me know if you need me to take down one of those guitars for ya." And, with a shake of his head, the tall man declines.

Ben steps through the doorway into the adjoining room. He glances over his shoulder to see if the tall man has taken his eyes off the three guitars, and the man has not.

White cinderblock walls line the adjoining room north and west. Along these walls, antique clocks, children's games, lamps, radios, tools, tables, chairs. Warm sunlight shines on these antiques and across Ben from the room's south side through three large square steel casement windows overlooking his town's Main Street. Alongside the square windows, a long, white wooden fixture from the doorway to the west wall, shelves stocked with rows of Betamax and VHS movies. He feels the sun burn hotter on his denim overalls' chest pockets.

"Wanna drive into the city later tonight, see a movie?" Ben hears Paul ask Annie in the other room, his voice just audible enough over Van Halen's "Ain't Talking 'Bout Love."

"I don't know if I can go back outside today, Paul. That heat is oppressive." Annie lifts her thick curls off the back of her neck and into the air. With a handful of napkins, she wipes gathering sweat from the back of her pale, slender neck. "How many more hours til sundown?" Annie says, looks over at a clock near the cash register. "Oh, god." She sighs. "It's barely three o'clock."

"Oppressive." Paul nods his Styrofoam cup of ice water to Annie as if giving a toast at a wedding. "Good word." Paul gulps from the half-empty cup and wipes his mouth. "Hey, Ben," Paul says. "Any good movies at the theater this weekend?"

Ben's walking along the row of wooden shelves, shouts to Paul, "*Jaws 2* could've been worse!"

Carefully, Ben stares at movies, each with its own rectangular box resting vertically against a white wooden shelf, each shelf with different movies, each movie box with its own distinct artwork capturing Ben's attention.

"Wait a second … " Ben hears Annie respond finally, "The shark's dead. The sheriff saved his town and blew up said shark at the end of *Jaws*, like, in a giant explosion. Impossibly but spectacularly and certainly. What in the world could a *Jaws 2* possibly even be about?"

"It's a different shark!" Ben responds.

Paul nearly spits his water, chuckles. He shrugs at Annie, lowers his voice to her, "It's a different shark, Annie."

Ben takes from the shelf a video box with an absurd image of a single hand on a white backdrop, the hand walking on two female legs wearing high heels, a U.S. military helmet atop one of two fingers flashing a peace sign. *M*A*S*H* under the high heels. Holding the movie, Ben calls into the other room, "If you still haven't seen it, though, *The Omen II*! The score's awesome!"

Ben hears Darla's startled voice. "The horror movie where the little boy is the Antichrist?" she gasps. "You actually saw that?"

"Yup," Ben responds, his voice carrying over music across both rooms. "Saw it at the movies last weekend with my dad." He returns *M*A*S*H* to its space on the shelf. "But he's not a little boy in this one. He's twelve now and, when the movie starts, Damien doesn't know yet he's supposed to be bad." Ben picks up *Butch Cassidy and the Sundance Kid*. "He only knows his parents died when he was a boy," Ben says. "That they left him to live with his rich aunt, uncle, and cousin, Mark." Ben places the video box back on the shelf, kneels to the shelf below it. "And, he's friends with Mark. Then, Damien's aunt and uncle send Mark and Damien to this military school, and these bad things start happening around Damien, like in the first movie. These mysterious awesome deaths, and he doesn't know why. And, then, it's kinda sad, because you think … maybe Damien doesn't want to be bad. Or, do bad things. The scene where he learns he's the Antichrist, he even runs from the school into the woods and screams, 'Why me?' I don't know. It's scary." Silence before an electric guitar announces the start of Van Halen's "I'm the One" across the store's speakers, the final song on the album's first side.

Still kneeling on the concrete floor, Ben takes a movie from the bottom shelf, and he hears Darla ask from the other room, disapprovingly, "And, your parents are okay with you watching these scary movies?"

Ben hears Paul chuckle again and respond to Darla, "Whatever, dude, when was *Rosemary's Baby*? Ten years ago? I was nine when I saw that scary shit in theaters. And I totally saw *The Exorcist* opening night the day after Christmas when I was like, what, 13?" Ben holds a movie close to his face, studies a video box with an American flag draped across the entire front, *Patton* written beside actor George C. Scott standing and saluting, dressed in full military regalia, as U.S. General George C. Patton.

"That's awful, that's just way too young."

"I'm with Paul on this one, Dar. My mom took me to a drive-in to watch *Texas Chainsaw Massacre* right after it came out, so I must've been 13. And, we also watched *The Exorcist* together at a drive-in, and that's when the scene where the little possessed girl is stabbing herself in the crotch with the crucifix, my mother turned to me and said, 'Annie, dear … this is a movie that hates women and women's bodies.' I told her I liked *Chainsaw* better, because Sally saves herself from the chainsaw guy at the end."

Ben places the *Patton* video box back on the bottom shelf, hears Darla say defensively to Annie and Paul, "I'm just saying, maybe nine or ten isn't an appropriate age for a person to be watching *The Omen IV* or *Texas Chainsaw Slaughter Ten*."

The *Night of the Living Dead* video box on the bottom shelf catches Ben's eye.

"Dude, speaking of," Paul says. "I just reread *Hansel and Gretel* in a Freshman English class last semester for an essay we had on fairy tales and myths. And, man, *Hansel and Gretel* is fucked up. Like … I had forgotten how fucked up. It's got cannibalism, famine, a crazy old woman trying to bake and eat children, kids pushing a witch into a stove and burning her alive. I mean, my dad used to read that shit to me at night before I was even in kindergarten.

And, I totally saw parents pass out *Hansel and Gretel* to their kids like it's trick-or-treat candy, man, and kids eat it right up, a story about kids and cannibalism. And, then, what's *Texas Chainsaw Massacre* about? Fucking cannibalism and kids lost in the woods. Might as well be the same story."

Paul's description of *Hansel and Gretel* amuses Ben. He grabs *Night of the Living Dead*, tucks it under one arm. Van Halen's "I'm the One" nears its conclusion, all the male band members singing in unison, "bop bada." Ben hears Paul say, "After *Chainsaw*, nothing's really scary about adolescent antichrists or pre-pubescent possessed girls. *Chainsaw's* fucked up, cause that shit's based on real life, on things that can actually happen, on, like, Ed Gein killing, eating, and wearing people in Wisconsin. All *Chainsaw* did was change Ed's name, give him a chainsaw, and move him to Texas. That's the scariest type of horror story to me, ones with real-life monsters, not ghosts or bogeymen."

Ben takes *M*A*S*H* from the shelf, tucks it under his arm alongside *Night of the Living Dead*.

"I don't know, man … my dad drove me home after we caught a midnight screening of *Chainsaw Massacre*. Opening weekend, and he's quiet most of the drive, but then he turned and said, 'war wasn't witches, zombies, or ghosts. Only evil doing what men do.' Literally, one of maybe barely a handful of things he's ever said about fighting in Dresden during World War II. And then, no shit, not another word for the rest of the ride."

Paul walks to the turntable, crackling from the record player on the store's speakers punctuating silence in the room. He stares out through the garage door windows at his town's Main Street as he takes the record from the turntable and flips it over.

"You know what. I think you're right," the tall man's words fill the store. "About horror stories. The scariest ones, I mean. About man, humans being the real monsters." Paul sets the record down on the turntable, moves the needle over the record. "Like, right now, I am holding a knife to this girl's throat." The needle drops from Paul's hand onto the vinyl.

Silence now a screeching guitar riff on the speakers, giving way to Van Halen's first verse of "Jamie's Crying."

The tip of the blade pierces only a first layer of skin on Darla's neck, just beneath her left ear, the hunting knife wobbling in the tall man's trembling right hand. A single stream of blood flowing from knife-point down Darla's neck, onto her shoulder, over her clavicle, and toward where her pale skin meets the white lining of her light blue tank top.

Paul stands with his back to the turntable. He can't move. Can barely breathe. No words pass through his lips. Too scared to close his eyes. He stares in terror at Darla, at the long wooden shelving unit separating Paul from Darla and the tall man, at three guitars on the wall precisely above Darla and the tall man, at the knife pressed against Darla's throat, the tall man's arm strong against Darla's chest, Darla's back pressed against the tall man.

Then, Paul's eyes lock, stunned, on the thing covering the tall man's face. The thing that won't stop watching Paul. A human skull, skeletal bones crusted crudely in white paint across a dark, black ski mask.

"Don't cry." The tall man's voice is guttural, hollow.

And, Darla swallows her cries, muscles tense in her face, veins distinct in her neck. She squeezes her eyes shut, too afraid to open them. She trembles, choking back tears.

Annie scoots slowly from the countertop, her blue eyes staring across the store. "Darla," Annie whimpers, her hands moving over her mouth.

"Whatever's in the register, man." Paul cannot believe he's speaking, knows only he has to say something. "Seriously. Whatever you want."

Beyond the red brick wall lining the store's west side, Ben hears Paul's voice. He's hiding along the wall with the three large steel casement windows, Main Street sunlit bright in front of him, the long wooden shelving of Beta and VHS video boxes at his back. Ben precisely a half-foot shorter than the five-foot-tall white wooden structure separating him from the doorway into the other room. He listens motionless against shelves, his head turned left so he can better hear, and then Paul's voice, "Just … please, put down the knife."

Darla winces at the mention of the knife, terrified to open her eyes, to look down. She feels the length of the cold blade pressing against her skin, knife-point digging slowly into her neck, the wound throbbing now, pain sharp.

Then, Darla feels the knife push down just below her left ear, stabbing through skin and muscles. Her teary red eyes jolt open, and Darla wails loudly over music. She hears Annie scream, "Darla!"

And, then the blade swipes across Darla's throat, cuts swiftly through skin and veins. She looks down through watery eyes, vision blurred, time standing still, her pulse quickening, and Darla sees her own blood gush down her neck all at once like a waterfall. She gasps, hears herself struggle to breathe, Paul's voice crying, "Fuck! Fuck!" Darla feels weightless. Time slowing. Her body collapses across the top of wooden shelves, her head smacking hard against wood. Ringing, the room hollow, noise muffled, screams echoing. Paul's barely audible, distant, "No, please!" Silence. Her vision splotchy and bloody, the store tilted at an angle. Men's work boots scrambling, thumping loudly in front of her, black boots pushing frantically through packages of vinyl records, the tall man lunging across the wooden shelf, over it. Paul's more distant, "Annie! Annie, run! Run!" Gurgling, blood in her throat, harder to breathe, the tall man running, knife raised at Paul. Everything slower around her. Paul's hand in the air to defend himself, turntable behind him, sunlit dust particles, the knife stabbing through Paul's palm, through the other side of his hand. Burning across her neck. Paul's muffled yelling, crying. The knife stuck in Paul's hand before the tall man kicks Paul hard in the chest and off the blade. Silence. Choking, salty tears. And, the tall man stabs the knife into Paul's chest again and again, Paul's blood splattering across his white t-shirt onto the windows. Nothing to breathe. Paul slumps against the garage door to the concrete floor. The tall man kneels beside Paul, stabs again into his chest. Darla gasps for another breath, and then she dies.

Ben's hands hard against his ears, his eyes squeeze closed, noises in the other room too much. He's paralyzed, too afraid to look around the corner of the wooden shelves, to see through the doorless entrance into the other room, to know where the tall man is now. Ben sees only darkness.

He scoots quietly along shelves away from the doorway toward the far west wall. Then, at the end of the shelves, he opens his eyes, his heart racing in his chest. No movement in the other room, no words, no screaming, only music playing on the speakers. Ben slows his breathing, places his hand over his mouth to keep any noise from escaping. His back to wooden shelves, he peeks around the corner of white wood, stares at the door frame, at the long wooden shelf in the other room.

No Darla or Paul or Annie or the tall man. Music playing on speakers. Records scattered across concrete floor.

Near the bottom left of the door frame, a pale, white arm reaches in front of the doorless entrance. Annie's thick black curly hair, her face low to the floor, and then Annie scooting on her stomach across concrete. Annie's eyes lock with Ben's when she sees him peeking from behind the shelves. She's shivering and, quietly, she raises her index finger to her lips.

Hush.

Ben nods, his hand still covering his mouth, and he blinks loose a warm wet tear. Then, Annie's body yanks back across the doorway, her nails scratching concrete floor, and she's gone.

Ben looks away from the doorway, his hand still over his mouth. Annie's halting screeching screams unbearable, following him from the other room as he scoots back where white wooden shelving separates him from the doorless entrance. A crunching sound in the other room, and then no more screams. His hands dart once more over his ears, his eyes bolt closed as he fights crying, his back against wooden shelves, a row of Beta and VHS boxes on the shelf over his shoulder.

His gray eyes open, filling with tears, widening in horror. Three large square windows in front of him. The blue '67 Chevy parking in front of The Music Store. Her favorite summer dress. Sleeveless. Lemon yellow and vibrant. His mother on the other side of dusty sunlit windows. Ben's stunned as she walks past the first large square window, his eyeballs trembling, his face quivering. He follows as she walks, the long, white wooden shelves full of VHS and Beta movie boxes behind him. She never glances at the store's square windows, only ahead, her dress blowing with the wind as she makes her way to the third window. And, Ben wants desperately to call out to her, to pound loudly on the glass windows, to warn her away from this place. Then, Ben can no longer see his mother, and he stands frozen in fear. The metal wind chimes tinkle above the door in the other room. He hears his mother's gentle voice say, "Ben?"

A loud, short bang in the other room.

Stella stands still. She remembers walking into The Music Store, saying her son's name. She knows she's just finished grocery shopping, that Ben's here in this store, but her mind grows foggy. Hair on her arms tingling all at once. Her chest numbing. She stares across the store and, finally, sees Darla's body splayed across a wooden shelving unit. Stella looks down to find the stinging on her chest. Her gaze finds only her yellow dress, and then a small spot appears and grows suddenly into a dark red circle the size of a baseball. Stella collapses to cold concrete.

Ben stands at the doorless entrance, screams with everything in him. He runs, shoes hard on concrete floor, past the glass garage door, past Paul's body, past the turntable, past his mother. Ben's hands push open the glass door as he runs into sunlight, one foot on sidewalk, metal wind chimes clanking, Ben's right hand reaching high into the air, and he cries out, "Dad!" A rough hand clasps his left arm, jerks him back into the store, and Ben's not sure the exact moment the blade stabs into his back, only that it has.

Ben does not move. He wouldn't know how. He stands still, and his eyes watch the glass door closing in front of him. The back of the *Jaws* poster, nearly as long as the boy is tall, blocks Ben's view of his town's mostly deserted Main Street. Loud footsteps moving away from him to the back of the store. Ben's knees weak, then his legs, and he's on the floor. His warm freckled face against cold concrete. His upper back numb. He sees his mother on the playground in her nurse's scrubs, singing to him. Plucking single strings on Teddy Bunn's acoustic guitar, Sidney Bechet's soprano saxophone from Bechet's "Summertime" playing on a turntable, the A-frame tool shed Ben's father is busy building. Oak trees, Nathan and Marc. How without Hank Sr., there's no Tulsa, no JJ Cale. And then, the music stops, and Ben is gone.

Gilligan's Island in black-and-white on the thirteen-inch television screen. Muted moving images of Gilligan and The Skipper standing on a raft, water everywhere, a white sail with S.O.S. in big black letters attached to the make-shift boat. A close-up of Gilligan and The Skipper arguing.

On a different black-and-white television screen, Rec blinks on the top right corner above a wide-angle view of inside The Music Store showing the glass garage door. A skull reflects faintly across the screen. The dark mask, white paint smeared messily across bloodstained black cloth. And, the tall man sees this reflection on the glass screen as he stares at the television set behind the wood-paneled checkout counter.

Stop appears in the top right of the nineteen-inch screen, the black-and-white image of The Music Store now blank blue.

A videotape ejects from the front of a videocassette recorder. "Saturday, July 1, 1978" written in thick black marker across a white label on the VHS tape.

Then, the television clicks off, fades black, leaving only the skeleton face on screen. The knife in his back pocket, his heartbeat slowing, videotape in his right hand, mask and gun in his left.

Chimes clank above the door, and he leaves the store. Bright, intense sunlight sweeps over him. Warm wind dries blood on his cheek as he walks.

On a metal car door handle, his hand trembles. The driver's side opens. He throws crumpled ten and twenty-dollar bills on the passenger side of a tan bench seat.

The door slams shut. Silence in the car. The back door opens, and a Gibson guitar hurls onto a pile of wrinkled, dirty clothes scattered across the backseat.

Engine turns over after three false starts.

The '72 Oldsmobile station wagon idles, then backs away from a spot on the pavement where, in a diagonal parking space, it's been dripping slick, black oil on the town's Main Street.

Dark red blood spills onto the sidewalk, flows steadily from inside The Music Store, just beneath the great white shark on the *Jaws* movie poster on the store's glass front door. Dry, southern wind blows leaves and red dirt across the sidewalk in front of the store. And, the leaves scatter tiny drops of blood across the pavement.

CHAPTER TWO

Breathe. Breathe deep. His blue eyes snap open, and he stares up at the inside of a tent, his back on thin plastic groundsheet and against hard-packed earth. Sam Ford is awake and, this morning, his mother is still dead.

Outside the small tent, the young man stands on a patch of grass, morning dew cold on his feet, hem of his light blue Wranglers at his ankles, campfire remnants in front of him. No sun yet, sky not completely dark, chirping birds in the distance.

Sam tilts a thermos over a toothbrush, spilling water on his feet, onto dirt. Mud between his toes. Warm wind across his bare chest and through his shaggy brown hair. He brushes his teeth barefoot, stares at stars in the twilight sky.

He sits under a tarp outside the tent, pulls a tan cowboy boot on his foot, pulls his other boot over a long scar extending on his left leg from his ankle to his shin.

He puts on a plain white t-shirt, brown chest hair through the V-neck. He gulps water from the thermos til it's empty.

He walks through the clearing toward a path leading into the woods, his hiking bag slung on his back. He glances behind him to their campsite, at a dark outline of a red Jeep parked beside two tents.

Time passes. He treads water in the middle of gray fog, forest at creek's edge, his head above the surface of natural spring water.

He's cross-legged on the creek's rocky shore, studying his reflection in crystal-clear water. With a steel straight razor, he shaves his cheek above a beard he's shaped to define his jaw. He rinses his razor, glances at his green hiking bag on a wooden picnic table. Behind him, a waterfall rushes over rocks into the creek.

He walks through forest, dark blue shading the woods. Branches breaking beneath his boots. His shaggy hair damp, his hiking bag on his back. His eyes follow a worn path winding through prickly-pear cactus, pine, and oak trees.

At the edge of a rocky cliff, he unfastens his hiking bag. Behind him, fog-covered valleys and mountains disappear into dark southern sky.

He kneels, reaches into his bag. A hawk squawks, drifts lazily past him toward sunrise. Sam wishes he were flying, too. That this task wasn't his, that he was anywhere but here. But, he's on this cliff, wooded green hills and prairie beneath him, his hometown no longer his home.

He pulls a silver urn from his hiking bag, then a photograph.

He looks at himself a year ago, sitting on a porch swing in front of his farmhouse with his mother. A place he can't go. His eyes dart to an eastern horizon.

He stands tall, lean, every bit of his six-foot-four body at cliff's edge, breeze on freshly shaven cheeks. All at once, he empties the urn of ashes. Gray dust swirling across a dark blue sky, the photo drifting over the green forest canopy.

And, he feels no better. And, the wind blows harder.

On the worn path through the woods, his backpack is heavier. He looks up at daybreak through leaves and trees, then to his boots and forest floor. He arrives at a clearing, sees the only other woman he's ever loved.

Wrapped in a knitted blanket, Sarah's sitting on a tree stump, a coffee mug in her hands. In front of her, campfire remnants. Her black wavy hair in a ponytail, red sunlight across her tawny brown skin. She looks up, sees her tall best friend.

Sam sits beside the stump, taking off his hiking bag. He scoots his bag behind him, rests against it, stretches his legs. He never looks at her, doesn't know what to say. He stares at his boots, into the woods.

She pours coffee from a steel saucepan into a ceramic mug, passes it to him.

Sam nods thanks, and Sarah clasps her blanket around her. Sam sips his coffee, and the two best friends sit for hours, saying nothing, watching the sun rise over the land.

Leaves canopy over a paved, narrow street, Sarah driving her Jeep down-hill through the woods. Sam grips a metal grab handle above him, the Jeep's windows and top down, his eyes following dense oak and elm trees he remembers climbing as a boy.

Sarah's red Jeep turns from the forest, passes a wood signpost, Now Leaving Chickasaw National Park.

Engine off, Sarah gone, her Jeep parked, Sam's in the passenger seat, waiting. Restless, he looks to a single key in the ignition. From the Jeep's passenger side, he searches across Main Street, Muskogee, once alive when he was a boy, now dusty, dry, quiet wasteland. Sunlight hot on his face. Empty diagonal parking spaces. He hates it here.

He thinks about lung cancer, how his mother never smoked. He replays in his head the last year of his life following her death—his farm work, the promise of a June wheat harvest. He tries to imagine another day on his farm, wants to find work out west. He looks to the key in the ignition.

A mud-splattered station wagon rattles into a parking space beside him. The Oldsmobile idles, coughs exhaust.

Sam leans back in his bucket seat, stares at the Jeep's hood separating him from an aluminum glass garage door with The Music Store written next to a neon Open sign.

He sees a young boy in denim overalls strolling past a large poster of Miles Davis' *Kind of Blue* album cover, the boy blowing an imaginary trumpet, like Davis. Sam grins, folds his arms, hears the Oldsmobile engine rattle to a stop, sees a tall man shut the driver's side door. Sam closes his eyes, tries to sleep, can't. The heat's relentless.

Van Halen's "Running with the Devil" blares suddenly on the street. Sam squints at The Music Store. Through the windshield's grimy film, a five foot nothing Sarah stands only a half-foot taller than the boy. Sarah kisses him on his forehead. Sam smirks.

His eyes close again. Engine turns over. He never looks at Sarah when he says with his deep drawl, "Gonna make my brother real jealous with that new boyfriend of yours."

"Whatever, man," she says. "Dylan's gonna love what I found for him." She reaches in her bag. "Check out this album cover art." She points to stark black and white font spelling *The Man Machine* on Kraftwerk's scarlet red record.

Outside the only diner in a neighboring town, Sam leans on a cinderblock wall, toothpick between his lips. A commercial ice machine humming steady between him and the diner door. Sarah's Jeep parked in front of him. He hears her laugh from inside the diner, "Yes, I swear! Next time we're in town … "

The diner door swings open, and Sarah's beaming.

Sam tosses his toothpick in a trashcan.

He lifts himself into the passenger seat. "Tend the radio," she tells him, driving from a gravel parking lot. "And, no more gloom."

They drive west past brick storefronts along the small town's main street, the road becoming a four-lane highway for miles through farmland and prairie.

Day gives way to dusk. Through the windshield, a green sign along the highway, Interstate 35 North and Okla. City.

Her Jeep turns toward an interstate on-ramp, a passenger side mirror reflecting a windblown Sam and distant rolling mountains.

He glances at Sarah's fingers tapping her steering wheel as if playing piano. Warm wind across his face. He looks west across the interstate where the sun's setting beyond the plains. Dark shapes of an oil derrick and trees silhouetted against intense white light bursting into tangelo orange and amber. And, the evening sky's on fire.

Two hours pass, and it's night.

Sam puts his camping gear on the ground, Sarah closes her Jeep's back door. "Tomorrow, then?"

"Bright and early," he says.

Her hand to his shoulder. "You did good today," she says. "Tell Dylan when he gets in I'll see him tomorrow morning."

"Yeah, sure."

Sarah backs her Jeep down a long, dirt driveway. Headlights shining on Sam standing beside his father's car. Oklahoma County Sheriff.

He watches Sarah's headlights disappearing on a dirt road in front of his farm. Then, his street's dark. To the south, silhouetted tall grassland, a first quarter moon in the night sky. He turns to his family's two-story farmhouse, sees only a single light in an upstairs window. His father's room.

He makes his way east of his house toward a barn. He tosses his bag to the ground. Crickets chirp across his yard. He brushes his hand across his horse's mane. "Hey, Brunhild."

Under a cottonwood tree, Sam sits in grass and dirt, his back against the barn. He slides a silver flask out from his hiking bag.

Brunhild neighs. Sam nods his flask to her, takes a swig. "To doing good." He looks to the light in the upstairs window, shuts his eyes.

An hour or two gone, his flask tipped over beside him, empty. Sam looks to the upstairs window, and it's dark. He pushes himself from the dirt.

Inside, he sets his hiking bag beside a grandfather clock. So, too, his camping gear. A familiar silence since his mother's gone. A mahogany staircase next to him. He leans on a railing, takes off his boots to the tick of the clock.

At the top of the stairs, he looks toward his room at the west end of a long hallway. He falls face-first onto his bed.

He wakes, turns quick to his open bedroom door, night shining across wood floors from a bay window on the other side of his room.

He's downstairs at a kitchen sink, filling a glass from the faucet, standing in his boxers and white t-shirt. He gulps an entire glass of water, refills it.

He walks barefoot past his camping gear, makes his way upstairs. He hears his father's loud snoring from behind a door at the east end of the hallway.

In his bedroom, Sam walks past his bay window. He stretches his arms. Behind him, unseen, a tall man stands in the shadows, his fists clenched, watching Sam.

Sam pulls back a sheet on his bed, looks to an alarm clock on a nightstand. three thirty a.m. flashing red. A giant canvas painting of Earth from the moon behind his headboard from floor to ceiling. Sam looks up, bedsheet still in his hand, and the two men see each other.

The bedsheet falls from Sam's hand the second he hears his father's snore at the other end of the hall. Sam remembers his brother's out of town til morning. "Oh, shit."

The two men stand across the room from each other. Sam takes a step forward, creaking floorboards, the tall man two steps toward Sam. They stop. From the corner of Sam's eye, he sees the bay window. Sam takes another step forward, the tall man another toward Sam. They stop again. Then, Sam dashes to the bay window, the tall man quick behind him.

Sam's foot busts through floorboards, wood scraping skin, tearing into his leg, and the floor collapses. He falls, crashing into his living room. His back slams against hardwood. He coughs blood, hears a man's muffled husky, "What're you doing out here, Sam?"

Sam shakes awake outside his barn, tasting red dirt. "Out here?" Piercing yellow light hurts his eyes. He sees the white outline of a broad-shouldered man standing over him. Sam squints. "Dylan?"

Sam's nauseous. His hand on dewy grass, cold clay dirt. His mouth dry. He hears a mower in the distance, too early. Sees his camping gear, empty flask beside him. The farmhouse, then back to his brother. He hears a car engine rev, sees the distant blur of a red sports car racing north on a street west of his farmhouse, dust rolling behind it. Dylan's hand grabs onto Sam's elbow and helps Sam from the ground.

"Guess I didn't make it inside, did I?" And, his words sound like a mouth full of marbles. Sam wipes dirt from the back of his pants. This is new. He's never done this, sleep outside without knowing. Couldn't have gotten that drunk, not to pass out outside. Did Dylan see his flask? "Wasn't ready to let go of camping just yet," and Sam looks behind him at his camping gear. Dylan smiles at Sam like he does, like the good one, the aw shucks one, the clean-shaven nice one with a handsome square face, neatly cropped hair, and Sam looks back at him and says, "What time is it?"

"Seven thirty."

Sam hangs his head, looks to the tallgrass field across the street behind his brother. Seven thirty. But, Sam was inside; he remembers going into the house.

"Go for a run after we throw our stuff inside and change?" Sam hears Dylan ask.

"Yeah, sure," and the words leave Sam's mouth before his brain has even a moment to process the question. A new phase of insomnia? Is this normal?

Wind rustles through tall grassland.

Sam's standing at an intersection, the tall grass beside him. He stares at street signs, Southwest 89th and Pennsylvania, his eyes following Pennsylvania til the long dirt road disappears into blue southern sky.

Dylan appears at Sam's side in royal blue basketball shorts, sky-blue sleeveless shirt, stretches his arm across his muscular chest. Sam glances at a black ink crucifix on Dylan's well-defined tricep. "Ready?" Dylan says.

"Yep," and the two start a steady jog from their farm on the dirt road. On either side of the brothers, endless green grass fields, sunlit and waving with warm wind.

So begins a variation on Sam and Dylan's morning routine. Wake up before sunrise. Meet at the intersection in front of their farm. Jog south five minutes, sprint five minutes, walk five. Repeat for three miles until South Tree, a name the brothers gave a particularly tall oak tree they discovered after their family moved to the city. Touch the tree's giant trunk, then its sprawling, twisted branches and head home, jogging, sprinting, walking til they arrive again at 89th and Pennsylvania. From boyhood onward, no matter what weather— rain, ice, sleet, or snow—this routine is theirs.

Sam's sprinting, his eyes on the dirt road, his brother at his side. He glances at Dylan's crimson baseball cap, backwards with OU embroidered in white. Sweat dripping from Sam's shaggy hair, and he's no longer sure how time moved so quick. South Tree in the distance. South Tree? Hadn't they just left his house? They slow to a walk, Dylan resting his hands behind his head, pacing to cool down, South Tree's leaves canopying above them.

Sam remembers the red sports car blur, rests a hand on each knee, catches his breath before he says, "Cristine's gonna fuck up her car if she keeps on with her engine like that."

Sweating, panting, Dylan chuckles, turns to Sam. "Yeah, well, not too sure Cristine's much a listening type on such matters." Dylan pats Sam's chest, starts walking back north.

Three bacon strips fry in a rustic iron skillet full of sizzling grease.

Dylan stands at a gas stove, holding a black plastic spatula. Grease crackles, pops. Smoke drifting from the stovetop to an open window above the kitchen sink.

Sam makes his way down the mahogany staircase, rolling up the sleeves of his plaid, peach pearl-snap shirt. His boots clunking with each step. A full chime sequence striking from the grandfather clock. The scent of hickory and bacon.

Pancake batter pours into a stainless-steel skillet, and Dylan sets a mixing bowl on the counter. Sam grabs a stack of plates from a cabinet next to a refrigerator, each plate clanking the next.

"Thanks, Sunshine," Dylan says from the sink, his back to his brother. He hears the screen door bang closed in the living room.

"Knock, knock." Sarah's at a wooden table near a gray brick wall lining the kitchen's west side. She sets her bag on the table, walks to the stove, examines the contents of the two skillets. She smiles. "Hmph. Not bad, Ford."

"Thank you, thank you." Dylan flips a towel across his shoulder at the sink, running water over a colander of oranges and apples.

"Pancakes even?"

"Mhmm."

Dylan leans over, kisses Sarah quick on the lips.

Sam carries a stack of plates in a narrow hallway through a laundry room, past a washing machine, a bathroom, then opens a back door. Bright sunlight shining across a field behind his house. He steps down from a deck, walks along a clothesline with bath towels blowing with warm wind. He walks to the east side of his house, past a tire swing at the end of a rope attached to the cottonwood tree. He puts his stack of plates on a wood picnic table he's built with his own hands.

On the picnic table looms an antique cathedral-style radio. Sam turns one of its three knobs. Static screeches, and he twists another knob til Seals and Crofts' "Summer Breeze" emerges midway through its first verse. Sam turns a different knob, the song a bit louder.

Juice squeezes from a fleshy peeled orange in Sarah's hand into a glass bowl. She scoops seeds from the bowl with a spoon. She grabs another orange from her backpack, squeezes. "Summer Breeze" drifts through the open window above the kitchen sink. She's sitting in a chair at the kitchen table, her bare feet suspended over blue slip-on shoes on gray brick floor. She looks up, smiles at Dylan, him with his back to her, standing at the stove in his white tank top and camouflage cargo shorts. He scoops bacon with his spatula from the skillet over onto a nearby plate.

"You get off work tonight?" Dylan asks, his back to Sarah as he turns off the stove.

"Yep." Sarah squeezes juice from the orange into the bowl. "Natalie's picking up my shift, and I'm working hers tomorrow night." She scoops out a seed.

"What you're saying, then, is I get to take my lovely, amazing girlfriend out on the town for a date?"

"Oh, is that what I'm saying?"

"Sure sounds that way."

Outside on the picnic bench, Sam sits shaded under dense leaves from the cottonwood tree. The opening guitar from Yes's "Roundabout" on the antique wood radio. He stares east beyond the cottonwood, past the barn and small round creek to a vast harvested wheat field. Above him through rustling leaves, morning sun warm on his face. Over his shoulder, Dylan and Sarah's words weave in and out of the other's. Silverware clanking against plates, Sarah and Dylan placing food on the table. A distant train horn. Dylan talking about his trip to the lake. An approaching, gruff male voice, "I feel as old as the man who shot Liberty Valance this morning."

At the other end of the table, Sam's father stands tall in his black sheriff's uniform, pours coffee from a pot into a thermos.

"Who is that?" Sarah says, then chuckles.

"Who's that?" Ryan's words hard, uneven. He sits beside Sam. "They don't even bother teaching y'all in school anymore?"

Dylan laughs under his breath, reaches for a plate of pancakes. "John Wayne? 1962?"

Sarah shrugs with a look of mock bewilderment.

Dylan pours syrup on his pancakes, stares at a plate of crisp bacon. "Jimmy Stewart? Vera Miles?"

"John Ford's best film," Ryan says, Dylan passing him the plate of pancakes.

"*The Searchers'* John Ford?" Sarah says, using a wooden spoon to stir orange juice in a tall glass pitcher. "Why don't I know this movie?"

Sam turns from the harvested field to the table, Sarah sitting across from him, beaming in a blue strapless summer dress.

Ryan smirks when Sarah looks at him. "John Wayne's this aging cowboy, Stewart this U.S. Senator home for a funeral, Vera's Jimmy Stewart's wife." Ryan twists closed a cap on his thermos. "At the start of the film, Stewart tells a newspaper reporter why he's home for the funeral, then the movie flashes back on how Stewart came to know Wayne's cowboy character, the man who shot Liberty Valance."

Sarah passes a plate of scrambled eggs across the table to Sam, smiles at him.

"We should say grace." Dylan extends his hand to Sarah, his other to his father.

Sam sets the plate of eggs next to the orange juice pitcher, Sarah's hand reaching across the table toward his. Ryan takes up Sam's right hand.

"Lord God, thank you for this morning's blessings," Dylan begins, his tone serious, resonate, sweet. "And, thank you for another day. We come to you humble servants, sinners no better than anyone. Thankful for this day of rest. Thankful for a wheat harvest."

For the first time, Sam's eyes open during grace, his brother speaking sincere, familiar words. Dylan's callused hand gripping Sarah's. Behind them on the brick farmhouse, sunlit chipped white paint.

"Keep us safe in your grace. Bless this meal as you blessed this land."

Sam glances at specks of gray in his father's short brown hair.

"In Jesus' name we pray, amen."

"Amen."

"Amen."

Sam's eyes dart from his father. Across the table, Sarah's thick lashes flicker, her brown eyes catching Sam's. He looks quick to his plate, then back to her, eyebrows raised. And, they eat.

Sam looks south across Southwest 89th Street at tall grassland waving with the wind, at a day eight years ago when he and his family arrived from their small town to this farmhouse. A ten-year-old Sam kicking hard at the dirt road with his boot.

"Why're you so angry, Sam?" says his mother's gentle voice.

He refuses to look up at her, stares at the ground, then the field.

"I'm not mad," he says, his words low, defiant, his eyes never moving from the grassland.

"You're gonna make new friends here. You and Dylan. And, we're gonna tend this farm together."

"I ain't much on making friends."

His fist balled-up, punching an older boy's mouth, his knuckles knocking out the boy's front teeth, five-year-old Sam's hand bleeding, the other boy's face gushing blood. This fight the first week of school after the older boy mocked Dylan's stuttering.

"It's just ... everything is moving so fast. Sometimes, it doesn't feel like me. It's as if nothing's real anymore."

His mother beside him, and the two stare past grassland to the southern horizon.

"Next time you feel alone, remember I'm here. I'm real."

A male DJ's voice breaks in on the antique radio, "K-O-M-A, Oklahoma City. It's ten o' clock."

A Pentax camera lens, Sarah's left hand adjusting, turning the black plastic focusing ring, her thumb and index fingers searching for the right number on the dial to let in the precise amount of light. Steady, Sarah holds her camera to her right eye, her right index finger waiting just over a shutter release button.

Through the lens, she sees Sam, wonders if anyone else really does. Through her camera, she watches him take another bite of eggs from his fork, focuses on his well-kept beard, his light peach skin, blue eyes, shaggy dark brown hair, the red barn to his left, the small creek behind the barn, the recently harvested wheat field extending east for acres across the Ford family's land where Sam, Sarah, and Dylan played inseparably as kids. An elm tree under which she and Dylan shared their first kiss. The horse eating at the barn door, cattle grazing in the distance. Sam looks up at her. Snap.

"What's this, Sarah, about you quitting school to take pictures? Traveling the state." Ryan wipes his napkin across his mouth. "Your parents know you're doing it?"

"Not quitting, Sheriff." Sarah clicks the metal exposure counter atop the camera. "Just putting it off a semester." She smiles at Ryan, then looks to Sam. "Do you know why you always blink when you take a photo?"

Sam glances up at her as if a deer in headlights, holds a piece of bacon at his mouth.

"The lighter the color of your eyes, the more light-sensitive you are, because there isn't enough pigmentation to buffer that light through," she explains, her tone careful, excited. "So, yeah, light blue-eyed people are just ultra-light sensitive. Even just stepping out into the sun."

Sam recalls waking up outside, bright piercing light, pushes away this memory.

Dylan puts his glass of orange juice on the table, turns to Sarah, smiles. "They'll pay you to teach classes."

Sarah sets her camera beside her half-eaten plate of pancakes. "I only know that from a *National Geographic* article I was reading the other day before my shift at work. Made me think about Sam always blinking in photos."

Sam takes a bite from his syrupy pancake stack.

"Anyway, this article talked about a photographer in mid-1950s Cuba. How she woke one morning, realized she'd lived in the same town all her life, so she just up and traveled her entire country, ends up documenting life in pre-revolution Cuba. Thought about how I'm 18, I was born here, lived on south side my whole life, same house, and I've seen less than half our state. I've never been to, like, the panhandle or any of that. So, the plan is to hit up as many towns as possible in all four corners of Oklahoma between now and spring semester. That'll give me time to take this little fancy robot guy on the road, get in some practice."

"I like it." Dylan smiles at her.

Sam nods in approval, gets up from the table with his empty plate.

Ryan watches Sam walk toward the back of the house. "You going to morning or evening service?"

"Evening." Dylan gulps the last of his orange juice. "There's a guest pastor tonight. Some guy from northeast side." He places his fork and knife on his empty breakfast plate. "Supposed to be good. You going?"

"Wasn't gonna." Ryan's walkie-talkie goes off at his hip. He turns down the volume. "Got stuff to tend to downtown. You gotta work tomorrow?"

"Yep. Seven a.m. Managed July 4th off Tuesday, though."

Sam returns to the table, takes Dylan's plate, then his father's, Sarah's. The Byrds' "Wasn't Born to Follow" on the radio.

"Sam'll be on the farm tomorrow, baling hay," Dylan says, pours another glass of orange juice from the pitcher.

Sarah points her Pentax at Sam as he carries plates to the back of the house. Her camera lens focusing on a new neighborhood far across the field from the Ford farm. Turning the dial, she can barely see an elevated new interstate just beyond the neighborhood. Wind blows hot on her skin.

Ryan folds his arms, finds himself staring at nothing in particular, lost in drums on "Wasn't Born to Follow." He looks at the other end of the table to the antique radio where his wife sat during these outdoor summer Sunday breakfasts.

"I don't think it got below seventy degrees overnight or this morning," Dylan tells Sarah as she snaps a photo of him snagging a bacon strip from a sole remaining plate on the table.

Music from the radio fades into a car commercial, promises extravagant July Fourth sales on pickup trucks.

A second commercial gives way to a third, then the DJ promises "another scorcher of a day."

Ryan watches Sam appear from the back of the house, walking to the barn, carrying two pails of water.

The DJ continues, a piano underscoring him, his voice as if he's announcing more big sales at a local dealership. "Oklahoma City weather is somewhere in the summer swelter. Few clouds floating over the city today. Gonna be hot this Sunday. Ninty seven the high. But, we haven't cracked it yet. Seventy five now at KOMA."

Near the barn, Sam greets his horse, pours water from a pail into a trough. He rubs her back as she starts to drink. "Morning, girl."

Sarah stands from the picnic table, stretches her hands high in the air. She picks up the pitcher, tilts it over her empty glass.

The DJ continues as orange juice pours into Sarah's glass. "And, as promised, details on a horrific Murray County tragedy where police discovered five bodies in what appears to be in Sulphur a mass murder robbery at The Music Store, a popular local business in the area."

"Oh, Jesus Christ." Ryan unfolds his arms. "Sulphur?"

Orange juice flows over the top of the glass and onto the wooden picnic table, between cracks, spills to the grass and mud. Sarah is no longer moving.

Dylan's startled. "Sarah?"

"The boy."

The pitcher smashes into wood tabletop, shatters into glass shards.

"Sarah?"

She says nothing, only stares.

Ryan bolts up, makes his way around the table to Sarah. "Sarah, what is it?"

Sam hears the commotion, starts running across the yard toward the picnic table, news on the radio becoming audible to him.

"Sarah, for God's sake, what the hell is it?" Dylan demands.

Sam grabs a near-catatonic Sarah's trembling hand. He looks to the dirt road in front of his house.

Sarah looks up. "We were there yesterday."

CHAPTER THREE

Derek Clover sits naked in bed, his dirty blonde hair swooping down his angular face. He strikes a match, smokes a cigarette, the only other light in the room a muted television on a mid-century dresser.

Beside him, his wife sleeps on her stomach, a white bedsheet covering her from thighs down. Her blonde hair across a white pillow.

Derek can't stop staring at the 19-inch television, his green eyes fixated on silent moving images, news reporters, flashing police lights, white words across the screen, "Sulphur Slaughter: An Unspeakable Evil."

He glances at an alarm clock on a nightstand next to Rachel's side of the bed. Four thirty a.m. Derek rests his face in his palms, exhales through his mouth, shakes his head.

He stands barefoot and naked in a bathroom, pissing and staring at a framed photograph above his toilet, his reflection beside the image of a white porcelain urinal signed "R. Mutt." He flushes, washes his hands with soap in a sink, splashes cold water on his face.

Plank wood creaks beneath his feet as he walks through a dark hallway. He hears distant barking dogs. In his living room, he checks a locked deadbolt on the front door. The door chain, too.

Back in bed, the TV off, he turns on his side, wraps his arms around Rachel. In slight protest, she moans, leans her slim body into his, pulls him closer to her. Derek kisses the back of her head, his arm across her breasts. He stares at glass French Doors separating their bedroom from the hallway. He looks to Rachel as he runs his fingers through her soft hair.

A ringing phone rips through silence, Derek's arm racing across Rachel to the nightstand.

"Hello," Derek whispers into the phone. "Yeah." Clears his throat, slides his other arm from under Rachel, careful to keep a spiraling phone cord off her. "Sure," his words full of agitation. "An hour, yeah."

Derek slides a glass door closed behind him, quiet, leaves space for the coiled cord into their bedroom. He stands in his boxers and button-up shirt, puts the rotary phone on a brick retaining wall surrounding the back porch of their

1920s bungalow. The phone receiver to his ear, he hears a man's groggy voice say, "FBI?"

"Yeah, man," Derek says, "they arrive Monday."

"Thought you said the three of us moved back to Oklahoma to get away from this sorta madness."

"I never promised you a rose garden, Charlie."

"Does Rachel know?"

"She's still sleeping."

"Your Sulphur article's about to be front page. You're welcome for helping edit it, Passive Voice King."

Derek looks over his shoulder at five a.m., darkness around him. He reverses his car onto a street lined with brick two-story four-plex apartments and empty bungalows, some with no running water, all built with oil money in the 1920s.

He drives east on Northwest 23rd Street along an abandoned movie theater and distressed shops. He passes under an unfinished interstate, a domeless state capitol building, a governor's mansion behind gates and shrubs. A succession of uninhabited brick storefronts, a nail salon with steel bars on every entrance and window. He turns left onto Martin Luther King, Jr. Avenue.

Driving north on this hilly avenue, he sees distant red lights flashing hypnotically on transmitters towering within an antenna farm. Jupiter his destination, he sees kaleidoscopic images of galaxies and gods above him through his windshield. Mars out his open window. Red Planet longing, spaceboy adrift. Venus, he's left behind, warm in her bed. Way out here, past a science museum and city zoo, past a Cowboy Hall of Fame on a hilltop full of trees, he's alone in the universe, stars his only companions in Jupiter's cosmos.

Derek catches a glimpse of himself in his rearview mirror, his left hand on his steering wheel, his other on his stick-shift. And, in an instant, he realizes, before he sat in his car, he never even bothered to check his backseat.

In a dark parking lot, a large lit sign glows in front of a nondescript brick building, OETA. Derek turns off his car, stares through his windshield at a giant satellite dish in a field behind the building, still hesitant to look behind his driver's seat, certain he's foolish. He takes his keys from the ignition, gets out his car, shuts the door, glances into his backseat at nothing at all.

Inside a small room, light bulbs buzz along a wide rectangular mirror. He sits, staring at his reflection, barely recognizes himself in his heather gray suit. Clothing he's worn twice, each time to two interviews securing his new job at *The Daily Oklahoman*.

A woman's hand puts a glass of water on a counter in front of Derek, startling him.

"Oh," she laughs. "Didn't mean to frighten you."

Derek smiles. "No worries. Guess I'm still half-asleep, apologies." He grabs his glass, nods it at her as she sets a black bag on the countertop. "Thank you."

"No problem," responds the middle-aged Black woman. "So, I'm Susan, and I'm going to be doing your makeup this morning."

"Morning, Susan. I'm Derek."

"Nice to know you, Derek."

He takes in the small room, its lack of distinguishing features, people in the mirror bustling back and forth in a narrow hallway outside an open door.

"Go ahead and lean back," she says, sweetly. "I'm just going to apply a light foundation, and you'll be all set."

"I can handle that, friend."

"First time on TV?"

"Yeah."

"It's nothing." She applies powder to his pale cheeks, his forehead. "Besides, you'll look good on TV. You have good cheekbones. And, a kind face. Pretty even. You ever been in front of cameras before?"

"Nope, unless you count Super 8 movies I made with friends growing up." In the mirror, he notices a slight smile on his face.

"We can count those if you'd like. Close your eyes, hun."

Silence around him, and he can hear indistinct chatter about coffee and lighting coming from the hallway just beyond the door.

"So, where did you grow up?" she asks.

"Here. In the city."

"Ah, nice, what part?"

"Mesta Park, Heritage Hills area. Went to Central downtown for high school."

"And, is that where you made your movies, then?"

Derek chuckles. "Yeah, mostly. There and whatever woods we could find. Where'd you go to school?"

"Douglass. On the northeast side."

"I know Douglass. We played you all in basketball. We'd even win once and a while."

Susan laughs heartily. "How long you been married?" she asks.

"Ten years," Derek says. "Married my Super-8 movie co-star day after high school, and we ran off to California with our comedy relief. How did you know I was married?"

"Wedding ring gives it away every time," responds Susan. "What's her name?"

"Rachel."

"That's a pretty name. Where're you calling home these days?"

"Mesta. Just bought a house. Didn't think we'd ever come back to Oklahoma but, well … Things just got too complicated."

Susan blends powder across Derek's tapered jawline, his narrow chin. "My sister tried her luck in LA," she says, "didn't make it a year. You, your wife, and your friend all came back together?"

"Yeah. Been back a couple weeks now. We made a pact to stick together. So, we did."

"That's real sweet. So, you think they'll catch who did it?" Susan asks, powdering his chin, the pad shaking, her hand trembling before she steadies herself.

Derek's eyes remain closed. All he sees is the front page of *The Daily Oklahoman* and his byline under "An Unspeakable Evil."

"That poor guy," Susan continues. "The husband, I mean. To lose your wife and only child in one day. Like that. I saw him on the news early this morning. Won't even look at the cameras. And, I don't blame him. I can't even imagine. You can open your eyes now."

And so he does, light in the room a bit blinding. His eyes follow Susan, studying her as she places foundation back in her black bag, his gaze settling on a wedding band on her ring finger.

"Do you have kids?" she asks, her back to him.

"No," and he thinks about the day before when *The Daily Oklahoman* called, sent him to Sulphur. Their other guy unavailable, so they sent Derek the New Kid. "You?"

"Two. A boy and a girl. Fifteen and Eighteen." She takes a pack of Marlboro's from her bag, pulls out a cigarette. "So, you think they'll catch him?"

Derek can see only deadbolts, Rachel sleeping soundly at home alone.

CHAPTER FOUR

On a color, muted television, Derek's talking, wearing his only suit, the morning sun casting its rays on a tan wall behind the TV and dresser.

A hand slides an 8-track into a player near a closet door. A bluesy jazz guitar strumming, and Nancy Sinatra's voice on "Not the Lovin' Kind" flows across the house.

At her feet, a phone cord she unplugged around 7 a.m., the nuisance which long ago refused to stop ringing, reporters calling, asking for Derek, television and radio stations wanting to know what he knows, what he saw.

In their kitchen, Rachel closes a refrigerator door, pours skim milk into a bowl of Corn Flakes near a sink.

She stands in a white bathrobe, leaning against the closed refrigerator, holds a ceramic cereal bowl with both hands. And, she stares at nothing. Nancy Sinatra and the refrigerator's steady hum in her ears.

She walks down her hallway into the bathroom, one hand on a champagne bottle.

Champagne pours into a flute half-full of orange juice resting on black-and-white checkered tile floor beside a white claw-foot bathtub.

Her white robe drops to tile, and Rachel dips a foot into steaming bathwater.

Each wall in the square bathroom is white with a small, rectangular window above the white porcelain tub where Rachel now sits.

A towel wrapped around Rachel's hair, and Sinatra flows steadily with steam throughout the room.

In her hands, a newspaper. She reads Derek's front-page story, and she's fixated on this story's headline—the word "evil"—and she's unsure exactly why.

She sips from her champagne flute, then sets it on the tile floor.

As she reads, drops of water fall from her fingers onto the newspaper. Her foot turns a knob at the other end of the tub, and hot water pours from the faucet.

Rachel turns the newspaper page, memories of trips to Sulphur on her mind, a younger Rachel in the fifties and sixties, summers with friends and family swimming beside a waterfall in the town's natural spring water creek, "Little Niagara."

And, she remembers playing Cowboys and Indians with neighborhood kids near the house where she now lives. Derek filming their Great War on his Super-8 camera, violence spilling from Mesta Park south into neighboring Heritage Hills with its great mansions, then across Northwest 13th Street into downtown Oklahoma City.

Rachel begins singing quietly to herself, "I was five, and he was six. We rode on horses made of sticks." Her voice soft, beautiful, accompanying Sinatra's. "He wore black, and I wore white. He would always win the fight, bang bang." And, on her back, she submerges her entire body, her blue eyes wide under warm water, towel wrapped on her head. She holds her breath, stares at air bubbles seeping from the corner of her mouth, at a torrent of water pouring from the faucet at her feet.

She comes up, wipes water from her face, runs her hand through blonde, wet hair, her white towel floating with her in the tub. She wonders if Derek tried to call.

She looks down at her breasts, her slim twenty-sven-year-old body, scrunches a green sponge in her wrinkling hands. She tosses the sponge into water streaming from the faucet.

She reaches down, turns the knob, and water stops. Sinatra croons, "Music played, and the people sang. Just for me the church bells rang."

She rests her arms outside either side of the tub, her wrists scarred with burn marks and each with a single cut resting on porcelain. "Aujourd'hui, je vais voir mon père. Aujourd'hui, je vais voir mon père. Oggi, vado a vedere mio padre." Holding her champagne flute in her hand, she says to no one, "I am going to see my father today."

* * *

Derek holds open a large wooden door, and Rachel walks through a tall, arched entrance into a church.

In front of them, people milling around a lobby in their Sunday best, talking in hushed sentences and serious tones, exchanging glances in a sea of strained smiles and somber stares. The evening sun sets through stained-glass windows.

Derek places his hand on the small of Rachel's back, the young couple walking politely between strangers. Derek in his slim-fitting suit, Rachel wearing tan pants and a maroon cardigan tied at her waist.

On occasion, older men he doesn't know nod at Derek, and he nods back to them.

Rachel stares at Bible verses painted across walls, ceiling fans swirling furiously above the crowded lobby, people wiping sweat from foreheads, drying eyes with tissue. Rachel flashes caring smiles, but few return this nicety.

An elderly woman whispers to another, "I heard FBI thinks it's someone from the city." Another wearing a sizable purple hat responds tersely, "Not surprised."

A frail old man wearing a brown three-piece suit stands beside a water fountain. He places his hand on a crying woman's shoulder, soothing her.

Inside the auditorium, two young Black boys sit on tightly woven wool carpet in the center aisle. Along the walkway, rows of empty chairs, and the boys move their toy trucks and sports cars across carpeted diamond-shaped patterns. The boys, Luke and Isaiah, recreate crashing noises and revving engines. Battering sounds echo across the spacious room's tall ceilings, the two kids oblivious to people filling the auditorium. Their mother, Alice, decides to let them play longer, exhaust their energy before the service.

Luke scoots his toy truck from one pattern to the next, looks down the middle aisle to the front of the auditorium to a wooden pulpit at the stage's center.

Alice's soft brown hand reaches down for Luke's shoulder. "Come now," her words warm, gentle.

"Where are we going?" Luke asks his mother, his tone respectful, inquisitive.

"To the front row, so we can watch your father deliver his sermon."

"Look, we made a racetrack!" Isaiah exclaims from the floor, tugs at his mother's slim black dress.

Alice smiles. "I see that." She leans over, tucks a strand of her thick black hair behind her ear. "Luke, would you mind helping your little brother move you guys' toys to the front row of chairs, please?"

Luke looks from Alice to his fire truck, Isaiah tracing his red racecar along patterns. Luke reaches out his hand. "Come on, Isaiah," and Isaiah looks up to his brother.

Isaiah can't take his eyes from his toy car, particularly its racing stripes, not even as he takes his big brother's hand.

"Thank you, Luke." Alice tousles Luke's thick brown curls, and the two brothers walk side-by-side in matching black suits to the front of the auditorium, toys in hand.

Walking in their suits, Luke and Isaiah have the auditorium's best view of the pulpit. From the aisle, they see three young men appear on stage from behind black velvet curtains, two of these young men with guitars slung across their chests, the third young man carrying drumsticks. Chatter fills the room. A young woman's emphatic, " … I did call last night … " A young man's, " … But, the Sooners, I don't know … " Another woman's " … God's purpose … " " … Supposedly, police … " "Sorry, I had to get gas … " " … Sarah Simpson, you just look lovely in that dress … "

"Sheriff Ford." A kind, authoritative male voice startles Ryan. He looks away from Dylan helping Sarah to her seat as an older woman compliments her dress. Standing in the center aisle near the front row, Ryan turns to a smiling, fair-skinned, middle-aged man in a brown sweater vest and blue button-up shirt. "Sheriff, I cannot tell you how happy I am you could make it." The man shakes Ryan's hand, his eyes noting Ryan's tan uniform. "Or, are you here in official capacity?"

"A little of both, Pastor." Ryan removes his black sheriff's hat, holds it at his side. "Forgive me, sir. Shoulda taken that off when I came through the door." He looks from Sarah and Dylan to the pulpit. "You doin'' alright, Jacob?"

"Sheriff, that's nasty business in Sulphur. What they did to that boy and his mom. Hard to say I'm alright after such senselessness." Jacob folds his arms. "You bring Sam? Been missing you two around here."

Ryan scratches his head. "Sam's his own man. Does what he does." His sheriff's hat at his side, Ryan nods to the pulpit. "Who's this fella preaching tonight?"

"Wait til you hear him, Ryan." Pastor Jacob glances to the three young men on stage, testing their guitars and drums. "He's just on fire."

The auditorium fills fast, people searching for any remaining seats, deacons scrambling, putting additional chairs at the end of each row. Parishioners stand along a back wall, fanning themselves with church programs—heat in the air nearly visible.

By the time a young man starts strumming his guitar, not a single seat's empty. Across the auditorium, dimming lights.

His guitar fades into a melodic opening of "Amazing Grace" with bass guitar and drums. An occasional sniffle and fits and starts of a crying baby the only other sounds.

From a projector at the back of the auditorium, lyrics for "Amazing Grace" appear on a screen behind the band and pulpit. Shades of blue and purple from track lighting illuminate the stage and screen. In a twangy, tenor voice, the lead guitarist starts singing, "Amazing Grace, how sweet the sound." The young man pauses, a deep breath. "That saved a wretch like me." Then, "I once was lost, but now I'm found. Was blind, but now I see."

The entire congregation joins him, sings the next verse in unison.

One by one, people stand, eyes closed, raising their hands into the air. So it goes for the next fifteen minutes of praise and worship songs.

As the final song concludes, Pastor Jacob walks on stage, his congregation enthusiastically applauding his arrival. Bursts of blue and purple light the entire stage around him. Clapping stretches for minutes, along with calls of "Amen," "Hallelujah," and "Yes, Jesus!"

Pastor Jacob's behind his pulpit, microphone in hand, a circle of white light around him, applause dying down.

"He is good, isn't He?" Pastor Jacob's face full of joy. "God is good."

Shouts of "Amen" across his auditorium.

"Yes, He is. His messengers are on this stage tonight, doing the Lord's work. And, ladies and gentlemen, aren't they wonderful? Can I get an Amen?"

"Amen!"

"Yes, Lord!"

Pastor Jacob smiles. "Yes, Lord, they are wonderful, and He is good."

The three musicians sit in chairs in front of their instruments, drinking bottled water, sweat pouring from their foreheads.

"We have a very special guest pastor with us tonight." Pastor Jacob's words ricochet across the auditorium.

Sheriff Ford slides his hat under his chair, hopes no one's noticed he's not sung a single song.

Pastor Jacob looks across hundreds of people gathered in his church. He glances behind him to a large mural across a wall. "A new church," he says, hands firm on his pulpit. "That's what I promised a year ago, that's what those bold words behind me read, and that's what we're building here together. We named it *A New Church*, because that's what we offer our city— a new relationship with God, opportunity to be born again, to find tranquility in Christ and grace in His Father, rebirth." He looks from words on the wall to his congregation. "I thank each of you for your devotion to this place, for being here, for the love and prayers you give my family. I'm in debt to your patience and kindness. Thank you."

They applaud knowingly.

Jacob holds his mic at his chin. "This weekend, we celebrate our anniversary. Three days of worship, community. Today, we saw our hard work bear fruit. Record attendance for eight a.m. and ten a.m. services. Tonight, we are, for the first time, standing room only."

"Amen!" he hears from the back of the room.

"This evening, a special welcome. My oldest, beautiful daughter, Rachel. Her handsome husband, Derek. A couple weeks ago, these two young people moved back to our city after a decade on our country's West Coast. As you might imagine, I'm delighted to have her and him home and here with us."

Despite herself, Rachel blushes, and her smile reminds Derek why he fell in love with her in the first place.

"Friends," Pastor Jacob says, improvises, "before I introduce our guest pastor, because Lord knows you heard enough from me this morning, I want to say thank you, Sheriff Ryan Ford and his family, for being with us tonight."

Nearly his entire congregation turns collectively, many in quiet disbelief, to Ryan, who wants nothing more than to sink in his seat, but who sits tall like nothing less than a pillar of strength, grit, and charm.

"Dylan and your lovely girlfriend, Sarah, my beautiful niece, my brother's eldest. Thank you both for being such a lovely presence in church this past year, for being incredible youth leaders and role models for your generation."

Sitting composed, Sarah scoots closer to Dylan, and he nods thanks to Pastor Jacob. All Sarah can see is holding open the door for young Ben at The Music Store.

"Ladies and gentlemen, we have a man of God with us." Pastor Jacob, sweat on his forehead, looks across his church's full auditorium. "Tonight, our one-year anniversary, breaking new bread, inviting our first, and hopefully not last, guest pastor to bear witness to our Lord's mercy."

At the back of the auditorium, a side door closes behind Sam as he slides beside an overweight woman fanning herself with her checkbook.

"It's my honor to bring to the far south side of our city a man who's led his church since the day he graduated high school eighteen years ago. I'm privileged to share a pulpit with such a faithful servant, a young father who lives the word of God. With great joy and a humbled heart, I introduce to you this evening's guest pastor."

Behind black curtains, Thomas stands, hand rattling change in his suit pant pocket. His other hand holds open the velvet curtain enough to see Jacob at his wood pulpit and Alice on the front row sitting poised upright, cross-legged in her slim black dress.

"Ladies and Gentlemen, Reverend Thomas Johnson."

He's on stage, bright lights bearing down on the young Black man, a mostly white congregation staring at him in utter silence. His brown leather shoes squeak as he walks across a hollow stage, sheer will propelling his body toward Pastor Jacob. At the pulpit, a firm handshake, Jacob whispering in his ear, "You got this, brother," just before he disappears behind curtains.

Thomas sees Alice's beautiful brown eyes and, for a moment, Thomas and Alice feel as if they're the only people in the room.

Thomas walks behind the tall oak pulpit and, in a calm, commanding voice over a few murmurs, whispers, "Everyone." The room quiets. "Everyone, please," he says again. "Thank you so much for visiting with us this evening."

He walks to the side of the pulpit, stands tall in a tailored navy suit, his short hair trimmed neat. He pulls an envelope from beneath a buttoned-up vest under his suit coat.

"I'm a preacher, and this here is my sermon." He stares down at sheets of white paper in his hand, his words matter of fact. "I won't take much of your time. My oldest son, Matthew, works after church service. And, I promised my lovely wife, Alice, not to drone on so we can have our two little boys, Luke and Isaiah, home before nine-o-clock bedtime."

From the back of the auditorium, through the crowd, Sam notices Alice glance at Luke and Isaiah enamored with their toy cars. Beside them sits Matthew, a light-skinned young Black man with a brown afro.

"But, as you see, the sermon I prepared is nearly five pages. And, since I'm not in the business of upsetting my wife, I'll save what I wrote for another day." His teeth shine bright through a wide, warm smile.

Throughout the room, laughter trickles.

"I hope you'll forgive, then, old-fashioned plain speaking," Thomas says, smiling, toneless, sitting on a barstool at the front of the stage. He tugs at a chain and pocket watch attached to his suit vest. His eyes move across the entire congregation.

"By now, you've heard stories about what's happened down in Sulphur. A boy and his mother. Three college students. Murdered for ninety dollars." He pauses. "This is the state of our state. This is our Main Street today in Oklahoma."

High above him, ceiling fan blades whoosh through air.

"Twenty years ago, I met your pastor on Oklahoma City's Main Street. At sixteen, I got a summer job as a dishwasher downtown. Back then, colored folk could work downtown, but we couldn't live or do business there," Thomas says, his words projecting to the back of the room. "One hot August afternoon, I left work, saw a Black woman leading a group of Black high school students down the middle of the street. So, I followed them up the street to Katz Drug

Store on the corner of Main and Robinson, and I watched them through the store's windows as they sat peacefully at a lunch counter, waiting for service that never came. I followed them every day they marched Main Street, and I watched them return for weeks to that lunch counter, enduring slurs and spit, violence and death threats, hot coffee thrown on them. Then, one day, I watched a thirty-six-year-old white youth pastor stand from his table and demand staff serve these young people he'd never met. Jacob's demand was as peaceful as offering to buy them lunch."

Thomas grabs a glass of water from the pulpit, drinks.

"Katz desegregated their counters, thanks to a thirth-five-year-old Black history teacher leading those students in that peaceful protest. And, I remember afterwards, standing outside the drug store, shaking Jacob's hand, introducing myself and thanking him for doing what I could describe only at the time as the right thing. I told him my father served as a pastor at an all-Black Baptist church on the northeast side of the city where we lived, and he invited my dad to come preach at his church the next week. I looked him square in his eyes, said, 'Boy, is you crazy?'"

Faint laughter across the auditorium, Jacob smiling in the front row, transported twenty years ago to summer 1958.

"Jacob's response was to laugh and say, 'you and your father meet me Sunday on Main Street. We're going to worship together.' The following week, my father and I met Jacob downtown. With a handful of elders and young folk from my father's congregation, we marched, hand-in-hand with Jacob, peacefully. Finally, when we arrived at Jacob's church, his pastor told us, 'God did not intend Negroes and whites to worship together.' Holding only his bible, my father told him, 'I will go anywhere people want to hear the words of Jesus.' So, he preached."

Applause, heat thickening as people fan themselves with church programs and whatever they can find in purses and pockets.

Thomas looks to Isaiah, his son's tapered fade haircut and toy truck. He folds his arms across his brawny chest, the auditorium quiet. "To everything, there's a season, and a time to every purpose. A time to be born, and a time to die; a time to plant, and a time to pluck up that which we plant."

His words flow across the auditorium, rhythmically, from one person to the next, to an old woman who's not stopped crying since she read Derek's news story with her Sunday morning coffee, to Sheriff Ford and memories of his wife, to Sam and thoughts of working his family farm.

"A time to kill, and a time to heal; a time to break down, and a time to build up. A time to weep, and a time to laugh; a time to mourn, and a time to dance. A time to cast away stones, and a time to gather stones together; a time to embrace and a time to refrain from embracing. A time to get, and a time to sew; a time to keep silence, and a time to speak. A time to love, and a time to hate; a time of war, and a time of peace."

Sam leans on wooden double doors at the other end of the auditorium, the back of his head against stained-glass, his eyes closed.

"Moreover, I saw under the sun the place of judgment, that wickedness was there; and the place of righteousness, that iniquity was there. I said in mine heart, God shall judge the righteous and the wicked; for there is a time for every purpose, for every work."

Dylan caresses Sarah's palm in his hand, her eyes on Thomas.

"I no longer understand this place where I live. Where we murder a child in our small towns. Katz Drug Store demolished, Main Street deserted, downtown abandoned."

Sarah grips Dylan's hands.

"Something wicked comes our way," says Thomas, "because we've lost *our way*. Until that Sunday morning downtown with Jacob and my father, I was lost. I started ministry work twenty years ago this Sunday and, for all these years since, I sat with God, watching with Him as our city killed our downtown with demolition and wrecking balls, promising skyscrapers and shopping malls, watching with Him elderly Black men and women who marched downtown with Jacob and me live today in houses behind metal bars on windows, afraid of Black gangs and drugs on their streets, scared in neighborhoods on a northeast side of our city they no longer recognize, the family under attack, and I asked Him why our children can no longer pray in school, heard Him weep for every baby a young woman kills in her womb, because no one teaches her wrong from right, wept with Him about men marrying men, because these are, in fact, the times in which we now live."

Thomas stands silent, stares stoically at a standing-room only congregation.

"It's time for a revival in our city," Thomas preaches, "for us to worship together and turn away from wickedness. A time to rededicate our city, ourselves to God, to His son, Jesus."

Thunderous applause across the auditorium washes over the crowd.

"Together, we offer this place rebirth." Thomas' hands clasp tight in front of him. "We can, once more, live right with God. We can be born again Christians."

Sheriff Ford scratches stubble on his chin, puts his hat on his lap, folds his arms.

"Our work begins tonight in this church," Thomas explains. "It starts with you standing and walking to this stage, dedicating your life to the true God, accepting His son, Jesus Christ, as your personal Lord and savior."

At first, only one or two people stand, then a young married couple in the back row. An elderly man with a thick white beard rolls his wheelchair down the center aisle. A teen in his sports letter jacket stands, offers to help the elderly man the rest of the way to the stage. The old man accepts. Then, one by one, more people stand, leaving purses under seats and church programs on chairs. Dylan sits holding Sarah's hand, awed watching people make their way to Thomas and the stage, becoming born again just as he and Sarah did a year earlier after his mother's death. Minutes later, hundreds of people surround the stage, standing between rows of empty seats, their hands in the air, sweat on their faces.

"Everything happens for a reason," Thomas tells them. "Every tragedy, His plan. Every blessing, also His."

Sam's fists clinch, palms sweating, balled-up fury. He feels unhinged. He turns to leave, pushes open one of the heavy wood doors with such force as he walks, the door swings violently back at him. He catches and slams it shut, banging it closed, cracks a stained-glass painting on the door where his head rested, a cracking thud reverberating throughout the church.

* * *

Two hours later, the steady hum of a vacuum cleaner is the only sound in the church auditorium. An older Guatemalan woman, the only person remaining, moves the turquoise Electrolux vacuum back and forth down the center aisle, where hundreds of people stood in exultation at the promise of new life.

On the oak pulpit sits Thomas' sermon and empty water glass. The first page begins, "I hope you will forgive, then, just old-fashioned plain speaking."

CHAPTER FIVE

Rachel sits on the red brick retaining wall surrounding the back porch of her 1920s bungalow. She stares into darkness at gable roofs on neighboring houses, at leaves rustling. A mile east, a horn piercing night as a train makes its way south across the city.

Through an open glass sliding door, Rachel can see inside their bedroom, a lamp dim yellow on the nightstand beside their bed. The train horn blares. From the porch, she watches Derek loosen his tie as he walks from a closet through a pair of French doors, disappearing into the hallway. Behind him, light flashes from the bathroom on the bedroom's plank wood floors.

Her bare feet on cool brick, Rachel clasps her cardigan around her, her back against a square porch column. She closes her eyes to the sound of Derek's voice carrying confidently from the bedroom.

"Right now, the Oklahoma State Bureau of Investigation is asking people around the area to keep watch for a '72 Oldsmobile station wagon," she hears Derek say on television to a newscaster. "They tell me FBI arrives Monday to assist OSBI and local law enforcement and, really, that's when we'll see this investigation expand statewide."

"I sound so nervous," Derek says from the bedroom.

"Yes, but it's charming," Rachel says.

Derek shouts over running water from inside the house, "What time's your new gig at the library start?"

"She said eight a.m. I need to check the schedule, though." Rachel glances into their empty bedroom.

"I can drop you off downtown on my way to the funeral. Did the mechanic say when your car would be ready?"

"Not 'til Thursday."

"I'm sure we can manage with one car 'til then. Feeling good about your first day?"

"Short an old-fashioned Bonfire of the Vanities book burning, I can't imagine anything too exciting," she says, an owl hooting nearby. "Basically, I'm babysitting a downtown library hardly anyone really seems to visit."

"Well, you're going to be the best babysitter this town has ever seen."

Rachel smiles, her eyes studying shadowy outlines of Red Oak and Bradford Pear trees in her backyard. Her thoughts drift to the sermon at her father's church, to Derek's front-page news story.

"How many people you think actually read *The Oklahoman?*" She looks to the open French Doors, waits for Derek to walk through them.

"Don't know," he answers. "It's statewide, and it's Sunday, so prolly a lot today. Why?"

"Just curious."

Warm wind blows her blonde hair, images in her head from church and the people watching Derek, introducing themselves to him, congratulating him, looking past her, smiling at him as if he were a celebrity. She's surprised anyone would even recognize the journalist who wrote the article, but then she remembers Derek's appearances all day on every local television channel, each broadcasting his name, his face, and the same phrase, "An Unspeakable Evil."

Faucet water stops, a television commercial the only sound in their bedroom.

Silence passes between them for some time.

Rachel looks out into the night, wants to ask Derek if the newspaper publishes his contact information, phone number, home address, wonders if the killer read Derek's story about the murders, saw Derek on the morning and evening news.

"What time's the funeral?" she asks instead, still sitting on the brick retaining wall, placing a blade of grass on her leg.

Behind her, light in the hallway disappears, leaving only a dimly lit bedroom.

She looks at French Doors, waits for Derek to appear, to say something. Instead, wind chimes and the television interview.

She stares at plank wood floors in front of a pitch-black hallway, waits for a creaking noise, realizes she has not heard Derek's voice since the water turned off in the bathroom, wonders again if the newspaper published their home address.

Floorboards creak, and Derek walks from the hallway into their bedroom in boxers and his button-up shirt, toothbrush in his mouth, and he turns off the television.

He looks to Rachel on their porch, toothpaste on his lips, his mouth full, slurring, "Did you say something?"

CHAPTER SIX

Dylan's in his driver seat, Sarah staring from her rolled down passenger window at a nighttime procession of headlights cruising 12th Street. Dylan's '68 Plymouth Roadrunner turns into a restaurant parking lot packed with automobiles. From his car's speakers, the rhythmic opening guitar riff on "Good Times Roll," its synthesizers, electronic drums, and lyrics filling the street. Speakers from the restaurant's roof blaring the same song. Across the roof, "Sonic Service with the Speed of Sound" lit on a neon sign. Dylan drives into a covered dining stall.

A half-hour passes, and Sarah's sitting on a metal truck bed, bites into a foot-long chili cheese hotdog, her legs dangling from the pickup's tailgate. A parade of vehicles disembark from the park surrounding her. High school boys hanging from car windows, coordinating on CB radios their destination, whooping and hollering at girls, automobiles by the dozens heading west, circling through Sonic's parking lot, then back onto 12th Street.

Headlights lull Sarah into a daze, blurring with Moore High School letter jackets stitched royal blue and red. Behind her in the truck bed, a gust of strong wind sways a muddied dirt bike strapped by its handlebars to both sides of a brand-new Ford Ranger. Shoepolished on a passing car, "Every tragedy His plan."

Their beers in hand, Dylan and Tate stand beside Tate's Ford Ranger, Dylan with his surfer-blonde bangs swept to the side, his crimson t-shirt with Greek fraternity letters and OU stretched across his well-built chest, Tate tapping Dylan's shoulder. Behind him, Dylan hears a car engine rev. He turns, sees Cristine's red Porsche 911 brake suddenly to a stop beside Tate's truck, its windows down, music loud.

"Well, goddamn, if I ain't never seen finer specimens of human beings," Cristine says with her country drawl. Her Porsche still running, she leaps from her car in a breezy summer dress past Dylan. She jumps, sitting on Tate's tailgate, scoots beside Sarah.

"These six-hour Sunday shifts," she sighs, her hand through her straight brown hair. "My boss schedules us at eleven, and the mall opens at noon, so no shopping before work." She grabs yarn from her knitting bag. "And, of course, we never leave til seven, and the mall closes at six, so no shopping after work, either. Meaning Sundays, which should be summer retail paradise, unlimited access to every imaginable store, I'm stuck finding fitting rooms, folding clothes, checking sizes, trying not to scream at terrible parents letting awful kids reenact the Battle of Helm's Deep at the Dillard's makeup counter."

Sarah bites into her chilidog.

"My reward?" continues Cristine. "Minimum wage, and a half-hour lunch break which, naturally, I took full advantage of today, got my ears pierced again."

Tate looks to Dylan, points to Cristine, holds up two fingers, plays a mock violin.

Dylan spits out his beer, and Cristine rolls her eyes. "That's easy for you to say, Tate," she signs to him. "You're deaf."

Silent, Tate laughs, and he looks to Dylan, traces his index fingers from his eyes down his cheeks.

For the first time since learning about the Sulphur murders, Sarah's face glows, a familiar reaction around Dylan and Tate, best friends since kindergarten. To help her son with stuttering—and, to prevent five-year-old Sam from further fist fights defending his brother—Dylan and Sam's mother enrolled Dylan at Sulphur's Oklahoma School for the Deaf. Tate's parents, first-generation

Japanese immigrants who moved from California to Oklahoma following the Second World War, found themselves surprised when their son, who was as shy as he was hearing impaired, asked after school one day if he could hike Arbuckle Mountains, swim Turner Falls with his new friend, Dylan, and Dylan's family.

The two boys grew inseparable—sports, playing war, four wheelers and dirt bikes, reading westerns and comics with Sam. Each summer after ten-year-old Dylan moved, his mother drove him to Sulphur to spend time with Tate and, eventually, Dylan brought along his new city friend, Sarah.

Watching Dylan and Tate tonight, Sarah wishes her camera wasn't in Dylan's car, Tate's wavy black hair shaping his elegant face, his build more muscular than earlier in the school year, his tank top with a young girl fishing from a wooden bridge surrounded with pink and white cherry blossoms, his golden brown skin in moonlight.

"Hey, will one of you gentlemen grab another beer for me, please?" Cristine's knitting needle weaves through yarn.

Tate shrugs, walks toward an ice chest at the front of his truck.

With a napkin, Sarah wipes chili from her lips, scoots closer to Cristine. "Lemme see your ears," she says, forces a smile.

"What're y'all fixin' to get into?" Cristine asks.

"You're looking at it," Dylan says, arms outstretched. "Living the dream."

Tate tosses a beer to Cristine, joins Dylan beside his pickup.

"Thank you," she says, smiles mid-catch. She flicks the cap spinning from her beer. "Good ole boys got themselves a bonfire going out in Choctaw. If y'all are interested." She nods her beer to Dylan. "Heard Sam freaked out in church tonight."

Sarah's eyes dart to Dylan and Tate.

Cristine shakes her head. "All this Sulphur shit's got everyone on edge, man."

"Oh, goodness, Sarah!" Tate interrupts, rotates his hand on his chest clockwise. His dark brown eyes expressive, he signs, "I'm so sorry. I completely forgot. Weren't you and Sam in Sulphur yesterday?"

Sarah looks from Dylan to a crumpled food wrapper in her hands. She signs back, "We ended up at Arbuckle Mountains, instead, decided to camp there."

"Thank Christ." Tate's hands clasp his heart. He signs, "I just, for a second ... I thought you two drove down there for your photo project."

Sarah signs back to him. "Good thing we didn't, huh?"

"Hmph." Cristine takes a swig from her beer, stares strangely at Sarah. "Lucky girl."

* * *

Half-past midnight, two wooden doors with stained-glass windows dissolve into an image of Jimmy Stewart's Scotty sitting in his suit at a restaurant bar. He stares over his shoulder across a bustling dining room with rose-colored walls.

Dylan and Sarah sit silhouetted in Dylan's car, his arm wrapped around her.

Through his windshield, rows of parked vehicles and a giant movie screen. A drive-in speaker attached to his windows, the sound of silverware clinking plates, conversations. On screen, a man wearing a tux sits across from Kim Novak's Madeleine at a candlelit table. Behind the movie screen, silhouettes of tall trees swaying in the dark.

Sarah leans over to Dylan, "I'm gonna grab some snacks, want anything?"

"No thanks, I'm good."

"Okay, be right back." She kisses him on his cheek.

Outside Dylan's car, Sarah walks to violins playing through speakers across the parking lot. She sees a young couple laughing in a station wagon, kissing. Sarah looks past them to Scotty on screen watching Madeline.

Sarah slips change into a coin slot, a payphone receiver resting on her shoulder. Behind her on screen, a close-up of Madeleine's face and blonde hair, the dining room's rose-colored wallpaper glowing red, Scotty trying not to stare at Madeleine, the soundtrack swelling with strings.

The phone picks up on the other end. Sam's voice startles Sarah. "You've reached the Ford residence," he says, first time she's heard Sam since breakfast. "Sorry, we're not home right now ... " She resists an urge to bite her nails.

She sighs after the recording stops. "Sam, it's Sarah. Just calling." She removes the receiver from her ear, then hears Sam's "Sarah?"

Behind the concession stand, a neon, forty-foot cowboy stands tall into the night. A rope of cursive writing spells out Winchester, then Drive-In Theater below, flashing green. Beneath the rope, a bright white sign reading, "Midnight Screening. *Vertigo*. Happy July 4! Thanks for 10 Years, Oklahoma City!" Beside these words, the cowboy in his brown boots, blue pants, red shirt. His hand waves into the night. In his other hand, a shotgun.

CHAPTER SEVEN

The speedometer flutters eighty-five, ninety—his cowboy boot hard on the gas. Sam's airborne in his pickup truck, his body in free fall, his stomach sinking, warm wind rushing his face, Sarah laughing lifted from a bench seat. His truck tires slam against asphalt.

His old pickup rips through night air, this sound his only respite from a pitcher of orange juice shattering to a wood table. His pickup roars up a next paved hill. He stomps again on his accelerator.

Out here, a dozen miles east of his city, the downtown skyline disappears, replaced with wooded hills and stars in the sky.

On these country roads, his mother taught him how to drive when he was twelve, four years after she taught him to drive a tractor and combine harvester.

He's no longer speeding, his hands at ten and two. Only headlights, yellow stripes, and darkness ahead.

Sam's walking with Sarah, gravel crunching beneath his boots. He rolls up the sleeves on his plaid pearl-snap shirt.

Sarah watches hundreds of people of all ages in western wear. Black cowboys, Vaqueros with belt buckles, starched shirts, pressed jeans, Native Americans in cowboy hats and boots. Her floral church dress waving with warm wind, Sarah looks above her at Spencer Rodeo in bold letters on a banner across a makeshift parking lot. Beside her, a Black teen girl gallops on a spotted horse.

Behind a ticket booth, flood lights shine on horses kicking up dirt, riders racing around an arena replacing images in Sam's mind of Sheriff Ford standing in the kitchen, Sheriff Ford asking Sam and Sarah to lie about being in Sulphur the day of the murders.

"That's right. Turn him loose," says a man across speakers. "Ride and swerve, cowboy, ride and swerve."

Behind a metal rail, Sam and Sarah walk through a crowd. Sam's thoughts racing to his first trip to Oklahoma City, the night his father took him to the National Rodeo Finals at the Oklahoma State Fair Arena. At age seven, Sam waits to see if Freckles Brown, a forty-six-year-old cowboy from Wyoming, can ride Tornado, an "unrideable," 1,600-pound bull, for a full eight seconds. Five years earlier, Freckles won a world bull riding championship, but not before a 2,000-pound bull knocked him to dirt and broke his neck. A young Sam listens to an announcer, " … on a bull never been ridden … if you believe he can, he will." Freckles and Tornado barrel out chute number two. Flash of a strobe-light camera. Tornado bucking, spinning violently. Freckles' fist in air, his body straightened on the bull's back, four seconds, five seconds. Six thousand people screaming, cheering to deafening applause. Whistle blows eight seconds. Freckles lands on his feet, Sam's fist in the air. Sam reads every news article he finds on the rodeo finals. The next three years, a daily exercise in how to walk, talk, and act like his cowboy hero. He learns Freckles reads, so Sam takes to books, everything from westerns to *X-Men* comics, classic literature, all to his mother's approval.

Thunder rumbles through gathering clouds above Spencer Rodeo. Sam twists the cap on his silver flask. Whiskey burns his throat.

The announcer's voice, "When that gate comes open, Oklahoma, put your hands together, make as much noise as you can for Matthew Johnson."

Sarah drinks from her stainless steel water bottle. She feels a drop of rain.

A gate swings open to shouts from the stands. A 1,500-pound bull spins furiously to Matthew's left, pounds the ground, kicks up dirt, sends Matthew's black cowboy hat through night air, six seconds, seven seconds, thunder through the arena.

Sam squints, his eyes fixed on the light-skinned young Black man on his back in dirt. Horn blows eight seconds.

Matthew scrambles to his feet, wipes dirt from his afro and face, his sleeveless shirt and well-defined arms. He leaps over a metal guardrail out of the arena to a cheering crowd, the bull behind him.

Sarah leaps to her feet, looks to Sam.

"Seven seconds, ladies and gentlemen!" the announcer shouts to applause, "And, a new record for Oklahoma City's own Matthew Johnson."

From the stands, Sam sees Matthew disappear into a crowd of handshakes and men patting him on the back.

Then, Sam recognizes him, Pastor Thomas' oldest son, the one who sat silently, wept at the end of his father's sermon.

CHAPTER EIGHT

Waking up, he hears steady raindrops tap his bedroom window. Sheriff Ryan Ford's eyes open, barely four hours of sleep. His back aches. A familiar pain in his right knee. His feet touch cold plank wood, then his hands. Half-asleep, fifty push-ups, a hundred crunches.

He lumbers in boxers toward his bathroom, splashes water on his face, stares at himself in an oval mirror, his hands on the rim of a porcelain sink. His blue eyes look back at his lean upper body, studies, as if for the first time, his toned, hairy chest, a knife scar long across his well-defined abs. His hand moves across his face, searches for the twenty-one-year-old who flew fighter planes in the Second World War, the thirty-year-old sheriff's deputy who married the love of his life, kept safe the streets of Sulphur. He finds, instead, this fifty-eight-year-old version of himself.

He shaves his cheek with a steel straight razor, just above his five o' clock stubble, just as he watched his father do. He wipes his face with a warm towel. He turns on water in a shower stall.

An alarm clock flashes on a nightstand, seven a.m.

In his black sheriff's uniform thirty minutes later, Ryan sits on his side of the bed. He takes a silver watch from the nightstand, glances at an old photo of her smiling with him, her name engraved beside his across a copper frame, Mary Mae.

In his kitchen, he pours a cup of coffee, his back sore from sleeping last night downtown at his desk, four thirty to five a.m., then driving home, sleeping for another hour. From the kitchen sink, he looks out the window at Sam trudging through light rain toward their barn. Ryan sips from his coffee mug. Nearly forty-eight hours since the Sulphur murders.

Driving south on I-35, Sheriff Ford passes over a barren river separating downtown from his city's south side. Rain falls from a cloudy blue sky on his windshield, evaporates soon as it hits glass.

From his rolled-down driver's side window, he stares through sepia-tinted sunglasses at two men on John Deere tractors mowing grass where a river once flowed, hot wind from the south carrying smells from nearby stockyards into his car, tastes in his mouth humidity and rain-cut grass, in his rearview mirror six traffic lanes of I-40 cut through downtown east-to-west, skyscrapers in a haze giving way to heavy-metal industrial sprawl, billboards, abandoned oil derricks, oilfield supply yards, one-story strip malls, fast food, pawnshops, strip clubs, gas stations, endless non-descript motels.

Motels.

He uses his police radio, sends a deputy sheriff driving along I-35 to motels between his city's downtown and the interstate's Southwest 89th Street exit, an invisible line where his jurisdiction as Oklahoma County Sheriff ends. Along the way, the deputy sheriff makes copies of every guest registry. If whoever committed the Sulphur murders is a drifter, which Ryan reasons is plausible, it's likely this person drifted from Sulphur into a motel on I-35, specifically somewhere between the ninty miles separating the small town from Oklahoma City.

This work requires cooperation with law enforcement in every county between Sulphur and the city. Ryan's certain he can coordinate such an effort through Oklahoma State Bureau of Investigations and highway patrol.

Then, the problem of I-240, particularly its possible hiding places.

Constructed in 1965 a mile north from rural Southwest 89th Street, I-240 forms Oklahoma City's southern-most border, four east-west traffic lanes separating new neighborhoods to the north from endless fields and the Ford family farm to the south.

Worrying Ryan, I-240 intersects with I-35 in the shape of a cross at Crossroads Mall. At Crossroads Mall, I-240 splits west along chain restaurants and car dealerships for six miles, turning north past an airport and forms the urban core's western border, then turns east shaping the core's northern border before reconnecting to I-35, creating a giant loop around the state's capitol city and its neighborhoods. Hundreds of square miles within Sheriff Ford's Oklahoma County jurisdiction.

Ryan thinks about Crossroads Mall, where 240 also splits east for thirteen miles through fields and rural suburbs developed in the late 1940s, past a General Motors factory and air force base where Ryan trained during the war and met his wife.

Police cars are parked along Muskogee Avenue, Sulphur's once quiet Main Street. Traffic cones set up between First and Fourth Street.

At the end of the blockade, an intersection where a four-story hotel once stood, a luxury hotel built in 1906 where Oklahoma's first governor lived during summers, where the wealthy and actors like John Wayne visited til the building burnt to ash in 1962.

At the other end of the blockade, an old two-story mansion built by a former Sulphur sheriff in 1924 across the street from a First Christian Church, the place where ten-year-old Benjamin Bullock studied two gold lanterns affixed to an arched wooden entrance a half hour before his murder.

Standing on steps leading to the mansion, Ryan asks two lone highway patrolmen, "Sheriff Garrett around?"

"He's out back, puking," responds a young patrolman. "Been puking all weekend."

The other patrolman slaps him hard on his shoulder. "Don't tell folk that."

"What? He's the first I told. It's true anyhow," the patrolman's thick Texas accent in each word. He rubs his shoulder.

"Show me where," Ryan says.

Trees surrounding him, Murray County Sheriff Bill Garrett spits in a creek. His arthritic hand against an elm, his other hand on his knee. He hears branches cracking.

"You seen it yet?" Bill asks, his words gravelly, rough. "Been in there?"

Ryan looks past trees to police cars parked along Muskogee. He takes a deep breath. "Yeah, Bill. I saw it."

Eighty-year-old Bill Garrett's eyes squeeze shut. "I was right there, Sheriff. Across the street. I'd been talking to Stella Bullock right before. I was right there." He blinks a tear.

"Bill," Ryan says, "I'll need you to walk with me to the church."

The two men say nothing as they walk along Muskogee til they reach the end of the blockade at First Street. In their silence, Ryan remembers patrolling Muskogee Avenue as Sheriff Garrett's deputy. He sees himself on a date with his wife, sharing a milkshake with her at a pharmacy diner, putting their bill on a monthly tab, walking their small sons to their first film at Carousel Theater. Then, an evening eight years ago, Bill asking Ryan not to move from Sulphur, not to leave the town the same way the pharmacy and movie theater left.

"Fifty uniformed officers in town the first night," Bill says. "Men from Ada, Davis, down in Dougherty. By two a.m., we flooded the area with search lights, put police shoulder-to-shoulder patrolling Saturday night, then again Sunday through dusk. Been out in the park with state boys, looking for clues, more bodies, they don't know what. Helicopters above our town past two nights. We're calling in another homicide unit, two more detectives, more detectives to do interviews, crime lab. We're pulling out all the stops."

Bill glares at the end of Muskogee, reporters and spectators gathering in front of a beige brick two-story First Baptist Church.

Ryan stops, turns to Bill. "And, John Bullock?"

Bill looks to Ryan. "In church about to bury his boy at noon, I reckon."

From back of the church auditorium an hour later, Ryan watches John Bullock, stares at his buzz cut, John's arm wrapped around his elderly mother, her winter white hair, a small wooden casket in front of a nave. "Blessed are they who mourn," says a young pastor, "for they shall be comforted." His words flow across 500 mourners standing along walls, sitting in pews. "Even so, it is not the will of your Father, which is in heaven, that one of these little ones should perish. Peace I leave with you. My peace I give unto you: not as the world giveth, give I unto you. Let not your heart be troubled, neither let it be afraid."

Inside the church following the funeral, Ryan signs "Ford Family" on a guest list in an empty lobby. Behind him, glass doors swing open to the sound of flash bulbs, sobs, reporters yelling questions on the church lawn to two FBI agents and Sheriff Garrett.

"Will Sulphur remain on nighttime curfew?"

"Yes," says Sheriff Garrett.

"How long?"

"Can't say."

"Any suspects in custody?"

"No."

"Any leads?"

"No, but Oklahoma State Bureau of Investigation agents started work this morning with FBI to check and cross reference criminal records. We also have crime lab specialists, searching the store for fingerprints."

"Any luck finding the knife used in the murders?"

"No."

"The gun?"

"No."

"Derek Clover with *The Daily Oklahoman*. Any leads on witnesses?"

"None we know of, Mr. Clover," Bill responds, "but detectives interviewed business owners on Muskogee, where one woman describes gunfire round about half past three. Nobody else, however, heard gunshots."

"Anyone see vehicles?" Derek asks. "Any leads there?"

"A business owner on Muskogee reports seeing a 1972 Oldsmobile station wagon with wood grain sides parked in front of The Music Store Saturday afternoon. But, no evidence exists connecting it to the murders."

A woman's voice, "Is it true officers are doing block-to-block searches in surrounding neighborhoods?"

"Within a two-mile radius, yes."

"Is it true the killer took a video surveillance tape?"

"Yes."

"Any other businesses have security cameras that might've caught something?"

"No, ma'am."

"Is it true Paul Hanson's father, Virgil Hanson, The Music Store's owner, posted a $10,000 reward that other businesses on Muskogee matched?"

"Not gonna comment on private matters, ma'am."

"Who'll be in charge of the murder investigation?" Derek asks.

"FBI Agent Adler Kenway, a longtime Murray County resident, will lead a three-agent task force, assigned only to this case with assistance from our city and county."

At the bottom of a steel staircase behind the church, Ryan listens to the news conference continue on the other side of the building. At the top of the stairs, John Bullock closes a metal door behind him, sunlight bright across his pale freckled face.

"Takes a funeral, huh?" John says, his words fragile, cigarette firm between his lips, first time he's seen Ryan in eight years. He removes his suit coat, strikes a match, sits on a steel stair shaded from the sun in his fitted button-up, black slacks, loosens his tie. He takes a long drag, stares with heavy bloodshot eyes at stairs leading down to Sheriff Ford. He senses Ryan can't look at him, and he's right.

Ryan remembers John Bullock at eighteen-years-old working at Carousel Theater. Deputy Ryan then, buying two tickets for his sons. Sitting on the steel stairs ten years later, John remembers cigarette breaks at the movie theater, talking his favorite New Hollywood and French New Wave films in the parking lot with high school sweetheart, Stella Stanley.

Staring at the distant forest, John says to Ryan, "Sorry to hear about your wife, Sheriff. She taught me to read." His hand trembles. He smokes quickly from his cigarette, flicks it to the brick church. "I was out on an oil rig, Sheriff. When it happened." He rubs his buzzed-cut hair. "How do you handle it, sir, everyone looking at you all the time?"

"Folk stare at me?" Ryan forces a smile, turns to green hills behind him, his eyes following a police helicopter over the forest. He realizes, until John Bullock, no one has ever asked him that question.

Through his windshield, the sky grows gray. Ryan drives to steady drops of rain pelting his police car. His back aches again, his thoughts drifting to Sam and Sarah. He turns on his police radio, his car heading north from the highway onto I-35.

* * *

The child stands barefoot in dirt, gray clouds thickening to the south, his father tightening a saddle to a horse in front of him. Cold rain drizzles on the boy's arm.

"Go inside, son," his father commands from his horse, his words tight-lipped, stern. The boy watches his father say something German in the beast's ear, and the two creatures take off, the horse stomping furiously south across farmland, kicking up dust toward a distant small town.

He hears a horn blare, the train sound the boy loves.

Rain falls sudden and heavy all around the boy, pings a metal roof on his house, batters the ground.

He's five, and his eyes remain obsessed with his father riding, the horse galloping in rain through dust and dirt.

Gray clouds darken, and warm air rushes upward. Wind sweeps from the south, roaring and rushing at him all at once with fence posts and branches. His mother's hand grabs his, yanks him toward her, strong winds silencing her screams. Behind them, thrashing charcoal-colored clouds reach down, cut violent into the earth.

In his home, he's pissing himself, frightened, pants wet, his jaw vibrating, floorboards beneath him loosening, grandfather clock levitating, his mother's body over his, wind hacking his skin, ripping his roof into a whirlwind of debris, his house carrying them into air.

"What's your name?" a man asks, his voice throaty, snaps his mud-crusted fingers at the child.

The boy stares blank, the night air still, the rain gone. His face plastered with filth and vomit, the roof ripped from his home the last thing he remembers, and he cannot find words to speak. So, he disappears into a yellow light staring at him. He says nothing when the man asks more firmly, "What's your name, boy?"

Half his town's dark, the other crackling on fire. He sits on a chair at a train depot. He hears the man say hoarsely, "Stay with him," a flashlight flicking off, ringing in the boy's head. The man's voice muffled, noises hollow on the train platform.

A warm, wet cloth on his forehead, wipes his left eyebrow, stings, sounds echoing, his jaw sore. Grown men confused and dirt-covered around him.

He can barely hear a woman's voice say, " … brave boy," Her hand wipes the cloth across his cheeks.

He hears the man again, " … over at the grade school," the man's hands at waist. He spits tobacco to the ground, wipes snuff from his mouth, his voice distorted and rough, " … clearing rubble … railroad repair yard gone … school kids buried … "

Another man, " … cyclone … night soon … coming back … " The boy's body stiffens from the neck down. He turns to the man.

The woman places her soft hand under the boy's chin, trying to force his head from the two men's conversation. He resists.

"Now, don't worry none about any of that." Her voice soothing. "Just you focus on the weight of my words," she says, turns his head slowly toward her.

Their eyes meet.

"Ford," he says, finally.

She grins, rests the cloth at a clear spot on his pale cheek. "Well, Ford."

"Ryan Ford," his little voice low, matter of fact. He bows his head to wood beams just beneath his muddied feet.

On a train to St. Louis three hours later, he sits fatherless with his mother, gauze bandaged across the entire left side of his face. "Sharecropper's son," he hears. "White trash, bastard, heading to southeast Oklahoma, coal mines."

The cyclone, he learns from train passengers, began at one p.m. in rural Ellington, a small town in southeast Missouri, where it killed a farmer. Fourteen minutes later, four more people dead in Annapolis, where it destroyed most of the town before traveling ninety miles to Biehle, a small village where German Catholic immigrants settled in the 1840s.

In Biehle, at two o' clock, the storm spun into two funnels and tore a roof from a church, ripped homes apart, killed another four people. At two thirty, the two funnels crossed the Mississippi River into Illinois, throwing golf-ball sized hail, then roaring into one massive cyclone, obliterating every building in Gorham, killing 37 of the town's 500 people.

The 12,000 living in Murphysboro had no warning when the mile-wide cyclone struck an hour later, set fire to the boy's hometown and collapsed a grade school into rubble on half its 450 students, killing over 200 people, including his young father.

From Murphysboro, the cyclone continued east another two punishing hours, into De Soto, then Bush, stabbing boards into the town's water tower, then cutting electricity to West Frankfort, a small mining community, forcing miners to climb to the surface from a 500-foot underground shaft.

The storm crossed another river into Indiana, having now traveled across three states and, with growing intensity, it twisted into three cyclones, reducing to ruins the town of Griffin, razing half of Princeton, Indiana to the ground before vanishing into clouds a few miles southeast of Petersburg. The whole thing, Ryan learns on the train, lasted just over three-and-a-half hours.

* * *

Rain taps his windshield. Sheriff Ford's in his driver seat, staring at his farmhouse, his sunglasses in his lap.

Time's slipped past. His brown hair speckled gray in his rearview mirror, two hours on I-35 gone. And, sitting here, he has only one thought: how, on one afternoon in 1925, one cyclone became three?

CHAPTER NINE

An electric motor cranks on. A pumpjack horse head nods up and down, up and down, pushing and pulling a long metal rod into the earth.

Behind the pumpjack, flat grasslands far west into gray cloudy sky. Dylan stares at rotating counterweights, rain hitting his hardhat and face.

How to keep Sarah safe? Dylan sees only the Sulphur murders. Brutality. The ten-year-old boy. How Sarah might've been in that store were it not for fate, for God. That God could take Sarah and his mother within the same year, he can't imagine. What if the Sulphur killer saw Sarah when she was in The Music Store? What about his brother? What if the killer saw Sam? Why'd Sam wait a year to scatter his part of their mother's ashes? Why'd Sarah go to Sulphur with Sam while Dylan drank beer at the lake, rode jet skis with his new fraternity brothers?

These questions punch Dylan in the gut each time he hears Sarah say, "We were there yesterday."

Last year—his first summer in oilfields as a roustabout—Dylan did grunt work. Helping with cleanup. Hooking up tank batteries. Threading pipe with a manual threader. After a month, Dylan starts work as a pumper, and his boss gives him a work truck. Reliant, competent, he drives across western Oklahoma, one rural town to the next in his new pickup, checking compressors and pumpjacks, checking water oil levels, gauging tanks, writing down sales and line pressure, bringing back information to his boss. If compressors at sites are down, he starts them. He calls in water trucks to haul, whatever else needs doing.

At age twelve, Dylan starts fixing cars at an auto body shop Sarah's father owns, learns to ride dirt bikes with Tate. At thirteen, he can change oil in any automobile. At seventeen, when he first steps foot on an oilfield, he has a complex understanding of combustion engines. At eighteen, Dylan watches rotating counterweights, worries about protecting Sarah, rain hitting his hardhat and face.

"Call me Sandra," an older woman says, her words raspy like a lifelong smoker. "Like the *a* in ant, not an *o* in on." Inside a job site trailer, Dylan walks past roughnecks huddled at his office manager's desk. "Today's your first day," she explains to the roughnecks. "So, I'll tell you the same as I tell all men their first day." Dylan slips his punch card in a tan timeclock.

He smirks, remembering her swearing at a trust fund kid from South Tulsa for mispronouncing her name.

"Have a good Fourth, Sandra," Dylan says, like the *a* in ant.

"Uh-huh, Ford. You, too." A metal trailer door bangs shut behind him.

Hours pass, Dylan's black Roadrunner parks in front of a beige brick building.

No other cars, no more rain. He walks under a steel gallery, its support columns framing the entrance to a two-story western wear store.

At an intersection, he crosses a wet street in work boots. He walks on a sidewalk along brick buildings selling saddles, prescriptions, and farm supplies. He drops change in a homeless man's cup, says, "God Bless you." Behind him at the intersection, a tall brick gate with a flat arch across a narrow street. Across the arch, "Oklahoma National Stockyards" and, "World's Largest Stocker and Feeder Cattle Market." At the arch's center, a cow's skull.

Inside a restaurant, Dylan waits, sits alone at a long wooden countertop. He hears steel guitars and a fiddle from Hank Williams, Sr.'s "Hey, Good Looking." From a barstool, he stares at his black coffee. In his head, football plays from his senior year of high school.

"You decide on something?" a young woman says, startling him.

He looks up at an attractive, redheaded waitress. "Haven't looked," he says, "Sorry."

She slides her pen and notepad in her apron. "No problem, Ford. Holler when you're ready."

He watches her refill his coffee. "Thanks," he says, and she disappears into a kitchen.

Steam rises from his mug, and he stares at air bubbles in his coffee. His thoughts on football and Friday night games. He's behind a defensive line at Moore High School on a brightly lit field. He crouches, football in his hands. He sees the Oklahoma Sooners rushing Owen Field in a sea of crimson.

Stevie Wonder on a radio behind the counter, "I was born in Little Rock, had a childhood sweetheart. We were always hand in hand."

Dylan knows this song. Saturday afternoon after a summer basketball tournament, Dylan sees Sarah for the first time. He's twelve, and no longer in the restaurant. He's following a distant radio and bouncing basketball into a dimly lit gymnasium.

He sees her at the other end of a basketball court, the only other person in the gym. The bouncing stops. The ball whooshes through nylon net.

At a free throw line, he stands arm's length from her. The ball thumps the court, back and forth from her left to right hand.

He hits at the ball, and she slides past him. The ball strikes the rim, falls through net.

He races down court, crisscrosses the ball between his legs, Sarah at his side. He stops for a three. She glides by him. He shoots, and she smacks the ball down to the ground. He chases her down court, his heartbeat heavy, his hair dripping sweat. She stops at the three-point line. Dylan slams the ball from her hands. He reaches at her, and she swipes the ball from him. In the stands, a radio plays Stevie Wonder's "I Was Made to Love Her."

For hours, Dylan and Sarah play basketball. They talk only to call fouls, keep score til Sarah's father arrives. She writes her number on Dylan's sleeveless shirt. At dinner that night, Dylan thinks about Sarah during grace. He's awake til three a.m., alone downstairs on a sofa, moonlight luminescent through his living room's bow windows. He replays their encounter. Next Saturday—right after his morning run with Sam—he calls her. She invites him to an outdoor court near her house.

He bikes from his farm on Pennsylvania, stares at dirt road giving way to asphalt. He passes housing construction a half-mile north from his farm, bikes under I-240, rides past car dealerships and chain restaurants along his city's new southern border.

Dylan bikes into a neighborhood north of I-240, ranch-style homes built during the sixties. He rides along Jefferson Middle School where he attends junior high, then neighborhood after neighborhood built on a grid system, turns at Commerce Street. He stops on a hill where a private Catholic school with gothic architecture overlooks his city.

They sit together on the Catholic school's lawn. He watches her skin glow in the sun. Behind her, the distant downtown skyline in a haze. They talk sports, vinyl records they own. Sarah's love for Stevie Wonder's album, *Songs in the Key of Life*, Dylan's for Neil Young, Parliament-Funkadelic. Dylan almost tells her about a song from another Stevie album, music flowing across a basketball court. But, he keeps "I Was Made to Love Her" to himself. She never seems to mind his stutter.

"Strip Sirloin, please." Gruff words force Dylan back into the restaurant at the counter with Cristine. He has no idea how long she's been sitting beside him, Cristine in her denim halter jumpsuit.

"Semi-truck full of bees spilled on I-35 this afternoon around the Purcell exit," she says. "Little fuckers were everywhere," she explains, "covering windshields. Beekeepers say they'll set 'em on fire once it gets dark. Turns out, bees become too aggressive at night. Jesus, can you imagine what it'll look like?"

"I'm gonna ask Sarah to marry me," Dylan says.

"I said bees, not locust plague."

"I'm serious."

"So am I." Cristine slaps Dylan's shoulder. "Chill. You just turned old enough to drive to Texas to buy porn."

"I made up my mind," Dylan says, still staring straight in front of him. "I'm taking whatever money from this summer, buying Sarah a ring."

"Betcha less dumb ways to spend your money, bro."

Dylan waves his hand. "I don't know why I said anything to you."

Her blonde bangs across her face, Cristine rests her chin in her palm, her elbow on the counter. She points a plastic straw at Dylan. "I'm being a dick," she says. "You told me, because I'm your girlfriend's best girlfriend. Dude, you can't be this freaked about starting OU next month? You killed it at the lake with my sorority and your fraternity."

"Has nothing to do with the lake this weekend, Cristine." Dylan watches Marjorie refill his coffee. "I'll take a T-bone, please." He hands her his menu. "Medium rare."

A bell clanks above a glass double door entrance into the restaurant.

From the corner of his eye, Dylan sees a dozen construction workers and roughnecks crowding through the door near a cash register, men in their late teens, twenties, early thirties. Some, he knows. Others, he doesn't.

Cristine leaps from her barstool, winks at a roughneck. "Be right back," she says. "That one owes me poker money from the other night." Cristine takes a step, turns, slides back on the barstool. "Shit," she says under her breath. "My dad."

Dylan's brow furrows. He looks behind him and, with a firm grip, Cristine's father shakes Dylan's hand.

"DA Curtis," Dylan says.

"Dylan." The fit, middle-aged man looks to his daughter, his one word flat. "Cristine."

"Dad."

District Attorney Edward Curtis turns to Dylan with his graying, clean-cut coiffed blonde hair, his horn-rimmed glasses tight on his face. "How's your father, son?"

"Well, sir."

"Good." Curtis nods behind him to a bald, portly man. "Agent Kenway, Dylan Ford, our county sheriff's boy."

The bell clanks again above the door.

Dylan shakes Adler Kenway's hand. "Nice to meet you, sir," Dylan's pulse quickens. He hears his promise to his father. Say nothing about Sam, Sarah, and Sulphur.

"My daughter, Cristine."

Cristine nods from the counter to Kenway.

"If you excuse us. Agent Kenway and I need to talk before he returns to Murray County." Curtis gestures Kenway to the front of the restaurant. "Gentlemen."

Dylan watches the two men—Kenway in a checkered blue seersucker suit, Curtis in fitted slacks, suspenders, and white collared shirt—the two men making their way through a restaurant full of oil-covered roughnecks, construction workers. "Shit's heavy," Dylan says, watching Agent Kenway and DA Curtis disappear into an adjoining room. "Your 4th of July party still on tomorrow night?"

"I don't know, man. I'd hate to interrupt your nuptials."

"Oh, ha ha," Dylan says, dryly, still staring at the entrance to the adjoining room.

"Yeah, man, we're on."

Marjorie puts two steak knives on the countertop in front of Cristine and Dylan.

An hour later, Dylan unlocks his car door, his stomach full. A car horn honks. Behind him, Cristine's red Porsche speeding past the beige brick western wear store.

Dylan drives from the Stockyards, his hand on his steering wheel. He passes over a dry Oklahoma River. His windows down, warm wind rushing across him. He tries to think about driving. But, his thoughts drift to people, parks, and places. He sees in his mind his mom showing him a sepia-tinted photo of his grandmother decades ago as a young girl sitting on a boardwalk at a black steel table near this river, tall trees with white lights surrounding her. His mother tells him, "That's her when she was six, wearing her favorite summer dress and bonnet."

From his window, Dylan remembers his mother describing the river's sprawling wooded shoreline, its floating wedding chapel and beer gardens, Oklahoma City's first zoo, a 3000-seat vaudeville and movie theater, its amusement park. He sees his grandmother here as a child in sepia-tinted photographs. He speeds past this place along a tan two-story Farmers Market building, its Spanish mission-style architecture disappearing into cloudy gray southern sky in his side mirror.

* * *

Dylan scoots under his car, cardboard beneath him scraping concrete. With a wrench, he knocks loose an oil drain plug. He looks at his engine, his arms sticky with sweat, his hand smeared black.

"Why'd you move down here?" Dylan says.

"Down here?" says a man with a baritone drawl.

"By the river."

"City started by the river."

Black oil spills from the drain plug, pours in a steady stream on a plastic pan beside Dylan. He tosses his wrench to concrete, wipes sweat from his eyes on the back of his arm. He squints, sees dusk through a half-open garage door. He thinks about Sarah, when she'll be off work, when he'll ask her to marry him.

He asks Sarah's father, "Why'd Pastor Jacob move to that new neighborhood behind our farm?" Dylan hears tools clank to his side.

"Never know why my brother does what he does. Says better schools."

Dylan twists loose an oil filter.

"Race riots spooked him," Sarah's father says, "back at U.S. Grant '75, right after busing integrated our schools in '71. South of that new interstate, instead of Oklahoma City, his kids attend public school in Moore."

Race riots spooked Dylan, too. He was fifteen in 1975, his father a sheriff's deputy on every local news channel, arresting a fifteen-year-old Black kid for murder only three miles north of their farmhouse at U.S. Grant High School, three miles south of the Oklahoma River and Stockyards where Dylan and Sam take their cattle to slaughter. "Can't you get the local news channels to stop showing his name and face on loop?" Dylan hears his mother say to his father. "He's a child, not a monster."

Dylan smears oil on a rubber casket along the filter, tightens it to his engine. His thoughts drift to riots at U.S. Grant, his city's public schools, its new rural suburbs, its exurbs. Edmond north. Moore south. Yukon and Mustang west. Midwest City to the east beside the air force base where his father met his mother. He imagines a suburban starter home with Sarah in such places—where their kids will attend school, where he'll keep them safe.

With a bar of soap, Dylan washes his hands in a dirty sink basin. Smell of motor oil and brake dust. His reflection in a grime-covered mirror and news-paper headline above it, "Capitol Hill: Opportunity for Sober and Industrious Mechanics to Secure Homes."

Following statehood, Capitol Hill became part of Oklahoma City, trolleys connecting its residents to downtown, trains taking them twenty minutes south across prairie for football games at OU.

Sarah's father is a stocky former linebacker with curly short black hair, a son of Irish immigrants hunched over a propped-up yellow hood of a '67 Camaro. Engine wrapped from years of over-revving. He doesn't speak about the Oklahoma panhandle, where he grew up, fighting overseas in the Korean War. For him, life began at age twenty-five when he bought a house near the river north of Capitol Hill. When he built an auto repair shop.

Staring back at Sarah's dad through the mirror, Dylan starts to tell him his daughter might be in danger.

Dylan turns off the faucet. "You were close to your parents growing up, right?"

"Mom, yes. Dad, no."

"You always do what they tell you?"

Sarah's father tosses a greasy rag to the floor. "Rarely. How's Sam's truck?"

"Still running," Dylan says, loses his nerve.

Dylan stands on a sidewalk later that night in front of the gray brick auto shop. He stretches his arm across his chest. He looks south to streetlamps lighting a bridge into Capitol Hill. He stretches his other arm, glances at a black ink crucifix he got on his tricep in North Texas his eighteenth birthday. A garage door rattles, Sarah's father banging it shut to the ground. On a sign behind Dylan, Jesse's Auto Repair.

Chrome hubcaps hang on a tall aluminum fence across the street.

Dread fills Dylan. Dozens of decorative wheel covers stare at him from the fence, shining under a streetlamp beside a parked, empty, dirty old station wagon.

CHAPTER TEN

"Working in the restaurant environment presents its own unique hazards," she says, the cadence of her words like a cheerleader, how a sorority girl speaks in beauty pageants. "Whether busboy, server, hostess, or cook, you have a responsibility to yourself and others to provide a fun, safe work environment. Wear slip-resistant shoes," she says. "Wear personal protective gear such as goggles and oven mitts to prevent workplace injuries. When using knives, wear cut-resistant gloves. Wash, rinse, and sanitize knives in a sink, like the one behind me. When handing someone a knife, always give them the handle, never the blade. Walk holding knives blade down, and never run with knives. Handle glasses carefully. Remember," she says, "cool liquids break hot glasses."

A nineteen-inch television reflects Sarah. "Here at Sizzlin Stockade, we value your safety," says the young woman with blonde hair. Tracking lines across the screen. The image jittery, blurs the woman's khaki shorts and wide smile.

Beside Sarah, a teenage girl chewing gum, slouched on a blue plastic chair, the only other person in the white-tiled room.

A pink bubble blows from the young teen's mouth. "Trainee" on her nametag.

A door slams behind Sarah as she walks into a hallway. Bright fluorescent lights across her from the ceiling. She pulls her hair into a ponytail.

She makes her way through a bustling kitchen–frantic cooks, fire flaring above a large industrial stove. She wipes flour from her black t-shirt. Surrounding her, clattering plates and conversations. A young man's, "Ticket yours?" "I don't know why she said that." "Corner!"

Sarah pushes open a metal door into a crowded dining area with wood panel walls, hears bass thump through the restaurant's speakers, disco. She walks past young people and families sitting at tables and booths, recognizing Thelma Houston sing, "Don't Leave Me This Way."

"You're the only one on now, Sarah!"

"Thanks," Sarah responds to a young woman at a host stand.

Sarah glances at glass double doors behind the hostess, sees headlights in the night speed across I-240. She walks along hanging heat lamps warming steak and sides at a buffet bar in the center of the dining room. She reaches in her apron pocket for a pen. She looks up at a circular clock on a wall, nine p.m.

Minutes later, Sarah stands in black shoes on wet red tile, scrapes scraps of ribeye and green beans to the trash. She stacks plates on a chrome countertop along a wall. She throws a steak knife and fork into a plastic bin of soapy water. She pushes a rack of glasses on a conveyor belt into steam rising from a stainless-steel commercial dishwasher. "Sarah?"

She looks around a corner of the large dishwasher to a young man behind it. Standing in warm steam, she squints, surprised. "Andrés?"

He stops spraying water on a rack of plates. "¡No mames!" He laughs, rips gloves from his hands. "Usted trabaja aqui?"

"What're you doing here?"

"Started this morning."

Sarah grins. "Nice hairnet."

Later that night outside an old church lit yellow with a streetlamp, Sarah and Andrés are sitting on a sidewalk, resting along the two-story red brick building.

Andrés bites into the last of his burrito.

Sarah stares at Commerce Street, the wet road in front of them lit red and green from a nearby stoplight.

"Sarah from the musicals," Andrés says. She looks at him, confused.

He wipes a napkin across his mouth. "Junior high. You looked like Rita Moreno, from *West Side Story*."

Sarah tosses a pebble across the wet street. "I'm half-Cuban," she says. "Moreno's Puerto Rican."

Andrés drinks from his Coke can. "So?" he says. "I'm Mexican and look a lot like James Dean. Take the compliment."

She looks at his brushed-up black hair, his black t-shirt, and work pants. A darker, more handsome Dean, she realizes. "I haven't seen you since eighth grade."

"I know, random, huh?" He cups his hands over his mouth, lights a Marlboro. "Where've you been?"

"I don't know, working. Texas."

"Since we were thirteen?"

"Construction, yeah. Farm work, too." He smokes his cigarette, looks down the street. "Never understood temperance growing up, patience. Prudence, really, either. Couldn't wait to quit school. Can't stay in one place. Love seeing the world. You Catholic?"

"Baptist," Sarah says.

"Good setting." He nods behind them to the church. She smiles.

"Still live south side?"

"Yeah, just north of the railroad. Between the river and downtown. No man's land, really. Love this part of town, though."

Andrés points his cigarette up the hilly street. "What happened to John A. Brown's department store?" he asks.

"Ms. Brown's family sold it after she died, the downtown store on Main Street, too. They call it Dillard's now at Crossroads Mall. Cristine works there. You remember her? Penney's left, too."

"So, our whole town moved south, huh?"

"I guess so."

"I started an exodus." Andrés smiles.

Sarah remembers an eighth-grade bully, Andrés short, scrappy, picking fights. But tonight, subdued. She hears a hooting owl, looks to boarded windows on Brown's Department Store. She worries a killer hides in its shadows, wants to tell Andrés why, can't. She thinks about a woman swimming above a great white shark on a *Jaws* poster at The Music Store.

Andrés asks, "Monday nights always that busy?"

"Every night since we opened," Sarah says.

"Ever think about stars?" Andrés nods to a break in cumulus clouds to a white waxing moon.

"Only when I remember to," Sarah says.

"I do all the time." Andrés ashes his cigarette. "Mi abuelita, when we were kids, she told my sister and me, Mexican Indians believe the moon's the left eye of God. Stars are family, because we come from the stars." He smiles, points to rolling cumulus clouds, "That's tio so-and-so, she'd say, your cousin, cousin's grandmother."

Sarah brings her knees to her chest. She looks to empty brick storefronts. "At night," Sarah says, "when I can't sleep, when my mind won't stop, I imagine ancient cave drawings from, like, tens of thousands of years ago, just to get out of a moment, to ground myself. Rhinos drawn with eight legs, so under torchlight, they look like they're are roaming alongside my shadow. Horses galloping on limestone walls, woolly mammoths beside bison. Everything in motion, but beautiful and still."

"You should see West Texas at night," Andrés says. "Stars painted across a dark desert sky. You'd love it." Andrés looks at his cigarette, his calloused hands. "I see you worrying about me, by the way, Sarah from the Musicals, but you shouldn't. I'm enrolled in welding classes at the city's new community college, World History even. I know all about Cuba now." Andrés waves an imaginary flag. "Remember the Maine. War with Spain."

Around midnight, Sarah walks alone across her backyard in her black t-shirt and work slacks, her Pentax camera at her side. Her small home with white vinyl siding and pointed turret on a corner lot. She walks along a chain-link fence and dim lit road along the edge of her aging neighborhood.

Across the road, a flat open field and distant tall trees to the east block her view of her father's auto shop. Capitol Hill across the railroad a few blocks south.

Red light dims across her in a tool shed. She rewinds a crank on top of her camera, the only noise in the room. She sits at a workbench, rotates a stainless-steel film-developing canister, this container clicking in her hands each time she moves it back and forth. Headphones covering her ears.

Along a concrete floor, a cord extends from her headphones into an eight-track player. She hums to the Beach Boys harmonizing, "Wouldn't it be nice, if we were older."

Sarah stands from a barstool, holds a 35mm filmstrip stretched out in front of her, studies each frame, the red room quiet around her.

Near her workbench, she stands at a sink, drains developing chemicals from the canister into a plastic container. She pours yellow stop-bath liquid in the canister. In her headphones, "God Only Knows."

Water drips from a faucet to the sink. From the ceiling, developed color photos hang on clothespins, eight-and-a-half by eleven-inch color prints strung along wire. Beach Boys singing, "Hang on to your ego," Sarah stares at senior year, friends at high school lockers, prom dresses, black tuxes, graduation. She thinks about thrift stores with Sam and Dylan on Saturday mornings across southside OKC, searching for cheap clothes and vinyl records, Dylan with his beautiful brown eyes, Sam hiking Sulphur's wooded green hills. She looks up at a photo from outside The Music Store through her Jeep's grimy windshield of Sam trying to sleep, his arms folded. In her mind, though, no matter how hard she tries, Sarah can't stop seeing herself lean down to kiss a young dead boy on his freckled forehead.

CHAPTER ELEVEN

That night, Sam's sitting in a tractor cab, turns his steering wheel, sweats in a sleeveless shirt. All windows open in the cab, engine humming. Country music on his radio. Through his windshield, headlights shine on a round bale of hay he's stacking on a semi-trailer with his tractor.

From his tractor cab, he unloads the round bale, steadies it with others on a flatbed. Alone out here, he thinks about the first humans afraid of the woods. He backs his tractor from the trailer, a vast harvested wheat field around him.

He's lying on his back in bed after an hour, his hands behind his head, listens to his tractor engine still humming in his head. He's staring up at his favorite image, the first color photo of Earth from the moon on a giant canvas behind his headboard from floor to ceiling. The moon's rocky gray surface across the width of his floor. Above the moon, the blackness of space surrounding Earth's white clouds and blue oceans.

He thinks about harvesting hay in June, round-baling alfalfa at night to avoid the summer sun, swathing it in rows. He thinks about threshing seeds and tractor combines, waiting in line at a grain elevator with a semi-truck full of wheat.

He looks from the canvas to his bedroom door. Staring at it now, he doesn't remember it open, but it is. The hallway dark through his door.

Sam's standing in a bar where he's never been. He knows he shouldn't be here, but he is. He looks at his boots and Wranglers, his hands at his belt buckle.

At the door, a man slides Sam's license under lamplight.

From the metal door, Sam hears a lion roar loud across speakers.

He looks over his shoulder where, in the dark, a sepia-tinted MGM trademark logo appears across the room's south wall. He sees men's silhouettes sitting at small round tables, standing along east and west walls, drinking beer, watching the lion emblem roar once more. He hears his heartbeat. He knows cops raided the place days before.

The man slides Sam's license back across the counter. "No names," the man says.

Sam's standing at a bar counter moments later in the center of the room. "Whiskey," he says again to a bartender.

Standing at the bar, he hears his heartbeat thump over the speakers, then a pool cue striking billiard balls on the north side of the rectangular room.

The bartender hands Sam a single pour of whiskey, and he hears a British man say low on the speakers, "I've been mad for fucking years, absolutely years, been over the edge."

Sam takes his whiskey tumbler, notices the bartender's silver wristwatch. On the speakers, he hears the thumping heartbeat, a cash register open, receipt paper ripping, rhythmically, repeatedly. "I've always been mad," he hears another man say over the sounds. "I know I've been mad, like most of us ... very hard to explain why you're mad, even if you're not mad."

At a pool table, he racks billiard balls. He hears a man's maniacal laughter swell into a woman's scream with all the other sounds on the speakers, collapsing as if in exhale into a guitar and melodic bass line, strumming the start of Pink Floyd's "Breathe."

Sam grabs chalk from a pool cue rack next to a dart board. Beneath the dart board on a table, his whiskey tumbler beside an ashtray and red lamp glowing gold in the dark.

Sam looks across the bar to a fading MGM logo, sepia-colored clouds appearing across the south wall, drifting behind words reading, "For nearly forty years, this story has given faithful service to the Young in Heart; and, Time has been powerless to put its kindly philosophy out of fashion. To those of you who have been faithful to it in return ... and, to the Young in Heart ... we dedicate this picture."

The south wall fades black, then becomes a copper-colored film image of a dirt road on a prairie. On the road, a young woman in pigtails and a dress, running alongside her dog toward a distant cloudy sky.

On the north side of the bar, Sam tugs at the back of his tucked-in pearl-snap shirt, airing it out, studying billiard balls. Behind him, a muted moving image of Judy Garland's Dorothy in close-up, looking anxious, holding and talking to Toto.

Sam stares across green felt, squints at a corner pocket and cluster of striped balls. His head lowered, cue stick balanced on his hand at table's edge, aimed like a rifle. Trying to focus. Worried he'll miss. Certain he won't. Across speakers, he hears, "Run. Rabbit, run. Dig that hole, forget the sun. And, when at last the work is done, don't sit down; it's time to dig another one."

A striped ball knocks into the corner pocket.

Warm air blows at his back from a large metal fan on a concrete floor—the room's only ventilation. He drinks his whiskey, studies the pool table, smells cologne, cigarettes, and beer, cue stick at his side. From the corner of his eye, men at the bar counter, drinking, smoking, laughing, the room becoming full. If police raid, arrest him, his home address published in *The Oklahoman* beside his name for moral complaints. Ten years in prison, if they convict him, says state law he's read at his father's sheriff's office when he's ten. A young man beside him playing darts looks at Sam, and Sam turns quick from him.

Tribal drums begin beating across the speakers, building repetitively, steadily. Sam eyes an eight ball near a side pocket.

"The time is in the street, you know?" says a man in spoken word across the speakers, speaking as if at an old Negro spiritual. "Us, living as we do, upside down. And, the new word to have is revolution." Sam rubs chalk on the end of his cue stick.

"People don't even want to hear the preachers spill or spiel," says the man over drums, "because God's hole card has been thoroughly piqued. And, America is now blood and tears, instead of milk and honey."

Sam tries to focus, think about math, his six-foot-four body at a forty-five-degree angle he's perfected at the pool table. Staring at the edge of his cue stick, he hears the man's words again say, "The youngsters who were programmed to continue fucking up woke up one night, digging Paul Revere and Nat Turner as the good guys."

Sam lowers his head, lines his shot, cue stick on the back of his hand. He glances past the pool table to the dart board on the north wall, a payphone beside it. From the payphone, he looks at the eight ball, sees Sarah in his head.

"We learned to our amazement the untold tale of scandal," he hears the man say, "two long centuries buried in a musty vault, hosed down daily with a gagging perfume."

The eight ball knocks into the side pocket.

Sam's standing at the bar counter again. "Whiskey," he says to the bartender.

"The present mocks us," says the man on the speakers.

From the bar counter, Sam sees Dorothy across the south wall, the scene muted where she sings on her farm to Toto, "Somewhere over the Rainbow."

"All I want is a good home and a wife," says the man over the drums, "and children and some food to feed them every night." The bartender hands Sam a single pour of whiskey, and he drinks it empty. "Another," he says. "Double and a Coors."

"What does Webster say about soul?" says the man over the drums. "After all is said and done, build a new route to China, if they will have you. Who will survive in America? Who will survive in America? Who will survive in America? Who will survive in America?"

The man stops. The drums, too.

Sam rolls a cue ball across the pool table, stares at the payphone, hears laser beams from *Space Invaders*, the arcade game lit bright beside the payphone in the dark, the metal fan beside it on the floor, blowing warm air. Across the pool table, he sees a jukebox lit up on the east wall, white buttons with numbers and letters, Pink Floyd playing again, their song, "Time," strumming the same guitar and melodic bass from the opening of the song, "Breathe." For how long, he's not sure.

Beside the payphone on a barstool, a nineteen inch television glows at him in the dark. Across the screen, a muted reporter speaking into a microphone in front of the downtown County Courthouse, then a close-up of the district attorney adjusting his horn-rimmed glasses above the words. "FBI, DA Curtis Discuss Sulphur Slaughter."

He reaches in his back pockets, looks at billiard balls behind Plexiglas along the side of the pool table. Behind him across the bar, Dorothy in close-up, gasping at a crystal ball, sitting across an old man in a turban dressed as a fortune teller.

Sam looks at his last dollar bills in his hand. He slides them back in his pockets, glances at a distant clock on a wood beam above the bar counters.

"Ladies and gentlemen," he hears a woman say, her words somber, guitars giving way to solemn piano music. "The time was one forty-five," she says, "closing's at two."

He walks along the pool table to the bar counter, drunk. Behind him in the dark, lamps glow gold on tables. "And, I am not frightened of dying," he hears a British man say on the speakers. "Anytime will do, I don't mind." Sam sees a silent image of a twister spin through a prairie toward Dorothy's house and farm, Aunty Em frantic on a porch, screaming with the wind.

"Why should I be frightened of dying?" he hears the British man say, "There's no reason for it, you gotta go sometime … "

Sam's walked past the bar counter. He glances at his boots, surprised he's no longer on concrete but wood floors. He looks up past men sitting in shadows in front of him.

"Coming to the stage," he hears the woman say, "her final performance, our Ms. Circa Club."

Across the south wall, Dorothy. Standing on stage in front of her, a full-figured woman, shaped like an hourglass, black evening gown sparkling, lit with a ray of light from the film projecting on the wall, her hair dark, big, and round, her skin umber brown.

Her lips, shaded purple, move in sync with a sudden sound of a woman wailing across the speakers over piano and drums, beautifully, painfully, orgasmically, melody without words, Pink Floyd's "Great Gig in the Sky." Her silhouette over a silent image of Dorothy frightened on the wall, running through her living room with Toto in her arms.

Sam starts to cry but can't, first time he's wanted to since he was a child.

On the bar's back patio, warm water splashes his face from a faucet. How's he outside? How long? He's kneeled against the building, water pounding the ground, mud on his boots, blurred music through the walls. But, after Sulphur, he had to know, he had to come here. "Why me?" he murmurs, his face pressed into hard brick.

Outside the front of the non-descript tan building, trucks and cars drive from a parking lot. Headlights bright on a gas pump across the street in front of an abandoned filling station and row of red brick buildings, mostly deserted, a highway sign on the road, Oklahoma, US 66. A block east, a wet road reflects a stoplight turning red at the intersection of Northwest 39th and Pennsylvania.

The air humid. He's still drunk, standing on a grassy hill on the back patio, watching red lights flash in the distance on transmitters towering into the night sky. Lost in thought, staring past a wood fence separating Circa Club from a beige brick two-story motel, losing himself in cars on I-44 barely north of the motel, headlights passing neighborhoods and a new outdoor shopping mall and drive-thru teller bank.

He turns around and sees a young man sitting on a stone bench, clean-shaven, staring up at wind rustling trees across the patio. Beside the young man, stone benches. Behind him, evergreen bushes. His face familiar, his skin bronze brown, his hair an afro, the cowboy at the Spencer Rodeo, the preacher's son. Their eyes meet.

"I'm Sam," he says.

"Matthew."

Red lights flash atop a transmitter tower. A half dozen transmitter towers flashing hypnotically across a flat grassy field on the far northeast side of town. Far from this place, the hovering sound of a helicopter. In the dark, Sam's pickup parked under an elm tree, engine off, chirping crickets, katy-dids. In the back of his truck, they kiss, terrified, hug tight, Sam's rough hand under Matthew's shirt, pressed against Matthew's toned chest, his other hand unbuckling his belt.

An hour passes, and they're asleep in his pickup bed beside each other under stars in a night sky.

The sun is in his eyes. He squints, hungover, his hand on his forehead, his hair across his face. He doesn't know where he is. He looks beside him, and Matthew's gone.

PART TWO

Perfect Day

CHAPTER TWELVE

Charlie's alone. He's in the dark sitting on a futon, stares out an open second story window, cigarette between two fingers. Cardboard boxes beside him across a concrete floor. Charlie written across boxes, Charlie Books, Charlie Photos, Charlie Kitchen, Charlie Living Room, Charlie Bedroom. A drag from his cigarette.

Hisses and pops punctuate silence in his apartment, his speaker boxes attached to an abandoned turntable on his living room floor. On his turntable, Louis Armstrong blowing into his trumpet, "West End Blues."

Another drag from his cigarette, Charlie ashes out the open steel casement window. He's lit the color of saffron from a nearby streetlamp, his chiseled face and big curly blonde hair lit gold. The air muggy.

On a cardboard box beside his turntable, a newspaper headline above the fold reads, "Sulphur Slaughter: An Unspeakable Evil." Next to the newspaper, typewriter paper stained with coffee. Written at the top of the first page, "Slaughter in Sulphur. By Derek Clover," then typed black words revised with red ink.

From an outdoor walkway outside his apartment, a three-legged calico kitten climbs a black steel chair, then scrambles up a table beneath his window.

"You again?" Charlie says to the cat.

The calico walks past Charlie onto his futon, then concrete floor, rubs against boxes.

Charlie puts his cigarette in an ashtray he's holding.

Standing from his futon, he says, "Alright," his words low. "I know this story."

Barefoot and shirtless, he walks past cardboard boxes, the hem of his corduroys at his ankles, the calico kitten following him to his kitchen.

At ten p.m., Charlie walks his bike in an alley between two-story brick fourplexes built in the 1920s, his helmet on his head. Above him, air conditioner units blow full-blast into apartment windows.

He's always late, nearly always broke. He's no longer walking, riding his bike along a chain-link fence and shrubbery separating him from a cemetery housing his city's founders. Trees surround gravestones and marble mausoleums where he's buried his parents and grandparents. At his handlebars, a flashlight wrapped with duct tape shines on the street. Behind him on the south side of the cemetery, a gray gothic cathedral stands above the neighborhood where he grew up. Biking in the dark, he glances up to the old building's eighty-foot spire topped with a Celtic cross.

Two miles north, he bikes across wet Pennsylvania Avenue at Northwest 39th under a stoplight turning green, rides along 39th Street's boarded-up brick buildings. He passes a highway sign, Oklahoma, US 66.

Charlie chains his bike to a fence post. Above him, trees rustle with warm wind. He looks at his wrist, a silver watch Ace gave him, 10:15pm. "A gift so you're on time." But, he tries not to think about San Francisco.

At a tan building's back entrance, Charlie removes his bike helmet. Glass crunches beneath his shoes. He stops.

He's arrived at work by routine, hasn't paid attention to anything around him. Confused, Charlie stares at a broken lantern on the wall, shattered glass across the ground.

"When did that … " Worried, he looks again to the lantern, a metal door beside it. The chirping of crickets and katydids across the back patio. Charlie reaches for a door handle, hopes it's locked.

From inside the building, loud thumping startles him.

"Paying customers!" shouts a man's muffled voice. Then, a pounding sound again. "Sign says ten!"

After midnight, Charlie's hands are in soapy water, washing shot glasses in a sink, beer mugs. He's sweating under red lights on wood beams above a bar counter, the air thick with cigarette smoke, dollar bills overflowing from a metal pail hanging beside him.

Behind him, Sam's at the crowded bar counter, tribal drums across the speakers. On the south wall, Judy Garland's Dorothy, the scene muted where she sings to Toto, "Somewhere over the Rainbow."

"Double and a Coors," Sam says to him.

"What does Webster say about soul?" says a man across speakers in spoken word.

Charlie's lost in tribal drums, Sam's light blue eyes. Then, he's pouring whiskey. Before tonight, he's never seen Sam, doesn't know his name, but he doesn't know any of the clientele's names, only they're construction workers, college students, farmers, lawyers, doctors, hustlers, handsome, muscular, masculine, feminine, all religions, all skin colors, ethnicities, every night.

But, no names, never names.

Behind Charlie, a young rancher at the bar counter, hiding under a black cowboy hat, drinking Tequila, smoking a cigarette, staring at Charlie.

The next morning, his bedroom dark, walls bare, Charlie's asleep, his arm across the back of a young man beside him, his air conditioner unit in a window whirring full-speed, the two men sleeping on a mattress and box spring on a concrete floor. Loud knocking in his ears, a muffled, "The time is in the street, you know?" from the bar last night. Charlie pushes his head in his pillow. On a nightstand beside his bed, a pack of Camels, black cowboy hat, and framed photo of Charlie in his Marine uniform. Clothes flung across his floor.

Fog shrouds a courtyard. Brightly colored stepping stones through mist and gardens to apartment doors. Across the courtyard, steel staircases zigzag to walkways along the building's second floor.

Knocking louder in Charlie's living room. Groggy, he rubs his eyes. He opens his front door to Rachel, her familiar smile, a champagne bottle and orange juice in her hands.

The dull sound of shower water echoes across his empty living room. Beside his open steel casement window, a black-and-white poster of automobiles driving between a bus and skyscrapers on a downtown street in 1940s Oklahoma City. Across a southern sky at the end of the street, Phillips 66 on an oversized highway sign. Progress beneath it. A sign across the top of a tall brick building for The Best Beer in Town. Across a billboard above the building's first floor, Blended, Splendid, Pabst Blue Ribbon. Another sign for Broadview Hotel, a different sign, Broadway Jewelry and Loans.

On the walkway beneath Charlie's apartment window, the calico kitten drinks milk from a dish.

From his hallway, Charlie walks into his living room, drying his curly blonde hair with a towel. Cardboard boxes across his floor. Through his open steel casement window, Rachel's on the walkway, watering plants along a railing with a clay jar.

Outside, Charlie sits at the small table beside his steel casement window. Behind him, his door open into his apartment.

"You should be proud," Rachel says, still watering plants, her back to him. "Your vegetables are doing lovely."

Charlie watches her study hanging macramé baskets and potted plants along his balcony, a hazy fog surrounding her.

"It's bright," he says.

She tilts the clay jar over purple petunias and blue periwinkles, plump red tomatoes. "It'll burn away soon," she says. "It's too bright to do anything else."

Birds chirp across his mist-covered courtyard.

She puts the clay jar on the steel table, sits in a chair across from him. She wipes soil from her hands.

He looks at her, earnestly. "Really think the tomatoes look good?"

"Mhm." Rachel smiles. "So do your rosemary and thyme." She pours orange juice into a Mason jar bubbling half-full of champagne.

Behind her through fog, sunflowers and sunny yellow gerbera daisies, ruby red begonias and pink impatiens, her hair at her shoulders, her blonde bangs across her face.

"Good," Charlie says. A bite of toast. He leans back in his chair. "Did you know Dante Alighieri was on city council in Florence?"

She shakes her head. "No, I guess I didn't."

Another bite of toast. "Won a term in 1300 as a local magistrate. Exiled in 1302. Wrote *Divine Comedy* in exile. Pain of death, should he ever return to his city."

"I'd forgotten," Rachel says. "But, he wrote *La Vita Nuova* first, though, right? Before his exile?"

"Yeah, before he was a magistrate."

"Such a beautiful sonnet," she says, drinks from her Mason jar. "Even if I don't believe people fall in love from first sight."

"Joyous, Love seemed to me," Charlie says, "the while he held my heart in his hand. And, in his arms, my lady lay asleep, wrapped in a veil."

Rachel grins. "I seem to remember it ending more sadly." She glances at Charlie's tank top, a hooded figure across the front cloaked in black with a mirror for a face.

"He woke her then," he says. "Trembling and obedient, she ate that burning heart out of his hand. Weeping, I saw him then depart from me."

Rachel hears an owl, realizes the cloaked figure on Charlie's tank top is carrying a flower bouquet on a sidewalk lined with trees and a stone wall covered with vines. "I remember when I first saw you," Rachel says. She looks up at Charlie. "You and Derek. Wearing your school uniforms to the public pool."

Charlie folds his arms. "Growing up in this place, I was certain I'd be a beat poet," he says. "All the beatniks and hippies here in our neighborhood when we were kids." Charlie savors this memory. He looks from the fog. "First day of third grade, by the way," he says. "That's the afternoon we met. Derek and I snuck swim trunks under our uniforms when we left for school that morning, August 1958."

"You two were handsome."

"We were sweaty."

Rachel notices a beige bandage on his toned bicep. "When do classes start?" she says.

"Tomorrow afternoon," Charlie says. He grabs jam and a piece of toast from a plate. "We're watching François Truffaut's *Fahrenheit 451* and reading the Dorothy Sayers' translation of *Divine Comedy* you found for me, comparing the two, then writing a three-point rhetorical analysis essay. Gotta finish the syllabus tonight."

"I wish you'd teach middle school, instead," she says. "You'd do so well."

"I cuss too much."

"They'd love you."

"How's the library?"

"It's fine," she says, sighs. "Dusting shelves, shelving books. Staring lazily out windows at an abandoned downtown."

"Do our days really have so much in common?" he says.

Her smile fades, her blue eyes worried. "Why didn't you come home for your parents' funeral?" she asks.

"Why would I?" Charlie says.

She looks down to a blade of grass in her hand. "Has anything unexplained ever happened to you?" she asks. "Something strange?"

"What do you mean?"

"I don't know. I've had these dreams," Rachel says. "Dreams I'd have before we moved from here. I've had them since the Sulphur murders." She looks at the clay jar.

"What sorta dreams?" Charlie asks.

Rachel scoots the blade of grass across the table. "About my mom's first husband, before she met my dad." She looks up at Charlie. "When we lived here, did you ever go to Marland Mansion?"

"No, but I know it," Charlie says. "'Palace on the prairie' an oil baron built in the roaring twenties, right?"

"Ponca City, yeah. North Central part of the state. My mom's from there."

"I didn't know your mom was from Ponca."

"In my dream, she's always sixteen. We're in a ballroom, dancing," Rachel says, "only I've never been to Marland Mansion. Everything glowing, crystal chandeliers with wrought iron bases. Exquisite gowns, a gold leaf ceiling. Her perfume's oakmoss, orange, jasmine. And, we're spinning across beautiful black-and-white symmetrical squares, terrazzo tiles. I look down, and she says she met her first husband in this ballroom. They ditched a field trip, played this game of hide-and-seek with friends across the mansion. Fifty-five rooms, including the ballroom. She hid under an upstairs bed. Six months later, one night soon after they're married, he strangled her until she fell unconscious."

"Jesus." Charlie folds his arms. "How long was she with him?"

"Two years," Rachel says, refills her Mason jar with champagne, then orange juice. "Once, he put her in an emergency room. Broke her ribs, choked her again. At the hospital, cops told my grandparents, legally, what he'd done was between a wife and husband.

Charlie slips a pack of Camels from his corduroys, cigarettes the young rancher from last night left on Charlie's nightstand while Charlie showered. "How'd she finally leave him?" Charlie asks.

"Without saying anything," Rachel says. "Left an emergency room at midnight, hitchhiked in her hospital gown to the city with a trucker. Didn't tell her parents, stayed at a homelessness shelter for weeks, wouldn't give her name til she got a job at John A. Brown's department store when it was still downtown on Main Street, perfume counter. When he couldn't find her, he divorced her."

"When was that?" Charlie cups his mouth, lights his cigarette.

"Late 1940s," Rachel says, "about a year before she met my dad, had me."

Rachel looks to her palm at the blade of grass. "After the ballroom," she says, "the dream's the same. I'm sixteen in mom's Volkswagen bug, the passenger seat. She doesn't say, but we're heading to take my driver's license test. I can't take my eyes from her. And, I realize I resemble her, physically, same posture even, where I sit up straight like her."

Charlie smokes, stares through fog at red begonias behind her, her jean jacket with its punk rock buttons, its cut-off sleeves over her lavender dress.

"My forehead slams the dashboard, and glass rips my face," she says. "My entire body feels the full force of this large truck, my bones shattering. Upside down, our car scraping across concrete to my mother's screams and high-pitched screech."

Charlie looks at Rachel's wrist, burn marks scarred with a single cut.

She notices. "I always knew about mom's first husband," Rachel says, her words with confidence. "She'd told me, when I was a kid, about how she got away. I never thought he'd find her. But, he'd never stopped."

"How?" Charlie asks.

She drinks from her Mason jar. "Not sure. But, since the murders, I wake up to an odor of fresh gasoline, and my eyes feel like they're filled with smoke. I see mom, unconscious, strapped to a seatbelt, our car in flames. No matter what I do, I can't reach her. Plastic burns my hands."

Rachel's stoic, the air still.

"He yanks me from the car, pulls my hair, drags me across rough asphalt. I kick, yell, 'let go, save my mom!' But, he won't, and he makes me watch her burn."

Charlie hears wood wind chimes from the courtyard. "Have you told Derek?" he asks.

"Derek doesn't know," Rachel says, a breeze across her face. "Something happened last night, Charlie, I need to tell you, something different in the dream." She looks from Charlie's silver wristwatch to his emerald green eyes. "When mom and I stop dancing in the ballroom, she smiles as she always does. This time, though, she kisses my forehead, then whispers, 'Why didn't Charlie come home for his parents' funeral?'"

Charlie puts his cigarette in an ashtray he's holding.

The calico kitten scampers on its three legs an hour later across a fog-covered street. The curved two-lane street wet. The calico stops at a parking meter on a sidewalk, scratches its ear beside a parked El Camino. Behind the cat, a trash can next to two garage doors boarded-up on a stucco building. "Jail" spray-painted across the boards, the neighborhood's public pool no longer there. Along the curved street, pastel-colored stucco buildings with clay roofs, abandoned Spanish revival architecture built in the 1920s. At an intersection on street signs, Northwest 30th and Paseo.

A block south, the calico chases a squirrel along the tan stucco building where Charlie lives, Charlie's corner apartment unit barely visible from the curved street. His balcony on the second floor with flowers, potted plants, and hanging macramé baskets, the steel table where Charlie and Rachel sat earlier empty.

A few blocks east, leaves canopy another street.

Charlie and Rachel walk under power lines and sycamore trees. Pine trees and bungalow homes along both sides of the street, Charlie with his hands in his pockets, Rachel's lavender dress fluttering with the warm wind.

"I read an article at our library," Rachel says, "an interview with the city's public works director, where he argues, 'people here don't want trees.' Bizarre."

Charlie notices a little Black girl across the street in a park, twirling a hula hoop around her neck.

"Derek tried to woo me here, you know," Rachel says, "impress me with how smart he was when we were kids. Long walks along this park, and he'd say, before we were born, his dad operated streetcars connecting these homes to downtown. He wanted to be an engineer like his dad and, when we were on walks in neighborhoods surrounding downtown, he'd point to grassy medians, 'this was a streetcar route,' or 'see rail still encased in the street, Rachel?' Then, he became a journalist."

Charlie grins, remembering similar lengthy childhood conversations with Derek.

"I lied all those years ago," Rachel says. "I told you the three of us should leave this place so you'd become a famous soap opera writer for *Days of Our Lives* or *One Life to Live*. We'd live in Los Angeles, I said, with Derek's aunt and, after a year, we'd be able to attend any California university tuition free. Derek, an engineer, me a librarian." Rachel looks to a tall pine tree beside them in the park. "Instead, the draft, war, Derek and you in Vietnam, Cambodia, me in L.A. with the Manson Murders while you're gone. My mom's first husband promised when they released him nowhere in Oklahoma would be safe—swore he'd kill me. That's why we left, and I should've told you the truth. Now, Sulphur, this new nightmare."

Charlie watches the little girl run to a playground. "Such confessions today," he says. "Worry not, Queen of Pain." His hand to his forehead, his chest, his shoulders left to right. "I absolve you, my child."

On a sidewalk lined with sycamore trees, Charlie and Rachel walk along the park, pavement cracked, a young couple playing tennis on a fenced-in court beside them.

"Did Derek and you write the headline for his Sulphur cover story?" Rachel asks.

"*The Oklahoman* copy editors changed it," Charlie says. "Guess you saw the draft at my apartment I helped him edit?"

"Such an incredibly irresponsible headline," Rachel says. "'Unspeakable Evil.' Removes the responsibility from whoever committed those murders, suggests 'evil' is something separate from being human."

"Evil was the Murray County Sheriff's word," Charlie says.

"Evil's the word Charles Manson used when he described his murders, arguing the devil made him do it."

"Manson is insane."

"No, Manson wanted us to think he was insane," Rachel says, "but he very much knew what he was doing. Literally, when he was a teenager, he even created what he called, 'The Insane Game.'"

"What?" Charlie chuckles. "I hardly know his story. What's the Insane Game?"

"Well, when he's five, his mom's in prison for robbery, so he lives with his religious zealot grandmother. He's always lying, blames others when he's in trouble. When he's eight, they release his mother, she remarries, and Manson starts running away, ditching school, and his stepfather sends him to a series of minimum-security reform schools. He breaks out, steals cars, commits armed robberies, gets caught, more reform schools. At a juvenile facility at fourteen, guards beat him, force him to work farm labor. Routinely, older boys rape him. So, Manson created the Insane Game. Contorts his face so he looks possessed by a demon, makes his whole body convulse to protect himself, all to make people believe he's more dangerous, scarier than them."

Charlie looks from cracked sidewalk to the young couple playing tennis. His hands in his corduroy pockets, he says, "You don't think Manson really believed his murders would start a race war, do you?"

"No," Rachel says. "But, his followers did."

"How many people did they kill?"

"Five. The first night at a house Doris Day's son once owned," Rachel says. "Actress, you know, from old Rock Hudson musicals. The next night, a married couple. Truly brutal," Rachel says, "but, alas, human."

They walk along apple trees in front of homes, peach and pear trees, the park disappearing behind them in fog. Beside them, yards with apricot trees reminding them they haven't lived here in ten years, Fuyu Chinese persimmons decorating lawns.

"Why haven't you unpacked since we moved back?" Rachel asks.

"Never seem to find the time," Charlie says, noticing apartments with Spanish mission-style architecture where, as kids, they played. "Managed a nice souvenir, though, from moving day." He nods to the beige bandage on his bicep.

They're standing moments later at the busy intersection of NW 23rd and Robinson, automobiles speeding past them east and west.

Charlie cups his hands over his mouth, lighting a cigarette, Rachel staring at a hazy blur of headlights, cars racing through fog on 23rd Street. From mimosas, she's a bit buzzed, runs her fingers through her hair. Charlie glances at his watch, eight thirty a.m., then at a stoplight. "Getting warmer," he says, slips his lighter in his pocket. "Fog's letting up, too."

"Told you it would. Still so bright out, though." Rachel looks across NW 23rd to a grassy median with sycamores disappearing down Robinson into her neighborhood. Then, she's halfway across a brick crosswalk, cars idling around her at the intersection. Asphalt stained with oil, grease. She glances behind her to Charlie's big curly blonde hair, to his white tank top disappearing into fog.

Sycamore trees guide her on a sidewalk along homes built in the 1920s with low-pitched hipped roofs and wide overhanging eaves, Prairie houses with American flags flying from wide square porch columns.

Rachel makes her way west on her hilly neighborhood street, walks along pin oak and birch trees in freshly mowed lawns, green and lush, lace bark and crepe myrtles, juniper trees shrouded in fog in front of craftsman-style bungalow homes, an old Laotion woman working in her garden.

As she walks, Rachel's dreams haunt her, sun shining through the haze on the neighborhood where she grew up, her childhood home sold, her father in a new house on her city's far south side. She sees an athletic young man shirtless on his morning run, a young mother on a sidewalk pushing her baby in a stroller, a golden retriever at their side. On Rachel's mind, Charlie and the hooded figure on his tank top.

CHAPTER THIRTEEN

Hector Ramirez straightens his tie. In an oval mirror, he's twenty-eight and Adonis, his thin black tie in a simple knot. His white button-up cotton twill. His shirt collar pressed. His five-o-clock shadow trimmed and edged. His manly face a bit sunken, cheeks clean-shaven. His dark black hair a classic fade, thicker on top, longer and tousled, tapered and shaved along the sides and back of his head. He slides a fitted black suit coat on his broad shoulders. His sister's obituary on a nightstand. Breast cancer.

Behind him across his bedroom, his son, twelve-years-old and four-foot-five, wearing a suit. Beside her son, a mother kneels. She guides him as he begins tying his tie in front of a full-length mirror. The standing wood mirror a half-foot taller than the boy. His reflection next to a painting on a wall, oil on canvas, a crowd assembled in a field under an oak tree, the *Surrender of Santa Anna*. Mexican General Antonio López de Santa Anna wearing a navy-blue shirt and white pants in front of wounded U.S. General Sam Houston, Houston reclining on a pallet at a tree trunk under dense green leaves, an evening sky painted purple, U.S. Colonel Juan Seguin watching with other men. The twelve-year-old boy's brown eyes following brush strokes across the canvas.

"Focus," his mom says. His eyes darting back to his striped silk tie. Scent of pomegranate from his mother. He's nervous, tries not to show it, his shoulders back, standing up straight. His reflection in the mirror.

But, in his head, his father's stories about Juan Seguin and the founding of Texas. He listens to his mom reminding him loop the wider over the narrow side of his tie. From the corner of his eye, the colorful oil painting and a framed faded newspaper with a row of people in photos above headlines, "No Regrets, Chicano Students Who Walked Out Say" and "'68 Protest Brought Better Education, Most Believe." The boy looks at his father in the newspaper, the photo of police staring down student protestors. Next to the newspaper, a diploma in Blackletter font, "Roosevelt High School, Hector Ramirez, Given at Los Angeles, California, 1968." Another diploma for "United States Air Force Academy, 1972."

In the standing mirror, the boy slides the wide end of his tie through a knot he's created. He centers a dimple in the knot, tightens his thin blue and white-striped tie. He studies his reflection, straightens his back, takes a deep breath.

"What do I say about Tia at her funeral?" he asks. "When someone there talks to me about her, I mean."

His mother looks in the mirror, smiles. Still kneeling, her hand on her son's shoulder, she brushes dog hair from his suit.

"Tell them what you're thinking," she says. "That you loved her," she says, her Spanish accent flowing through her English. "That you're sad she's gone, too, and you're here to listen." She brushes a last strand of dog hair from his shoulder. "Mostly, people want someone to listen, to share their grief. Try to be that person for them," she says as her husband fastens a cufflink to his shirt. He looks over his shoulder at his wife.

The boy's hand slides in his suit pockets, his mother and his reflection in the mirror. "I think I might cry, though," he says.

She pushes back tears. Her son taller than she remembers, older, his voice deeper, breaking. "That's okay, if you do," she says.

He slides his foot from carpet into a black leather shoe.

"Why's her funeral on Fourth of July?" he asks.

"Important people die or have funerals on the Fourth of July," she says.

The boy slips his other foot into his black shoe, wobbles a bit, steadying himself. "Important people?" he asks.

Watching herself in the standing mirror, Josefina clasps an earring in her ear. "Jefferson and John Adams died within hours of each other on the Fourth," she says, "fifty years to the day of our country's founding." Josefina clasps another earring in her other ear. "President Monroe, too," she says, "only five years later. So, that's three founding fathers, and over a million people attended President Perón's funeral in Argentina on July Fourth." She studies her reflection in her lace shift dress with its short lace sleeves and lace overlay, black and knee length with its fit and flare silhouette, her wavy brown hair to her shoulders. She watches her son grab from the bed a bottle of cologne.

"Two sprays on wrists, Enrique," she says. "Just two." She turns from the mirror. "Hector, would you fasten the back of this dress for me, please?"

Wanting coffee, Hector stands from a chair in front of the credenza. Thinking about the ten-hour drive ahead of them, he rubs the buzzed hair on his son's head, then rubs his eyes.

Enrique sprays cologne a second time, tosses the bottle to the bed, rubs his wrists together, then along each side of his neck, cedarwood and musk, cinnamon and sage. He looks across the bedroom to his parents, his father behind his mother as she lifts her hair from her shoulders.

Hector's hands on her arms, he kisses Josefina on her neck.

Their pickup heads north on I-35 through Hill Country, Texas plates on their truck. Early morning dew glistening on green grass and wildflowers along the road.

In a camper on the back of their truck, Enrique shakes his inhaler. Beside him on a beige blanket, his sleeping German Shepherd and beef jerky. Enrique presses his inhaler, breathes slow. He unbuttons his suit coat, stares at a small rectangular window looking into the truck cab. He holds his breath, counts in his head to ten, remembers his mom saying unbutton his suit coat's bottom button when he sits at the funeral, or when he sits generally.

In their truck cab, a Styrofoam cup of black coffee shakes in a console between Hector and Josefina. Calm piano music plays from their truck's radio speakers along with a hypnotic drumbeat—haunting, simple. Hector reaches for his coffee.

Four hundred miles north of the Ramirez family, the same calm piano music plays. Along the interstate, east of its shoulder, a woman walks in wavy grass, a car door opened to the driver's side of her mud-splattered station wagon. Behind her car, a thicket of trees in a dense grove. Reluctant, she trudges up a grassy incline, hesitant toward semi-trucks and cars speeding on the interstate. Her high-rise stonewashed jeans pulled above her waist, her white t-shirt tucked into her dirt-stained jeans.

From her open car door, a man on the radio sings, "Just a perfect day," his sullen words with the piano, "feed animals in the zoo. Then later, a movie, too, and then home." Her hood raised on her '72 Oldsmobile. On the passenger floorboard, a black ski mask smeared with crusted white paint and blood into a human skull.

Confident, she stands at the interstate, thumb raised, worried, her arm out stretched, hasn't showered in days, cars racing past her. "You made me forget myself," she hears from the radio. "I thought I was someone else, someone good."

She waits. The chorus of Lou Reed's "Perfect Day" blending with the rush of traffic, blaring with her thoughts.

Hector glances to his dashboard, six hours gone, one pm. His wife asleep against the passenger window on her pillow. His face depression. Awake. In his console, his empty, coffee-stained Styrofoam cup.

Through his windshield, a green exit sign for Purcell/Lexington near an off-ramp. Hector yawns, drives under shade from an overpass. His eyes close. Then, a woman at the side of the road. Her car broken down behind her. Alone. He imagines his wife. Or, his sister four days ago before her death. He glances at Josefina, sleeping.

He clicks on his truck's hazard lights.

Josefina's eyes twitch, bright sunlight, groggy, her mouth dry. Half-asleep, she massages her shoulder. Her other arm jerks from the passenger window, hot glass. She rubs her throbbing forearm, looks to an empty driver's seat, the truck cab quiet, her husband's suit coat folded on the steering wheel. From the dusty windshield, Josefina sees Hector walk along the front of their truck to the young woman standing beside a muddy station wagon. Hector rolling up his sleeves.

Standing in warm wind, he squints, shakes the woman's hand, his other hand shielding his eyes from the sun.

Josefina puts her pillow on the console. She grabs a crank on the passenger door, rolls down her window, heat rushing from outside across her as if from a furnace. She hears a steady drone of Dog-day Cicadas, the young woman saying in a bland, Midwestern voice to Hector, "Just stopped working."

Silence in the truck cab. Her mouth still dry. In her rearview mirror, a reflection of the rectangular window into the camper. Josefina looks through the windshield, "Purcell," and an arrow pointing east on a distant green exit sign, the promise of water at a gas station, a bathroom break. She looks over her shoulder into the camper, their German Shepherd sleeping beside Enrique who is passed out in his suit.

"Where y'all heading?" shouts a man, gruff, guttural, startling Hector and scares Josefina.

From her passenger seat, Josefina sees only Hector and the disheveled young woman with brittle straw hair, her hood raised on her mud-covered station wagon. Josefina scans the grassy incline, sunlight bearing down on the land from a blue sky, the tall man with shaggy hair walking from dense trees behind the broken-down Oldsmobile, a shorter man at his side in a baseball cap.

Her hand to her heart, Josefina feels her stomach drop.

At the hood of the car, warm wind across Hector, his eyes sizing up either man on the other side of the station wagon, maybe in their late twenties. He realizes how far he is from his wife, child, and truck, thinks about the sloping hill behind him.

"Where y'all heading?" shouts the tall man again with his drawl.

Silence between them. At his waist, Hector's clenched fist, his hunting guns in his truck camper, the warm air suffocating. He stares down the two men, says, "Wichita."

"Wichita!" says the tall man. "Wichita. I've been to Wichita." He reaches out his hand to Hector, his hair slicked, parted to the side. "Thanks for stopping to help us."

Hector looks to the tall man's hand, feeling like a bullied kid at recess, trying not to show it, his shoulders back, angry at himself, wanting to refuse but shakes the man's hand.

"Wichita," says the tall man again. "What's in Wichita?"

Hector glances behind him, sweat stinging his eye, his wife staring back at him from their truck up the hill, her face full of worry.

"Sister's funeral," Hector says.

"Sister's funeral," says the tall man. He spits smokeless tobacco. "Hate to hear it," he says, wipes snuff from his chin and thick black mustache. "This here is my brother," he says, throws his arm around the shorter man's shoulder. "Sure would hurt something awful anything happened to him."

Josefina watches from her passenger seat, her pulse racing. She thinks about Hector's hunting guns, his .357 Colt revolver she gave him for his birthday, his .22 caliber pistol, his .22 rifle, 150 rounds of ammunition, all locked up in their truck camper with their son. Engine off, she looks to keys in the ignition.

"What kinda work y'all do?" asks the tall man, staring at Hector's suit pants and white button-up shirt, Hector trying not to overreact.

"Look, if you don't need … "

"What kinda work?" Agitation in the tall man's words, his eyes wide at Hector, the young, disheveled woman backing away from him.

Hector looks to the grass, rubs his hand on his mouth. He laughs under his breath, forces himself to stay calm, his face reddened. "Air Force Technical Sergeant," he says.

"Air Force Technical Sergeant!" says the tall man, flashes a smile. "Fuck, Grady, you hear that?"

The shorter, scruffy man nods from beneath his baseball hat.

"Air Force Technical Sergeant," says the tall man again. He spits tobacco on the station wagon's raised hood. "How about that? How lucky to have his help?"

Hector looks from the ground to the two brothers sizing him up, sweat drenching his undershirt, the young woman staring past Hector to his pickup truck.

"And, after this funeral of yours?" asks the tall man.

Hector's fists clench to his hips, his posture mirroring the tall man's, heat rushing across him. "Fireworks display in Pauls Valley," Hector says.

"Pauls Valley!" says the tall man, a mischievous grin on his pearl white face. "Goddamn, Vera. How about that?" he says, chuckling to the young woman next to him. "Fireworks in Pauls Valley, Oklahoma."

Vera brushes her brittle black hair from her greasy cheeks, a hint of a smile on her thin lips, her husband at her side in his untucked western shirt and black jeans.

The tall man looks away to dense trees where he hid with his brother. He turns, moves closer to Hector. Their eyes meet. "I killed a Paul once."

A bullet rips Hector's throat, his hands to his neck, warm blood gushing from his mouth down white cotton twill, a semi-truck roaring across the interstate, drowning Josefina's screams from their pickup, Hector drowning in his own blood.

Grady grabs a .38 caliber gun from his brother, runs up the hill to the truck, his eyes fixed on a shocked, horrified Josefina.

Hector stumbles to the tall man, can't breathe, dizzy, his hands on his neck, swings his fist and falls to the ground, his head slamming against the open station wagon door. The tall man kicking him in his face with his work boot.

Josefina grabs the window crank, crying. Grady rushes up the hill toward her. Her hand on the window, he shoots, shattering glass. She screams, staring at her hand bloodied from glass, hears her son yell from the camper, "Mom!" Josefina hides beneath the window, a bullet firing past her, her hands over her ears. She turns, looks at keys in the ignition.

Bullets ping the side of their pickup, spiral through air, cars speeding south and north across the interstate. Josefina reaches across the console for the keys, wipes shattered glass from her face, glass cutting her cheek and hand. She turns the keys, engine revving.

Hector on his back in grass beside the station wagon, gurgling blood, struggling to breathe, thinking about his son and military school, staring at the blue sky. He dies.

Josefina grabs for the steering wheel, pulling instead Hector's folded suit coat, a bullet slashing her cheek, stinging, burning, bleeding. Her hand over her cheek, her face streaming with tears, snot from her nose. She hears the whir of traffic and her son banging on the rectangular window into the cab. She's trembling, reaching for the steering wheel, and another bullet tears into her throat, her mouth filling with warm blood, seeing in her mind a locked camper door, hearing their dog, barking, growling. Then, nothing. Her body slumps.

The tall man looks to Vera, then past the grassy incline to the pickup. He slides a hunting knife from his back pocket and marches stealthily up the hill.

Traffic flows north and south on I-35, power lines parallel to a service road. Standing at the back of the pickup truck, traffic rushing past him, the tall man punches his hunting knife into the camper door.

Enrique's eyes widen, terrified, staring at the blade cutting through the camper, his dog barking furiously at sunlight piercing aluminum with each stab. Enrique scoots from the camper door, shivering in his suit, turns to a duffle bag beneath the window into the cab, remembers his dad's hunting guns. The knife pounding, stabbing into the camper like a battering ram. His breathing heavy, Enrique scrambles across the truck bed past his inhaler on the beige blanket, his dog barking, snarling behind him at stabbing sounds. Blood sprayed above him across the rectangular window into the cab.

Sunlight pouring on him, sweat dripping from his slicked shaggy hair, the tall man stands in blazing heat, single-minded, punches his knife into the camper, saws a jagged shape of a rectangle into the camper door. He stops, knife at his side. He looks through a hole he's ripped into the camper, sees the boy, shouts to his brother, "Bring the gun!"

Enrique unzips the duffle bag. All at once, he realizes, guns in the bag are unloaded, chambers empty of cartridges.

Grady tosses the .38 to his brother, and the tall man points his gun barrel through the hole he's cut into the camper. He stands with feet shoulder-width apart, his hand high on the handle of his revolver, his other hand tight around his grip on the gun. He slides the barrel of the revolver back and forth across the rectangular hole, firing it into the camper. Gunfire flashes across the enclosed truck bed. Enrique digging frantic through the bag, sweating, sobbing, his dog barking violent, bullets blasting, ricocheting off metal, ripping through Enrique's hand.

The tall man slams shut the driver's side door, sits behind the steering wheel in the pickup truck, his adrenaline racing. He wipes blood from his face on the back of his hand. Grady and Vera sitting at his side in the truck cab. Behind them in the camper, the dog barks relentless, growling, engine revving, and the truck speeds from the shoulder, swerving north onto the interstate.

CHAPTER FOURTEEN

Sam paces in the hot sun, nervous, stares down the long dirt road. He stretches his arm across his bare chest, glances at familiar street signs above him, Southwest 89th and Pennsylvania, his eyes following Pennsylvania until the dirt road disappears into blue southern sky.

He's sprinting, his shaggy brown hair dripping sweat, grasslands surrounding him, sunlit as if on fire. Warm wind across his face, the dirt road in front of him, his foot on the ground, then his other, leg down, foot down, leg down, faster.

The more he runs, the more nervous he becomes. The thud of his running shoes on dirt, cicadas buzzing with chirping birds through grassy fields. His breathing heavy, rhythmic, his heartbeat quicker. Alone in a distant field on the west side of the dirt road, South Tree's sprawling, twisted branches, the old oak tree's dense green leaves canopying the road up ahead in a haze of heat.

An hour later in the high noon sun, Sam wipes his sweaty arm across his face, dirt from his forehead. He's squatting in green grass, tying electric poly rope to the bottom of a wood fence post.

Cattle flood across the wheat field by the dozens when he's done, grazing grass and weeds. He watches cattle move past him, some he's birthed as calves. Flies buzz as manure bakes in the sun. Bales of hay consume his thoughts. He counts cattle in his head, how much hay his farm will need to feed their cows in the coming months.

The grandfather clock begins its full chime sequence at the bottom of the mahogany staircase, its melody striking across the farmhouse. Framed Ford family photos ascend along the wall down the staircase. The sheriff's bed made upstairs. The framed photo on his nightstand of Ryan in his sheriff's uniform, smiling with Mary Mae, their names inscribed on the frame. The door to Dylan's room closed on the north side of the hallway. Short rope hanging outside Dylan's room from an attic door in the ceiling. The door at the west end of the hallway open to Sam's room, sunlight across his bedroom's wood floors, the cloth color photo of earth from the moon hanging above Sam's headboard, chimes downstairs concluding Westminster Quarters.

Sam's in the kitchen, pulling a plain white t-shirt over his head, his hair still damp from his shower.

The grandfather clock chimes from his living room again, then once more. Two p.m.

A spiral cord dangles from a yellow phone attached to gray brick wall lining the west side of the kitchen. The window closed above the kitchen sink beside the gas stove. Two cast iron skillets clean on the stovetop. A note on the fridge, "Missed you this morning, brother. Dylan." Sam rubs his beard, studying the note. He looks to the window above the sink, thinks about Sarah, the red barn out the window where he passed out the night of the Sulphur murders, the small creek behind the barn, the wheat field disappearing east behind the creek.

He looks to his side at the quiet narrow hallway through the laundry room north of the kitchen. He slips another note from his back pocket, holds it for a moment, worried, glances again to the window above the sink.

Sam picks up the phone, contemplating numbers on a circular dial. He's memorized the note he's holding in only six hours, hears a dial tone on the phone, imagines turning the finger wheel, but can't.

Moments later, the dial tone stops.

Sam clears his throat, waits, anxious, the phone to his ear, the note in his hand. A young man's voice picks up on the other end, "Hello?"

"Matthew?"

Violins swell an hour later at the start of a song Sam's heard before but can't name, soulful jazz as he stares at a movie poster framed on a rust red brick wall. A vibrant golden image of a polished metal robot, shaped like a woman, staring back at Sam from the bottom of the bronze poster, tall art deco skyscrapers behind and above the robot, drawn in crisp, clean lines, *Metropolis* above the buildings in art deco lettering. At the bottom of the poster, "Ein Film Von Fritz Lang."

Then, a woman's mournful, raspy voice starts to sing "This Bitter Earth." Sam backs from the poster, remembering the lyrics, a rhythm and blues album he found with Sarah in a thrift store. "What fruit it bears," he hears her sing. "What good is love, that no one shares?"

Across the room, Matthew's hands fold thin paper used for making cigarettes, sides of the paper pinched in one hand between his thumb and pointer fingers, his other hand sprinkling marijuana.

Sam studies cherry wood bookshelves along the brick wall, a reflection of waves across the brick, the bookshelves four rows each of four stacked squares. Sam's cowboy boots clunk with each step on the concrete floor.

Matthew clusters marijuana in the center of the thin paper, focused, folds the paper over the weed.

In front of Sam, Plato's *Republic* on one of the square shelves, Saint Augustine's *City of God* next to Plato and Aristotle's *Poetics*, author James Baldwin beside the Bible, Hegel. The wood shelves sparse with books and antiques, vinyl records and potted succulent plants.

Matthew twists the bottom end of the joint, shakes it to pack weed in the paper. He glances across the room at Sam, still faced away, at Sam's shaggy brown hair, at his Wranglers, then back to the rolled joint.

Violins swell again on the song, and Sam notices an ink drawing on the brick wall, a clown holding a balloon with one hand, a cigarette in the other.

"Lord, this bitter earth," he hears the woman sing again with the violins. "Yes, can be so cold."

Matthew lights his joint, leans back in a pallet of pillows on his concrete floor. "Today, you are young," he hears the woman sing. He closes his eyes, smokes, listens to violins and rhythmic bass guitar across his bedroom. "Too soon, you're old."

Sam looks from the ink drawing to Matthew across the room, Matthew's brown afro, Matthew's eyes still closed, Matthew's lips moving silently to the song.

"But, while a voice within me cries," the woman sings, "I'm sure someone may answer my call. And, this bitter earth." Matthew mimics. "May not be so bitter after all." Sam looks back to cherry wood bookshelves, thinking about Sulphur.

Along the south side of the bedroom, sunlight shines through a wall of windows. Waves from the pool outside reflecting across the room's red brick walls.

With his eyes still shut, Matthew holds the joint in the air. "You smoke?" he says.

"Sure," Sam says, looking again at the ink drawing.

Matthew hears Sam's boots on the concrete floor, feels a breeze from a ceiling fan. He passes the joint to Sam, not looking at him, blows smoke circles through the air.

Sam sits on one of the pillows surrounding an antique wood trunk. He grabs another pillow from the floor, puts it against the wall, and leans back on it with his long legs bent in front of him, his arms resting across his knees. "Like it out here?" he asks, smokes the joint.

"Out here?" Matthew says.

Sam stares across the small rectangular room, feels smoke fill his lungs, exhales slow. "This was the pool house, right?" Sam says.

Matthew rests his hands behind his head. "My grandfather and I rebuilt this place into a bedroom over the summer when I was fourteen," Matthew says, "when my youngest brother was born. We needed more space in the house. Seemed a fair setup. You got brothers or sisters?"

Sam watches smoke drift through sunlight. "Twin brother," Sam says. He passes the joint to Matthew. "We don't look alike, though. Fraternal."

Matthew looks over to Sam. "Y'all close?"

"Close enough," Sam says, looks to the fan swirling on the vaulted ceiling, not noticing Matthew looking at him, thinking about Dylan's note, how in eight years since they've lived in the city, until this morning, the two brothers had never missed their morning run together.

Matthew stands, barefoot in brown plaid pants. He walks to the bookshelves, slips a lighter from his back pocket. "My grandfather used to talk about architecture and housing, how it was for his father growing up," Matthew says, "how families were closer, two or three generations living together in the same house, that it'd changed by the time grandfather was born. He wasn't sure if that was a good or bad thing."

Incense burns from the bookshelves—sandalwood—and Matthew slips his lighter into his pocket. "When we worked on this place, grandfather told me his father was first in our family to live on his own." Matthew kneels to the bottom bookshelves, flips through vinyl records. "His father moved to the city, apparently, around turn of the century," Matthew says, "lived east of downtown, long-term lease in a rooming house during one of the city's first construction booms, when the railroad was bringing jobs." Matthew slides Led Zeppelin's *III* from a shelf. "Lots of young men like him renting from rooming houses, hotels, having arrived mostly from small towns, single guys in their teens and twenties, living by themselves for the first time, looking for factory and construction work, building the city. Grandfather's father got work as a brick mason," Matthew says, standing up with the Zeppelin record. "Your people from here?"

Sam looks to an oak wood drafting table along the wall of windows. "Dad grew up in southeast Oklahoma," Sam says. "Little Dixie, down around Robbers Cave. Wasn't born here, though."

Matthew places a needle from a turntable on the record, and the first song plays. He smokes, nods his head to a relentless opening staccato riff. He mimics silently to himself the singer's wailing howl, flips over the album's cover art to look at the back. "What about your mom?" Matthew asks.

Sam looks from the drafting table to dense trees outside, blowing with the wind. "She passed last year," Sam says. "Cancer."

Matthew turns from the bookshelves, sees Sam still sitting against the brick wall, staring out the windows. "Sorry to hear that, man," Matthew says, his words sincere. "She from here?"

"East of here," Sam says, watching the trees. "Choctaw. Out past Spencer."

Matthew grabs an ashtray from his drafting table. He walks along a futon mattress sprawled on his floor, straightens his short-sleeve, gray button-up utility shirt. He sits on pillows surrounding his antique wood trunk, passes the joint to Sam. "I know Spencer," Matthew says.

Sunlight across his face, his hands clasped at his knees, Sam looks from the windows. He smokes, glances at Matthew. "I've seen you rodeo out there," Sam says.

Smoke flows from the joint, and Sam passes it to Matthew, the ceiling fan swirling above them, the Zeppelin song the only sound in the bedroom.

"Wanna go for a walk?" Matthew says.

Outside in warm air, Sam and Matthew walk on a quiet neighborhood street, a circular driveway on a corner lot in front of Matthew's two-story red brick house disappearing behind them.

"The secret to summers here is shade," Matthew says, his hands in his pockets, walking on a street winding between ranch-style, modern, and contemporary homes built into canyons and wooded green hills. Mature tall trees shading each side of the street, blackjack oak in sloping yards.

As he walks, Sam folds his arms, glances up through canopying leaves at shimmers of blue sky. Matthew smiles, and Sam notices.

"I walk or bus everywhere," Matthew says, thinking about design, his eyes following mid-century modern architecture. He looks to a basketball goal in a driveway. "I walked to Circa Club last night," he says, "not so bad, four-and-a-half miles, took about an hour. Gives me time to get my mind right. Mostly, I walked 50th Street, which is nice, because 50th runs alongside some of our city's oldest neighborhoods. Hardly any sidewalks, though." Matthew turns to Sam. "Where'd they bury your mother? If you don't mind my asking."

"We scattered her ashes where I grew up," Sam says, "down in Sulphur."

Still with his hands in his pockets, Matthew thinks about the murders, his father's fearful sermon. "After working as a brick mason, grandfather's father started his own funeral business," Matthew says, "built it himself, back when Oklahoma's first state law segregated everything—including cemeteries. Our family business," he says, looks up at flashes of sunlight through leaves.

His arms still folded, Sam looks beside him to blue lilies in a garden sloping down a yard. He hears in Matthew's words a careful drawl, a familiar cadence Sam remembers from Pastor Thomas' sermon Sunday evening, more measured, calm. He hears a helicopter hovering, trailing off toward downtown.

At the southern edge of his neighborhood, Matthew looks to a stop sign, a minivan driving from 50th, turning into his wooded housing addition. Matthew still with his hands in his pockets, shade from trees giving way to sunlight and warmer air.

About a mile south of Matthew's neighborhood, the rattle of a wooden roller coaster sifts through trees as Sam and Matthew walk up a hill through dense blackjack. Sam follows Matthew, hears the roller coaster trudge on a wooden track up a lift hill, branches crunching beneath Sam's boots. Seconds later, screams fill the wooded forest, the coaster plummeting fifty-five mph down tracks through the woods, people on the ride suddenly visible, then gone.

They arrive at an amusement park, a Ferris wheel towering from a distant midway, a young family of three in front of them steering motorboats on a small lake.

The wooden coaster whips past them again, racing down a sixty-foot drop to a rush of crying and cheers before disappearing into the woods.

Ducks float in the lake, a young boy in the two-seat motorboat pointing out the ducklings' every movement to his mother, the boy's father watching from another boat.

The west side of the amusement park's quiet, clear from rides, faint screams from the roller coaster fading east through the trees.

Matthew slides his hands in his pockets, looks at Sam, and says, "Shall we?"

Sam shrugs, a wry, puzzled look on his face. "Why not?"

The pair walk in silence along the lake, a lighthouse in the water near the shoreline, the grassy shore giving way to an open field behind them of shrubbery and trees.

Sam looks across the lake, notices on the north side of the park a large group of people gathered under a shaded picnic pavilion, carrying ice chests and covered food, greeting each other enthusiastically.

Above the lake, whispers and gentle laughter from a sky-lift ride carrying passengers over the water, Matthew watching the Alpine Skyway moving riders north to south across the amusement park. He looks over to Sam, who's still focused on the gathering under the picnic pavilion, people of all ages.

Skee-Ball minutes later, Matthew rolling a miniature bowling ball up the game's incline ramp, Sam sliding coins into a Skee-Ball machine next to Matthew's, noting his score.

"Practicing already for second, huh?" Sam says, glances over his shoulder to Matthew's machine totaling points.

Matthew smirks, rolling another ball up the ramp, adding another fifty points, grabbing another ball from the machine. "Second's gonna look a lot like first here a minute when you actually start playing," Matthew says.

Sam's Skee-Ball machine releases a torrent of heavy plastic balls in a queue, colorful lights flashing across the game.

Outside, "Play Skee-Ball: A Bowling Game, 9 Balls for 5 cents" written across an aluminum building's open garage door entrance, the Ferris wheel behind the building spinning in place.

Matthew rolls another ball up the ramp, fifty more points.

Sam walks through a whiff of fresh popcorn, hears splashing, bells from games. He looks behind him through the crowd to colorful images of an octopus, sea lion, and dolphin leaping from water atop a building. Beneath these animal images, Sea Aquarium above Mysterious Underwater World. Written on either side of the aquarium's entrance, Performing Porpoises and Reptiles.

Sam notices a line in front of the wooden roller entrance, Fun House across the same building alongside Auto Skooter and Rifle Range. He watches people through an entrance into Auto Skooter crash their bumper cars into each other.

Inside the funhouse, curvy mirrors distort Sam's reflection, his tall thin body suddenly shrunk. He walks through a mirror maze, no longer sure where Matthew's gone. Sam's boots clunk concrete floor, echoing through the quiet room, Sam's reflection along a hall of mirrors shifting, multiplying, fragmenting. He hears a baby start to cry, the child's mother shushing it somewhere in the funhouse.

Sam's standing alone sometime later at the bottom of two slides in a basement, the length of the polished wood slides disappearing above him in the darkness.

Silence in the basement. Sam can barely see his own hands. He looks to his boots, hears a cranking sound, a wheel on the floor eight feet across lit up all at once with a white spotlight on a wall, the rest of the room still dark. A half dozen people visible suddenly on the wheel with Sam, an elliptical hump at the wheel's center.

Matthew looks across the room at Sam, the two of them standing on the large wheel with a couple young kids and teenagers. The wheel begins to spin slowly, nearly knocking Matthew to the ground before he regains his footing. He smiles across the room to Sam as the wheel turns its steady spin.

The two young kids, a brother and sister, watch each other across the wheel, standing in place, having dared the other to stay on longer, the sister's red hair in two braids. They sit, following the lead of three laughing teenagers, the brother's palms firm at his sides on the spinning wheel, his eyes still fixed on his sister.

Sam starts to kneel, stumbles, balances himself. He sits, the last to do so, the spinning picking up speed, his palms on the wooden wheel. He notices the boy beside him do the same, never taking his eyes from his sister. They spin faster, and Sam looks to Matthew, who's grinning at him from the elliptical hump at the center of the wheel.

Matthew turns to a teenager beside him, spotlight on the padded wall whooshing by, velocity increasing, pulls everyone toward the edges of the room, more difficult to stay on the wheel, centripetal force slamming two of the teens into the padded wall, then another, the boy beside Sam still staring at his sister.

Sam steadies himself, turning faster, can barely hang on, palms sweating, Matthew sliding from the elliptical hump, rushes past Sam in a blur with the girl and her brother.

They eat in midway around six o'clock. Sam takes a bite from his Indian Taco, watches lights illuminate arcade games, hears bits of passing conversations. He eats another bite of fry bread from his plate, smells cotton candy and greasy corn dogs.

Matthew wipes powdered sugar from his shirt, eats another bite from warm funnel cake on his plate. He wipes a napkin across his mouth.

The two of them stand in the middle of midway, each holding plastic cups and plates of food, staring off through a growing crowd.

Sam drinks lemonade, kids running in front of him toward a merry-go-round and wishing well, a windmill turning behind him. He glances but looks away from Matthew's brown eyes.

The Ferris wheel lights up behind Matthew. He eats another bite of funnel cake.

They're on a city bus, the sun still up, Sam watching out a window as a seemingly endless row of abandoned brick buildings pass him by along hilly Northeast 23rd Street.

Matthew's in an aisle seat beside Sam. He looks to a brown grocery bag near his feet, whole wheat bread near the top, an egg carton, an older Black woman with gray hair, probably in her eighties, standing in the aisle alongside the bag, her wrinkled hand gripping a metal bar above her. The bus fairly full, other passengers sitting, standing.

Matthew hears conversations happening around her, the old woman's gaze focused from the middle of the bus on traffic through the windshield. She looks only forward, and Matthew wonders what she's hearing, how she's always standing when he sees her ride, courteous but never talkative. He looks to a white sidestripe on his brown hi-top Vans, his hands clasped between his legs.

The bus brakes at a bus stop, conversations continuing onboard to the sound of the braking system releasing air.

From his window, Sam watches two Black teenagers stand from a bus stop bench. A reflection of deserted brick storefronts along the bus window. The two young men boarding the bus, leaving behind cracked sidewalks with grass growing through pavement. Sam hears behind him a young mom ask her daughter about their science museum trip, the third grader describing how she climbed through a jungle gym shaped like a crystal molecule.

Matthew looks up, hands still clasped between his legs, the older Black woman gone, carrying her grocery bag in the aisle past other passengers, walking steadily, wearily, conversations around her, traffic and the state capitol over a hill through the windshield.

From his window, Sam looks to a tattered metal awning above an entrance to another abandoned business, a barbershop, the one-story brick building's windows covered with a welded wire mesh security guard, a vacant lot beside the building. He hears the bus closing its doors.

The bus arrives at another stop, braking to the same sound of air released from the brake system. Through the windshield, a three-story red brick church, Matthew on the bus walking in the aisle, staring ahead of him at arched wooden doors at the bottom of the church's neo-Gothic tower.

Sam stands at an intersection, the bus idling, a young Vietnamese couple walking past him on a sidewalk, holding hands, Robinson and Northwest 11th on street signs.

"Thanks," Matthew says to the bus driver, stepping down to a curb.

They head south, walking alone along the church, the bus driving past them, Matthew's hands in his pockets, Sam's arms folded across his chest.

Behind the church, the setting sun, all the church's stained-glass windows lit with fading orange and brown sunlight.

A red brick wall surrounds concrete stairs to the church's arched wooden entrance, and Sam tilts his head up past the wall to a similarly arched stained-glass window at the center of the church.

"That Baptist congregation's been here since the 1889 Land Run," Matthew says, nods behind him to Sam, "back during Twin Territory days."

On the west side of the road, they walk south across an intersection on Robinson, Matthew looking down 11th at an evening sky colored with pink clouds, the Baptist church an entire city block to the next north south road.

"The church building's newer, though," Matthew says, almost to himself, "built somewhere after statehood, early 1910s, maybe 1912, the chapel and gym, I think, early fifties. The courtyard's later, too."

Sam looks back to the church.

"I think often about church as physical spaces," Matthew says, "places for education. Love learning church history, talking theology, religious history, wish we had more of those conversations at Sunday school. Did you know first Christian churches were in the home," Matthew says, "with women cooking and leading discussions on scripture?"

Sam walks with his arms still folded. "Guess not," he says. "Why women?"

Matthew looks to a distant downtown skyline at the south end of Robinson, thinks about his grandfather's stories. "Everyone thinks the divide between Christians and Jews is whether Jesus was the son of God, prophesied Messiah who would liberate Israel, but that wasn't the debate," Matthew says. "The debate was over which parts of Jewish law would define Christianity, this new religion born from Jewish beliefs, whether early Christians could discard parts of God's law and Judaism, keep the rest, which foods God wanted them to eat, kosher rules for eating at the heart of the fight."

Beside them, a vacant grassy lot along the west side of the road, and Sam looks past power lines and two recently cleared city blocks to a towering red brick building on a hill, several stories tall, St. Anthony's Hospital. "Why's food so important?" Sam asks.

"Because, early Christians thought of Heaven as a food banquet," Matthew says. "Meals were the ritual early Christians shared in common, thought of the Eucharist as an actual meal, not symbolism, that God comes to us as food. At the time, you don't necessarily know where your next meal's coming from, when you'll eat next." Matthew looks up the street to a gigantic gold dome atop a First Christian Church at the next intersection, stained-glass windows wrapping around the dome. "Early Christians held communal meals in the home," Matthew says, "so, the head of the household, sometimes the father but, often, the mother, led house churches, home already a social space at ease with women's authority."

"What changed?" Sam asks.

"The church changed," Matthew says, walking past a fire hydrant and detour sign. "The church reshaped to resemble the structure of city government, trying to bring order to what some saw as a chaotic, disorganized religion."

Sam looks across the street to the three-story First Christian Church. He notices on the gray building a gold dome, a smaller dome atop a tholobate with limestone columns lower on the church's north side. "Why city government?" Sam asks, staring up at a statue of a religious figure within the columns.

"Helped them think through how to centralize house churches under a single authority," Matthew says, "a congregation modeled as a city, a bishop modeled after an administrator." Matthew stops at an intersection, a couple cars driving past him, closed garage doors on the first floor of a two-story maroon brick building built in the twenties, an automotive warehouse. "You should all follow the bishop as Jesus Christ did the Father," Matthew says, glances to a stoplight, "follow, too, the elders as you would the apostles, and respect the deacons as you would God's law." The stoplight turns yellow. "He who pays the bishop honor has been honored by God," Matthew says. "But, he who acts without the bishop's knowledge is in the devil's service." He looks at Sam. "Quoting scripture and old religious thinkers are two of my many specialties, by the way," Matthew says.

"Many specialties?" Sam says.

"Skee-Ball, for instance." Matthew smiles.

They're halfway across a crosswalk, Sam looking behind him to tall columns lining the top of a wide staircase to three sets of double doors into the First Christian Church, streetlamps turning on around it.

The sidewalk on the west side of Robinson becomes a blush red brick walkway with trees and lit streetlights. Sam looks to public housing across the street, an American flag flying from a pole in front of an Episcopal Church Center across from the apartments. Beside them, Sam sees their reflections along the west side of the walkway in glass windows on the first floor of a tall brick office building. Then, another vacant lot. The walkway paved concrete again.

At the next intersection, Central High School, Matthew glancing up at windows along the gray five-story Collegiate Gothic-style building, a car parked parallel beside him in front of a parking meter.

"You plan on being a preacher like your father?" Sam asks.

"Not a preacher," Matthew says, "an architect." The downtown skyline closer. "And, if I were, not one like him."

Sam hears a curious blend of confidence and sadness in Matthew's words, scratches his beard. "Where's school to study architecture?" Sam asks.

"New York University," Matthew says with his hands in his pockets. He looks to pavement. "I leave this fall." And, in an instance, Sam wants to leave with him, his stomach dropping as if he's racing his truck down rural roads where his mother grew up.

Sam folds his arms. They continue walking in silence.

They walk along the new Murrah Building, a nine-story structure of granite and glass stretching a city block to the next north south street, the space south behind it opening to an elevated, tree-filled courtyard. South of the courtyard, a five-story federal courthouse across the next intersection, Northwest 4th Street.

On the east side of Robinson, a Methodist church, limestone and brick, Sam staring at the church's bell tower, thinking about his parents' religious denomination. He looks to the federal courthouse, elevated figures almost floating from the east side of the granite and limestone building, three English settlers with a Native American man and woman, seemingly ethereal above a sidewalk.

"Church Row. That's what grandfather and older pastors call this street," Matthew says. "He'd bring me downtown when I was growing up, take me to diners, restaurants, to see movies at the Criterion on Main Street after church service on Sundays. You ever gone to the Criterion before they razed it?"

"Never got the chance," Sam says.

Matthew sighs. "This beautiful French revival building," he says, "Velvet walls, two orchestra pits and a built-in organ, 1,900 deep-cushioned seats, ushers, people dressing up to go to movies. Saw all kinds of first-run films with my grandfather," Matthew says. "*Chinatown, True Grit.* Like walking into a palace."

South of the federal courthouse, they walk along the city's first post office, Matthew studying the three-story limestone building's neoclassical architecture and arched windows, its red tile roof, pilasters, and ornate shallow balconies, bushes and shrubbery along the sidewalk.

"Surprised this building survived recent urban renewal implosions," Matthew says, staring up to a tall tower at the center of the post office, balustrades along the building's second and third floors. "Grandfather and I went to several of 'em over the past decade, the implosions. Saw old Biltmore Hotel come down, thousands of people there. Never seen grandfather cry til then. Not like that," Matthew says.

They wait at the next intersection for a Ferrari to pass, the Ferrari's small-engine consuming Sam's thoughts as it heads east, taller buildings and skyscrapers ahead of them, the post office extending west behind them an entire city block.

"Why'd your grandfather take it so hard?" Sam asks.

They walk across the intersection. "Alzheimer's," Matthew says. "Doctors diagnosed him last year."

Sam lowers his head, his arms still folded. "Sorry to hear it," Sam says.

"Thanks, man," Matthew says, unsure what to say next. He glances up, instead, at windows of varying shapes and sizes along a thirty-story skyscraper east side of Robinson. South of the new skyscraper, a ten-story red brick building at an intersection, Baniff on a vertical sign along the corner of the building.

They walk along a plaza on the west side of the street, south of another recently built skyscraper, sixteen stories, Matthew still looking up at a new corporate headquarters for Kerr-McGee oil and gas company.

Sam turns from trees in the plaza, notices Matthew staring at a new park south of Kerr-McGee. Barely anyone's downtown, Sam realizes, the park empty, streets uninhabited.

Matthew squints at a statue in the park, a sculpture of a young boy on a horse, his rifle strapped to his saddle, his horse's head down, the boy's father wearing a cowboy hat, kneeling with a stake in the ground and a hammer mid-swing in his other hand. Matthew looks from the sculpture to a train stopped on a bridge at the east end of 2nd Street.

"Grandfather went to school other side of those tracks," Matthew says. "And this street's where my grandfather's father became first in our family to live on his own." Matthew's gaze follows 2nd two blocks til it disappears under the bridge. "You listen to jazz?" Matthew asks.

"Some," Sam says. "Mostly with my brother and his girlfriend."

Matthew looks from the train to skyscrapers and high-rises on either side of Robinson. "I love jazz," Matthew says, "improvisation. Grandfather's stories always involve jazz history. He was born at the turn of the century, soon after his father arrived in the city. His father helped build Oklahoma City's first public schools, even an all-white elementary, Webster." Matthew looks from the twenty-story Petroleum Building to a taller tower south of it, his thoughts hazy, rambling, worrying, focused again. "Sometime before statehood," Matthew says, "the County created an all-Black school district on the other side of those train tracks, turned Webster into an all-Black school, Douglass High School. When we'd come downtown, grandfather would talk about his walk from East 2nd to the corner of Walnut and Reno, walking every day across Walnut Bridge to high school."

Sam turns to Matthew, confused. "The school was in our old warehouse district?"

"That whole area was a federal military outpost for a year or so after the Land Run," Matthew says. "Feds gave it to the City, made 'em build a park along the river and school. Rest of the area became the warehouse district. Grocers, hardware, furniture companies, wholesalers setting up beside the railroad, agriculture and cotton, industries like that."

"Why's it abandoned?" Sam asks, realizes they're in the heart of their city's downtown business district.

"The Depression," Matthew says, notices Sam staring up at the thirty-three story Ramsey Tower on the east side of Robinson. "They ever tell you about the skyscraper race between those two buildings?" Matthew nods south of Ramsey to an art deco skyscraper across the next intersection, First National Building.

"My dad mentioned something," Sam says. "Never details, though."

Matthew's thoughts grow hazy again, blurring, sentences stammering in his head. Closes his eyes as he walks. He focuses on each breath, every sound around him. His mind calming, slowing. He opens his eyes.

Robinson and First on street signs, they walk in the shade of skyscrapers, downtown still empty of people.

Matthew looks to the U-shaped Perrine Building, thinks about Perrine's widow designing the thirteen-story building in 1927 with ventilation and lighting in mind, how the Perrines secured this spot two years after the Land Run, how the family once operated a horse stable and funeral parlor where the skyscraper sits today.

"Zelia Breaux taught grandfather jazz," Matthew says, "to appreciate it." Matthew looks to orange and brown sky. "Ms. Breaux's father owned Aldridge Theater in Deep Deuce," Matthew says, "back when it was an all-Black neighborhood during Jim Crow, Black-owned businesses, barbershops, grocery stores, hotels north of the warehouse district. You ever seen the *Negro Motorist Green Book*?"

"No, what is it?" Sam says.

"List of places Black folk could go for service in the thirties, forties, fifties, sixties," Matthew says. "Grandfather had a copy, bought one for my father in the fifties when he was a teenager and got his first car. Addresses for businesses in all fifty states, service stations where it was safe to stop for gas, hotels, restaurants. I read my dad's copy," Matthew says. "He kept it in his glove box. It was an actual green book. This post office worker in Harlem wrote it," Matthew says, "Victor Green. Guess that's how it got its name."

Sam smiles, his arms folded again, his gaze moving from gray-black marble and aluminum art decorating First National Building to Matthew's bronze skin, toned triceps, and chiseled jaw. Sam forces himself to look at art deco designs across the first five stories of the skyscraper, an entrance adorned with silver lanterns, cherubs, peacocks, and swans. The first building as a kid he saw from the downtown skyline. Then, Matthew again.

"Grandfather frequented Zelia's after returning home from the First World War," Matthew says. "Had a room near his parents' place around the corner from her dad's theater. He'd tell me stories about getting drunk every night at Zelia's, describe himself as an eighteen, nineteen, twenty, twenty-one-year-old there, wouldn't even call the place 'Aldridge,' because he saw it only as hers. Saw Billie Holiday and Duke Ellington perform. Charlie Christian. Told me Billie and Ellington traveled with the *Green Book*, too."

Sam sees cleared city blocks ahead of them, construction stopped on a six-story building, a crane above the unfinished structure.

"Grandfather despised how our city integrated our schools, though," Matthew says. "Forced bussing back in '71. Thought it destroyed our neighborhoods."

Sam furrows his brow, still walking with his arms folded. "How so?" he asks.

"Zelia became music supervisor for all our Black public schools east of the tracks," Matthew says. "Same year grandfather returned at the end of the First World War. She put a music teacher in each school, made sure all students learned music theory and history, classical music. She headed Douglass' music department after grandfather graduated, but he heard her work every night on 2nd at Aldridge. Her students brought Deep Deuce to life," Matthew says. "Because they knew music so well. What they learned in their classes, they played in churches and, from it, helped create jazz with New Orleans. Charlie Christian and Jimmy Rushing were her students."

Sam looks to Matthew, notices him walking with his hands in his pockets, wonders if he's walked this way all day. "Before forced bussing," he hears Matthew say, "teachers and principals lived in the neighborhood, cafeteria workers, support staff. If you got in trouble, wasn't long before your parents heard. Steal something from a nearby store, and the owner made sure your parents knew, because those businesses actually lived in the neighborhood, knew the neighbors they're serving. And, that's how community works, grandfather said. Busing students to schools twenty minutes across town ended that," Matthew says. "Shoulda just funded our schools proper, invest in our neighborhoods' infrastructure needs."

They walk along a dirt pit on the west side of Robinson, Sam staring at work-site trucks, construction trailers. "Why'd your grandfather fight in the First World War?"

"He talked more about when he returned," Matthew says. "Was horrified what he fought for abroad didn't exist at home. Saw lynchings. Towns with signs and unofficial laws warning Black people not to be seen there after sundown. Deep Deuce segregated from downtown and the rest of the city. Strangest thing," Matthew says.

Sam looks from tractors in the construction site to Matthew.

"Grandfather showed me copies of our city's weekly Black newspaper he'd kept during and after the war. Talked about how he and other veterans read *Black Dispatch* daily at Zelia's, the paper's editorials advocating respect for rule of law, promises President Wilson made about why we were fighting. He'd even read 'em to me sometimes as a kid. The Bible, too. "For those are the cornerstone of democracy," Matthew tries to recall, "Wilson says we go out to make the world safe for democracy … But, democracy means, if we would breathe the 'pure air' of which Wilson speaks … segregation, Jim Crow, and mob violence must die. That, in its stead, must rise justice and fairness." Matthew looks up the road, past the dirt pit to a lone skyscraper remaining at the end of Robinson, the city's first. "All I want is a good home and a wife," Matthew says, his voice mockingly deeper, "and, a children and food to feed them every night." The hint of a smile fades from his face.

Sam hears a playful wit in Matthew's words, melancholy.

They walk in silence. Matthew's thoughts drift before urban renewal to all the other tall buildings once surrounding the fourteen-story Colcord Hotel, the state's first building with steel-reinforced concrete, the vast dirt pit along Robinson surrounding it now.

"I read this news story," Matthew says, "this seventeen-year-old. He walked different. So, one afternoon, he's walking home from school, and these guys chase him. People in his town didn't care for the way he walked. The guys chasing him threw him from the roof of a five-story building, an old mill on the outskirts of town. He died."

Sam looks to Matthew.

"My father reads his Bible different than grandfather and me," Matthew says, staring up at the Colcord. "So, I made an agreement with my dad start of senior year. He'd allow me to accept scholarships to attend architecture school at NYU, if I attended therapy til I left. And, I have for the past year," Matthew says, looks from Colcord to pavement, his hands still in his pockets.

"What happens at therapy?" Sam asks, scratches his beard.

"They show me photos from a slide projector," Matthew says, "images of men holding hands, hugging, kissing, two men together. I sit in a chair and watch. When I see those pictures ... " Matthew stops, thoughts hazy, breathes. "We do sessions every weekday. An hour at church or my parent's house."

Sam walks with his arms folded beside Matthew. They walk past the pit in the shadow of the Colcord. "Sounds miserable, man," Sam says.

"Was the only way I could convince them to let me leave for architecture school," Matthew says. "Grandfather taught me to read, interpret, and think for myself about the Bible, made sure I knew Socrates, Erasmus, the Protestant Reformation, Martin Luther, taught me debates between denominations, how kings and queens for a thousand years during the Dark Ages forbid people to read the Bible for themselves, how kings burned people alive as heretics for having different biblical interpretations. My father doesn't believe in interpretation," Matthew says. "But, grandfather asked me to read the Holy Bible as if each word has a deeper meaning. Reading with him, I felt as if the Bible were lit up with a new light," Matthew says, smiling, half-quoting a 19th Century Presbyterian minister he's read more than once, one of his favorite pastors. His smile fades again.

Robinson and Sheridan on street signs, scattered colored clouds across the south side of the city, another dirt pit south of Sheridan.

Sam and Matthew make their way across the street, Colcord behind them at the intersection, the top and first floor of the fourteen-story hotel lit with white light.

The sun's setting across them, honey orange and brown sunlight painting downtown, Matthew focusing on the dirt pit in front of them where Biltmore Hotel once stood. He sees in his thoughts an architect standing ten years earlier with city leaders over a ten-by-twelve-foot design of a promised downtown, "City of the Future." Matthew tries to imagine the plan's proposed gardens stretching west from Robinson along the two city blocks south of him, complete with a crystal bridge botanical tube and pond in a park resembling Tivoli Gardens in Copenhagen, Denmark. But, Matthew's thoughts become hazy, blur. He sees, instead, him and his grandfather watching the thirty-three story Biltmore implode where the hotel would've overlooked the planned gardens.

Biltmore gone, mud across two city blocks, stagnant water in two different dirt pits, a single bench on cleared land.

The pair walk west on Sheridan along the dirt pits to the distant sound of fireworks. They sit on the bench, Matthew clasping his hands between his legs.

Sam looks north across Sheridan to four cleared city blocks, almost all the businesses and buildings once a block away along Main Street gone, City Hall beside an eleven-story County Courthouse staring back from two blocks away on First. Sam folds his arms.

"Back in the early twenties, your grandfather lived in Deep Deuce, police raided this man's home, this Black fella, last name Chandler," Sam says. "Officers found where he and his dad made moonshine six miles north of town, got in a shootout, Oklahoma City police. Chandler's dad died. So did a deputy sheriff, federal Prohibition agent, another deputy wounded." Sam rubs his beard.

Matthew listens curiously to a story he's never heard.

"Cops arrested Chandler, jailed him," Sam says, folds his arms again. "Rumors reached other side of those tracks. Three men, no masks, took Chandler from his cell. Bunch of Black men met on East 2nd, armed themselves, thought through how to stop those fellas from lynching Chandler. Police arrived on 2nd with Oklahoma City's mayor. Mayor and police let three carloads of Black men from the crowd chase after Chandler, disarmed 'em first all of their guns. Two Black officers went with 'em. Searched all night til noon next day." Sam stares across the dirt pit to the County Courthouse. "They'd shot him twice," Sam says. "Found his body beaten five miles west of here, hanging from one of four trees in a field on Reno Avenue and Council."

Matthew leans back on the bench, Reno a block behind him on the south side of the dirt pit.

"I read about that arrest after I moved to the city," Sam says, "found files buried in boxes in my dad's office. When he became sheriff." Sam looks from the County Courthouse to the red beacon atop a distant First National Building. "*Black Dispatch* was in that box, too," Sam says. "Stories about an undertaker taking Chandler to Deep Deuce, people gathering there to view his body. Paper wanted to know where the sheriff was, why he hadn't stopped those men from kidnapping Chandler."

Matthew looks to Sam staring off, despair across Sam's sunlit face, a gleam in Sam's light blue eyes. Matthew unclasps his hands, places one on his lap, the other between him and Sam on the wood bench. He closes his eyes.

Fireworks boom in the distance. The sun still setting.

From the corner of his eye, Sam sees Matthew's hand on the bench, Matthew's eyes still closed, Sam wondering what Matthew's seeing. He looks away to the distant Oklahoma County Courthouse. They sit on the bench together, silent.

CHAPTER FIFTEEN

Two drumbeats, then strings start a song at the top of a Cherokee Gothic building. Fireworks explode in succession across the twilight sky, fizzling, crackling, bursting again. College students on the rooftop, dozens of them, conversations and laughter in pastel polos and summer dresses. A DJ standing over a turntable beside big audio speakers.

Dylan's distracted beside Cristine, Cristine laughing loud at a fraternity brother's joke. "No, dude," Cristine says, interrupts her own laughter. "So, I get in this wreck … "

"Cause you're a shitty fucking driver," Dylan says.

"Cause you can fuck right off this roof," Cristine says with a sardonic smile, winks at two sorority sisters.

Dylan smirks, drinks Budweiser, slips his hand in a front pocket of his khaki shorts. He turns from Cristine, finds Sarah through the crowd. At the edge of the rooftop, she attaches a camera mount to a tripod, beautiful in a sleeveless brown turtleneck and picnic-red plaid skirt he's never seen, Tate beside her, holding and studying her camera.

Sarah turns from her tripod, two sorority sisters watching Tate adjust her camera's focus ring.

"He's quite handsome," Sarah hears a sorority sister say. "August, he's official. And, if you did come here and pledge with us in spring," Sarah hears the other sister say to her, "Dylan's fraternity is like family to us ... "

From across the roof, Dylan's brown eyes meet Sarah's, fireworks behind him, the sorority sisters not noticing Sarah's sly smile to Dylan. Dylan furrows his brows, slack-jawed, wide-eyed, making faces, pretends he's hung himself with a rope.

Strings on the song reach a crescendo, collapsing into a psychedelic funk and swanky guitar riff at the start of Isaac Hayes's "Walk on By."

"But, I put it in reverse in the old Plaza District," Cristine says, "thinking it's in drive. Middle of the night, and I slam the holy fuck into this parallel-parked car. Say to myself, shit, car's gotta belong to some squatter in one of these abandoned duplexes."

Sarah positions her Pentax on her camera mount. She watches Tate sign to her, "Trees are old here on campus." She signs back to Tate, "I saw that." Gone, sorority sisters trying to recruit Sarah. She glances west of the university at dense trees in neighborhoods.

Sarah signs to Tate, "The elm behind you is my favorite. Nice colors in the sky, too." Tate looks behind him, a blue beam across the northern sky.

Through her camera lens, Norman, Oklahoma—a college town Sarah's seen only on television til tonight. Behind the elm, an American flag flying in a landscaped campus lawn along an oval drive. Sarah waits til Tate's truck comes into focus, his muddied dirt bike strapped at handlebars to either side of his pickup truck bed, Sarah's thumb and index finger turning a dial on her camera, Tate's '78 Ford Ranger lit under a streetlamp. Snap.

"But, that's what I'm saying." Cristine's hands move passionately. "Central planners can't know everything, everyone's needs, the level of supply, individual preferences."

Dylan finishes his beer, his hand in his front pocket caressing an engagement ring. He looks from the roof's makeshift guardrail, partygoers below in a courtyard dancing, talking. Suddenly, he's less sober, trying to focus on crimson brick and green ivy on another Cherokee Gothic building across the courtyard. "Individuals know what's best for them," Cristine says with sincerity Dylan's heard since sophomore year. He turns from blurred crimson and green ivy to Sarah and Tate across the roof signing, Tate looking through Sarah's camera. Watching his childhood best friend with his girlfriend, Dylan realizes Tate should officiate their marriage. Propose now?

"Society should want an efficient economy," Cristine says, two sorority sisters excusing themselves in coral pink dresses, chatting, laughing about an after-party on Chautauqua. Two fraternity brothers beside Dylan, following Cristine's every word.

"What're you studying?" Cristine asks.

"Landscape design," says one of the fraternity brothers, his accent Deep South, Dylan contemplating the young man, wonders if he was a linebacker in high school.

"Finance," says the other fraternity brother, Dylan recalling the lake last weekend, the wealthy banker's son saying he's from western Oklahoma—wrestling scholarship.

"Perfect." Cristine grins to the finance major. "You've read *Road to Serfdom*, then? *Wealth of Nations*? Government should never interfere with prices," Cristine says. "You only intervene in a market-based economy when a market failure occurs, when a specific externality exists. Pollution, for instance," Cristine says, "a monopoly. Marketing's a problem, too, because early economists never took seriously how marketing distorts an individual's understanding of products and prevents us from making rational, informed decisions."

Dylan looks at his beer bottle, realizes it's Coors, sees Mickey Mouse ears through the crowd, a fraternity brother wearing the familiar cartoon silhouette on his head, bragging about an internship, about a new way to drill shale rock for oil and natural gas.

"But, we don't need a federal government," the finance major says.

"That's the Articles of Confederation, friend," Cristine says, "not our Constitution."

"States should govern themselves, though," says the finance major, defiant, confident. "That's why we left Europe, to get rid of kings and central governments."

"Doctrine of Discovery is why Europeans left Europe," Dylan hears Cristine say, Dylan's hand in his pocket, grips his engagement ring. "Hear ye, hear ye. Official edict. Search for souls and gold." Dylan looks down to the courtyard. "Invade, capture, vanquish, and subdue all Muslims and pagans whatsoever, and other enemies of Christ wheresoever placed, and the kingdoms, dukedoms, principalities, dominions, possessions, and all moveable goods whatsoever held and possessed by them and to reduce their persons to perpetual slavery. Wherever you place your European flag, Christians, this land is your land. Pope Nicholas V to Portuguese King Alfonso V, 1452."

Dylan finishes his fourth beer, debates a fifth, watches the two fraternity brothers listen to Cristine. He glances to a clock tower west of the campus library, eleven p.m.

"Have you read Edmund Burke, yet?" Cristine asks.

"Burke?" says the finance major.

"Bro, read Burke," Cristine says.

"What're you gonna study?" the finance major asks Cristine.

"Law."

Tate signs to Sarah, "Cooler tonight. Still muggy, though."

"Humid," she signs back to him. She drinks from a plastic cup of water.

Tate smells savory chili in the air, spices drifting past them. He wonders if the flavorful scent made its way to Sarah.

Instead, his skin balmy, he signs, "I started swimming this summer. Every morning," his hands as if wading water, his index finger across his forehead in the shape of a claw.

"I still swim each morning," Sarah signs. "Force myself up around six, make my bed, drive downtown to the Y." Her hands create a rooftop. "Hate waking up early. But, water feels so good." She pauses, confused. "How do you say," she signs, spelling with her hand, 'rejuvenated.'

Tate gestures, and she signs back, "Thanks." For the first time, Sarah notices Tate's toned biceps when he signs, an Oklahoma flag across his sky-blue tank top, the battle shield of an Osage warrior across his shirt, the shield covered with an olive branch and peace pipe. Sarah signs, "After I swim, I feel rejuvenated, accomplished. My whole day ahead of me, only seven a.m."

Sarah notices wrinkles around Tate's eyes, his familiar smile faint. She sees his eyes widen a bit, his brows drawing together. "What's wrong?" she signs.

Tate takes a deep breath. "Town's on curfew," he signs. "Nightly, seven p.m. to seven a.m."

Sarah's thoughts rush to Sulphur, The Music Store door, Ben Bullock. Her hand to Tate's shoulder.

"Please, forgive me," Tate signs. "I must sound like a child."

"Nothing to forgive," Sarah signs. Behind Tate, Mickey Mouse ears on a young man flirting with someone Sarah can't quite see. "How's your little sister?" Sarah signs to Tate. "She okay?"

"She's alright. I can't take her fishing evenings anymore." Tate pauses, a bit buzzed, sees in his mind police cars on Main Street in Sulphur. "Creepy under curfew," Tate signs, "unable to leave my house after dark. Haven't really slept the past three days."

Tate's asleep a few hours later in his truck cab, uncomfortable across his pickup's bench seat, a bunched-up shirt his pillow. He dreams in silent black-and-white, his father through fog in a fireman's uniform, waving from a firetruck on neighborhood street. "Don't be afraid," Tate sees Sarah sign, then Dylan in the dark sitting beside a phonograph at the front of an empty classroom. "Sometimes, I stutter when I speak," Dylan signs. "My br ... "

A cop taps his nightstick on the driver side window, waits, Tate asleep across the bench seat. Tate's hands around the shirt beneath his head. The cop taps his nightstick harder against the window. Around the cop, dawn the color of orange marmalade.

Tate sits up sudden, hungover, his eyes wide seeing the police officer's dark shades, hat, and expression-less face.

Tate signs, "I'm deaf, one moment, please," his hands to his cheek and ear, his heart.

The cop gestures roll down the window, his gun in his holster.

His eyes heavy, Tate grabs his window crank, his mouth dry. The cop points his nightstick north, and Tate turns to his windshield. He sees the long oval-shaped drive, the landscaped campus lawn. The cop motions his nightstick north again, and Tate points to his khaki pants for his keys, then the ignition.

Tate's driving on the interstate. He scratches his choppy-layered black hair, wishes he had mouthwash. Barely awake, he yawns, wonders if he's still sleeping, his head pounding, seven a.m. on his dashboard clock. He needs to piss, looks to his windshield, no restroom stops. He looks to the floorboard for a plastic cup or bottle, nothing. He opens his truck console, grabs his crotch, certain he's about to piss himself. From his windows, he sees only trees and flat farmland. In the distance, a closed car dealership along the east side of the interstate. Tate looks to his dashboard clock, 7:02 a.m., won't be able to hold his bladder, hopes to find a diner or gas station in town when he reaches the dealership exit. He starts to speed.

Tate's Ford Ranger is parked alongside the interstate south of a green exit sign, Purcell. Surrounded by trees, Tate's pissing with his eyes closed to intense relief and sound of a passing train he can't hear. Sulphur still an hour's drive.

When Tate's eyes open, he looks down to leaves, fabric from a lace shift dress, a bloody hand sticking out of bushes. His eyes widen, terrified in silent disbelief. He steps from the bloody hand, can't see if it's attached to anyone, still can't hear the passing train. He realizes suddenly someone might be watching him. He slips, falls to the ground.

Stumbling to his feet, never taking his eyes from the bloody hand and lace fabric, Tate starts to run, almost backwards, pulling up his pants. At his pick-up's passenger door, he fumbles for the handle, his other hand in his pants for his keys, his little sister's fishing pole and bait box behind him in his truck bed beside his muddied dirt bike.

CHAPTER SIXTEEN

Sheriff Ford stands in the middle of an interstate, early morning air hot, muggy. Behind him, his police car, its lights flashing blue and red, parked across a northbound lane, blocking traffic south into a single long line for miles.

"Two bodies shared three bullets," Ryan hears his deputy sheriff saying. "Shot 'em in their throat." Ryan looks down a hill to the mud-splattered station wagon, its hood raised. Behind the broken-down car, dense trees and bushes. He's numb.

"How'd the woman's body find itself up the road a half mile?" Ryan points north. "If it happened here?"

"Not too sure, Sheriff," says the young deputy. "Both bodies aren't in a bad way, couldn't have been here long. Since maybe early morning, sometime yesterday."

Sheriff Ford looks up the road to the dealership, the green exit sign, Purcell. He tilts back his black sheriff's hat, rubbing his forehead. "Maybe she fucking crawled," Ryan says, wanting to hit something, feeling defeated. "You touch anything?"

"No, sir."

"Good." Ryan hears a helicopter hovering toward them. He looks at his wristwatch, eight a.m. "Where's Tate Tanaka?"

"McClain County Sheriff's Office, sir."

Ryan sighs. "I'll call his parents."

"Already taken care of, sir."

Ryan lowers his head. "Shouldn't been him."

"Sheriff?" says the deputy, confused.

"Nevermind."

"Sheriff Ford!" yells a deputy in the distance. "McClain County's asking for ya."

Ryan turns to the young deputy beside him. "Search this station wagon for bullets, weapons of any kind, this whole area. No one else gets in here."

"Sheriff!" yells the other deputy again.

Few moments later, Ryan reaches into his police car from his driver's side window. "Ford," he says into a two-way radio.

A woman's stern voice answers. "OSBI provided identification on a magazine label one of your deputies found. Hector Ramirez," she says, "Air Force Technical Sergeant."

Ryan turns from the radio, not sure he can keep listening, hears the woman say, "Word from San Antonio is that's his wife, Josefina Ramirez. They would've been heading to Wichita in a blue F-150 for a funeral—Mr. Ramirez's sister. You copy?"

Sheriff Ford glares at pavement, his eyes following road flares and traffic cones.

"You find their dog and twelve-year-old boy, yet? Would've been traveling with 'em," he hears the woman say.

Ryan's heart nearly stops at the news. His two-way radio drops to his side.

"Sheriff?"

CHAPTER SEVENTEEN

Derek jumps into a Buick's passenger seat, frantic, slams his car door. "Go!" he yells to an intern turning the key in the ignition. "Go! Go, go, go, go, go!" Tires screech. Derek bites his nails.

Rachel's six miles away, sliding on her cotton white bathrobe. She grabs a remote from a white comforter on her unmade bed. Morning sun pours through glass doors from the balcony into her bedroom. Rachel points the remote at the TV on the dresser. Barefoot, she walks across creaking plank wood toward glass French Doors into the hallway, the television flickering on behind her.

The Buick squeals from a parking garage, its undercarriage scraping concrete, races from a thirteen-story gray building where Derek works for *The Daily Oklahoman*. Derek's face red, his fist to his mouth, knows Rachel's unplugged their phone.

Hot water pours from the faucet, steam from the porcelain white clawfoot tub. Sitting on the side of the tub, Rachel watches in her robe, her feet and champagne flute on checkered black-and-white tile floor. She reaches for her mimosa.

The brown Buick speeds along grassy fields on the far northeast side of town, Derek in its passenger seat wearing his heather gray suit, pushing back tears, his dirty blonde hair swooping down his angular face, his fist squeezing tighter at his mouth. "Come on!" he yells at the driver. "Fuck!"

Rachel dips her hand in warm water, looks to white square tile walls, sunlight through the small rectangular window above the tub. She starts to remove her robe.

A woman's voice booms suddenly, startles Rachel, blaring, "Anita Bryant is a former Miss Oklahoma, a pop singer with three gold records to her credit." Her hand to her heart, Rachel catches her breath, wonders why her TV's on its loudest setting. "Until just lately," Rachel hears the woman say, "she's been identified with nothing more controversial than orange juice."

Engine revs, the Buick speeding past a semi-truck on a rural two-lane road, Derek's fist tighter at his mouth. His other hand covers his fist, the driver accelerating into the passing lane.

Water pours into the tub, steam rising from porcelain. Rachel's in the hallway, tying her robe around her waist. She walks to the glass French doors opened into her bedroom. "Extremely religious," she hears the reporter say, "Anita says she feels God singled her out to spearhead a crusade to prevent admitted homosexuals from teaching her children."

Out his passenger window, construction speeds past Derek's blurring eyes, tractors, workers, and cranes constructing an interstate dividing northeast from the northwest side of Oklahoma City, the new highway connecting downtown to the northern suburb of Edmond the way his father's trains once did. His thoughts focused on the phone unplugged in his and Rachel's bedroom.

Slowly, Rachel walks through open glass doors, a piano playing from the television across her sunlit bedroom, a woman's cheerful voice singing, "What a wonderful change in my life has been wrought, since Jesus came into my heart."

Her bedroom's empty. On TV, a close-up of a woman with hoop earrings and curly red hair, the woman singing into a microphone in front of a church congregation. Rachel grabs the remote from her bed, points it at the television. She's confused, pressing buttons, trying to change channels, trying to turn it off, nothing. She moves closer to the TV, presses more buttons on the remote, nothing.

"Jesus came into Anita Bryant's life eight years ago," the reporter explains, Rachel pressing buttons harder, "and, since then," the reporter says, "visits to churches to extol her reborn faith have replaced USAO tours to Vietnam with Bob Hope."

The doorbell rings.

The Buick speeds toward vehicles waiting at an intersection. "Go around them!" Derek demands. He looks over his shoulder, sweating, the Buick squealing to a stop. "Reverse! Put it in reverse!"

Rachel unlatches the door chain, unlocks the deadbolt, opens the front door.

"Hi, I'm Emily," a young girl with a blonde bob says, standing on the porch. "Wanna buy Girl Scout cookies?" The young girl smiles at Rachel. "Why's your TV so loud, lady?" the Girl Scout asks, looks past Rachel into the living room.

The Buick backs up. "Hit 'em, if you have to!" Derek yells, the car reversing, Derek looking behind him for traffic, the Buick speeding onto the shoulder of the road, swerving through an intersection across Northeast 50th Street, dodging cars.

Silently, blue and red lights flash from a police car driving north through the intersection of Northwest 13th and Robinson, from police cars speeding north a block west through the intersection of 13th and Harvey, from police cars at Hudson and 13th, at 13th and Walker, 13th and Dewey, 13th and Lee, 13th and Shartel. Dozens of police cars driving in rows from downtown on tree-lined streets along the mansions of Heritage Hills.

"Thanks!" says the blonde Girl Scout, skipping from the porch down steps leading through the lawn, a mailman waving at Rachel from a sidewalk.

"Morning!" Rachel waves back to him.

The brown Buick races past bungalow houses and trees on either side of Robinson, Rachel and Derek's home a mile away. "Go!" Derek yells, points at the windshield.

In her bathrobe, Rachel walks down the stairs sloping through her lush green yard, the mailman at the bottom of the steps in a blue shirt and shorts, sifting through envelopes, the Girl Scout skipping past him, grass glistening.

Police cars speed past mansions with similarly sloping yards, past Sycamore trees, homes built in the 1910s and 1920s with low-pitched hipped roofs, wide overhanging eaves, Prairie houses with American flags flying from wide square porch columns.

Rachel looks at crepe myrtles, freshly mowed lawns surrounding her, juniper trees in front of craftsman-style bungalow homes, a park with a playground across the street.

"Here you are," says the mailman, Rachel taking two envelopes from him.

"Thank you."

The Buick speeds through another intersection across Northwest 23rd Street, nearly hitting a city bus and motorcyclist.

Rachel walks up the stairs in her yard, looking at two envelopes, one addressed to Derek and her, no return address. Confused, she slides her finger beneath the envelope flap. She opens it, reaches inside, a slip of paper.

Police cars speed silently around the corner.

Rachel hears screeching tires. She turns, seeing a Buick speed to a stop in front of her house, police cars surrounding the neighborhood park and their home, Derek leaping from the brown car. "Rachel!" he yells. "Rachel, stop!"

Rachel looks from Derek and the cops to the white slip of paper in her hand, realizing it's stained with blood. "To the reporter and his wife," handwritten across it. "$5 Gift Certificate, The Music Store. I am murder."

Rachel's eyes widen in horror, her bloodcurdling scream echoing across the park and through her neighborhood.

CHAPTER EIGHTEEN

Church bells toll from far away, trees swaying in sunrise around the limestone city hall building. Across the street, news vans along the County Courthouse. Reporters talking with cameramen in a courtyard along the west side of the courthouse, broadcast journalists sitting on benches, scribbling notes, walking past a miniature metal replica of the Statue of Liberty.

Inside the courthouse, Sheriff Ford walks from his office. "I'll let you know when we need anything else," he says, the mailman from Rachel's neighborhood shaking Ryan's hand.

"Thanks, Sheriff," says the mailman, adjusts his mailbag across his shoulder, his youthful face distraught as he walks down the hall. He passes Rachel sitting on a wood bench, can barely nod at her.

From his office door, Ryan hears footsteps across terrazzo tile floors, conversations, a glimpse down the hall at Rachel.

"District Attorney Curtis received one, too," says the city's police chief into a phone on Ryan's desk. The chief hangs up, a cigar in his other hand.

Derek looks from his wood chair to the police chief, then to Sheriff Ford still standing at his door, his back to his office.

"Curtis has himself a shotgun and rocking chair," the old police chief's rough voice says. "Has since he was knee high to a turnip truck. He won't mind none, sitting on his front porch, shotgun in hand."

Derek's eyes heavy with worry, he watches Sheriff Ford stare into the hallway.

"Homer Hanson's got himself a similar piece of mail down in Sulphur," the police chief says. Derek leans back in a chair he's certain has been in the courthouse since the county built the building during the Depression.

"Wasn't it our young reporter there," Sheriff Ford says, "wrote about Homer Hanson having himself a $10,000 bounty for the killer?" Ryan turns from the door, glares at Derek. "Wrote yesterday in a statewide paper about DA Curtis calling for the death penalty regarding a case Curtis ain't even took to court, yet. Front page," Ryan says. "Same on Sunday when he first wrote about the Sulphur murders. Here we are on Wednesday."

Derek lowers his head.

Ryan scratches his chin, looks across his cluttered desk at the police chief. He huffs. "Any word from federal boys or OSBI when they're planning to find twelve-year-old, asthmatic Enrique Ramirez, his family's pickup truck, all the guns in their camper?"

Rachel massages her wrist—scars, burn marks, and cuts. She's alone in the hallway, sitting on the wood bench. She looks up, her reflection in framed photos along the wall, a history of the county's sheriffs. She looks back to her wrists.

Derek closes the office door, Sheriff Ryan Ford written across glass behind him. The row of framed sheriff photos beside him. Rachel down the hall. He sits with her in his heather gray suit, his tie undone. "You okay?" he asks.

"Not at all," Rachel says in her jean jacket with cut-off sleeves over a purple dress, her bare arms folded. She glances at Derek, then to the wall of sheriff photos. "You know, I knew this was coming?" she says. "That poor boy."

Derek looks to terrazzo tile. "The second the District Attorney called saying I might be a target, I raced home. You are not alone, Rachel. We're all here with you." He twists his black wedding band. "We're going to take you someplace safe."

"Oh, yeah?" Rachel chuckles, her eyes watery. "Where's that?"

"I don't know, but we're gonna take you there."

Rachel sighs. "Half of Oklahoma City's police force surrounded our lawn," she says, looks from the sheriff photos to Derek. "You feel safe?"

Sheriff Ford walks through double doors into stifling hot sunlight, puts on his black sheriff's hat, reporters rushing him with microphones, cameras, notepads. Behind him, the eleven-story concrete county courthouse towers with silver art deco designs above the set of double doors.

"Sheriff Ford!" reporters shout. "Sheriff Ford!"

"No comment," Ryan says, stern.

"Any word on the missing boy?"

"When did District Attorney Curtis receive a letter from the killer?"

"Will Oklahoma City go on curfew? Declare a state of emergency?"

"What're you doing to keep Oklahoma City safe?"

"How're you coordinating efforts with Murray and McClain County?"

"Are the Sulphur and Purcell murders work of a serial killer?"

"Are police still questioning motorists on I-35?"

"Is it true a clinical psychologist is working with police detectives to create a profile of the killer?"

Ryan walks from the courthouse steps, journalists chasing him on a narrow sidewalk, yelling questions. He stops, turns abruptly in his cowboy boots and black sheriff's uniform, face full of contempt. He's shaking, his blue eyes wide at suddenly stunned reporters. His clenched fist to his mouth pushes back words, silence between him and the crowd. A tear falls from his eyes. He turns, walks away, his boots clunking pavement.

At a nearby intersection, Ryan waits for a stoplight, sees in his mind Sarah, his two sons. He rubs his fist, rush hour traffic driving north and south past him.

"Learn the laws and obey them," Ryan hears a man say, his words calm, direct. "Abraham Lincoln."

A fit, middle-aged man stands behind Ryan, removes his horn-rimmed glasses, breathes on one of its lenses.

"Sheriff Ford," the man says, "do you know the history of vice in our city?"

His back to the man, Ryan rolls his eyes. "I know enough, Curtis."

"Law and order, Sheriff," Curtis says. "Safety and security." He slips a hand-kerchief from his crisp cotton khaki suit pants pocket. "Keep our people safe, our neighborhoods secure. Prosecute crime in pursuit of justice for those touched by evil." Curtis wipes the cloth on one of the lenses. "What, after all, is more important than the administration of justice and the execution of civil and criminal laws?" He wipes the cloth on his other lens. "That's Alexander Hamilton, by the way." Curtis nods to engraved words over his shoulder along the second floor of the courthouse.

Ryan doesn't notice, doesn't care, glares across the street at city hall, waits for the north south stoplight to turn red. Curtis puts on his glasses. South, he sees four cleared city blocks, mud from Reno Avenue to First Street. East, the morning sun rising between Ramsey Tower and First National Building.

"Hell's Half-Acre," Curtis says. "This area of our city, 1889-1907, from our founding Land Run to statehood. Nearly two decades of debauchery and sin. Saloons and gambling on Main Street, liquor 24-hours a day, brothels, madams, venereal disease. Your wife and you ever read *Saturday Evening Post*, January 1955, Sheriff?"

"No," Ryan says.

"Drugs, crime, abortionists, teen prostitutes, homosexuals." Curtis adjusts his glasses. "Vice. Juvenile delinquency. Welcome to Oklahoma City, wrote *The Post*. On God's green earth, who'd want to work and live in such a place? Raise a family?"

Ryan looks at his wristwatch, nine am, then to the red stoplight.

"Nevermind *The Post* was factually inaccurate," Curtis says. "Nevermind the article's primary source was a state legislator who later admitted he exaggerated. Nevermind the article's authors paid the legislator for his exaggerations. As District Attorney—as a devout Baptist—I've dedicated every election to cracking down on vice." Curtis turns from the sun. "My daughter's a gambler. Poker. Quite good, I hear from informants. Cristine's a renaissance woman, Sheriff, modern, full of ideas from continental philosophy. She'll learn."

The stoplight turns green.

"Do you know the history of my name, Sheriff, the story of King Edward and his son, Edward the Second?"

Ryan starts across the intersection, Curtis beside him with his coiffed, graying hair, his suspenders over his fitted white button-up shirt.

"Unfortunately," Curtis says, "as always, one can't tell the story of a son without speaking of his father. My namesake, King Edward, removed his crown at his coronation because of his father, said he wouldn't wear it again til he regained what his father lost. Specifically, Scotland and Wales. Respect for England. Newly king, Edward persuaded his subjects to tax themselves to support military campaigns to restore England's authority over Scotland and Wales. Ruthless campaigns," Curtis says. "Then, brutal occupation."

The rising sun behind them, Ryan and Curtis reach the west side of the road.

"Edward created new punishments for a new crime," Curtis says. "Treason. For rebelling against England, Edward had horses drag the Prince of Wales to his execution. First person in history put to death for crimes against a king. For killing noblemen, they hanged him. For committing murder on Easter, they castrated him alive, disemboweled him, burned his entrails. For committing crimes across the kingdom, they hacked his body, distributed pieces across the land. Same in Scotland with rebel William Wallace. Tortured and hanged, disemboweled, quartered, beheaded. A warning what happens when one crosses Edward, 'hammer of the Scots.'"

To the sound of splashing water, Ryan and Curtis walk in a plaza along a fountain beside city hall.

"Real story here's Edward the Second," Curtis says. "Smart, strong, tall, handsome like his father. But, Edward the Second shunned pastimes of princes, refused to hunt, preferred instead common pursuits of the working class, music, swimming, boat building, rowing, riding horses." Curtis clasps his hands behind his back. "At Edward the Second's coronation sat his childhood friend, Piers Gaveston, an English nobleman," Curtis explains. "No one knows the precise nature of their relationship, but Piers wore purple robes to Edward's coronation, not traditional gold. And, Edward presented Piers with his wife's wedding presents and jewelry. Oh, how did his contemporaries describe it? 'Love that surpasseth the love of a woman.'"

A helicopter hovering in the sky, Ryan looks from the plaza south to his sheriff's car parked parallel beside a ten-story brick building with a limestone cornice along the top.

"I do remember to have heard one man so loved another," Curtis quotes from a favorite historian. "Jonathan cherished David, but we do not read they were immoderate. Our King, however, was incapable of moderate favor and, on account of Piers, was said to forget himself."

The plaza behind them, the two men walk on a narrow sidewalk under the shade of green cloth awnings, Ryan realizing the ten-story brick building beside him is one the only remaining structures from the 1920s to survive urban renewal in the 1960s and 70s, Hightower Building engraved in limestone. He sweats under his sheriff's hat.

"They exiled Piers," Curtis says, "threatened Edward the Second with civil war, told him to end his relationship with Piers. But, Edward returned Piers to his side, and Piers mocked nobles with contempt and clever nicknames. Edward and Piers fled," Curtis says, "Edward abandoning his pregnant wife. All the same, the nobles caught Piers. With no trial, they murdered him.

Heartbroken, Edward the Second led troops into a battle where he abandoned them to die."

His parked sheriff's car beside him, Hudson and Main engraved along the Hightower in stone, an abandoned Main Street stretching several blocks west, Curtis turns to Ryan.

"Because, he swore an oath to confirm the laws of England," Curtis says, "the nobles enacted a cruel punishment for Edward the Second. They held down their king and forced a hollow instrument like the end of a trumpet into his rectum, thrust a red-hot poker through the instrument into his bowels, burning his intestines."

Ryan's reflection beside Curtis in windows along the Hightower's first floor, a crest on the building's limestone with a castle, knight's helmet, and Christian cross at its center.

"You have an election this fall, Sheriff," Curtis says, calm. "We will protect our people from evil, because that's our oath. Your promise to them."

CHAPTER NINETEEN

Noon. "Tell me," Sam hears a young British woman's gentle voice saying, "that number you wear, what's it mean?"

"Oh, Fahrenheit four, five, one," says a man with an Austrian accent.

Sam watches from his desk two characters on a movie screen, a medium close-up of a man clad in black walking beside a young woman, her hand across her stylish brown coat, her hair a short blond bob, her skin milk white. As they walk, an elevated, silent, futuristic train speeds across a cloudy gray sky.

Sitting in the classroom's back row, Sam's stunned. His leg bounces beneath his desk, first day of his summer college English class, the Circa Club bartender from the night he met Matthew suddenly his professor.

"Why four, five, one," says the young woman on screen, "rather than eight, one, three, or one … "

"Fahrenheit four, five, one," interrupts the man in black, "is the temperature at which book paper catches fire and starts to burn."

On the young woman's face, a worried smile. She looks to the ground as they walk. "I'd like to ask you something else, only, I don't really dare."

"Go ahead," says the man.

"Is it true, a long time ago, firemen used to put out fires and not burn books?"

"Put fires out?" he laughs. "Who told you that?"

"Well, I don't know, someone," she says. "But, is it true, did they?"

"Oh, what a strange idea," he says. "Houses have always been fireproofed."

"Ours isn't," she says.

"Well, then, it should be condemned one of these days," he says, no longer smiling. "It has to be destroyed, and you will have to move to a house that is fireproof."

"Too bad," she says. "Tell me, why do you burn books?"

Sam looks to his professor focused on the movie screen, his professor's hands relaxed behind his head, the bartender's familiar curly blonde hair. How many whiskeys? Enough to remember Sam? To tell his father? Did he see Sam leave with Matthew?

"Well, it's a job like any other," Sam hears the man in the movie say. "Good work with lots of variety."

Sam forces himself not to think about Matthew, his father, turns to the screen, loses himself in the film's bluish gray color palette, then back to the bartender.

"Monday, we burn Miller," Sam hears the man with the Austrian accent say. "Tuesday, Tolstoy. Wednesday, Walt Whitman. Friday, Faulkner. And, Saturday and Sunday, Schopenhauer and Sartre. We burn them to ashes and, then, burn the ashes. That's our official motto."

Sam looks back to the screen, a chalkboard behind it.

"You don't like books, then?" the young British woman says.

"Do you like the rain?" the man asks.

She smiles. "Yes, I adore it."

The man in black shakes his head. "Books are just too much … rubbish," he says. "They have no interest."

"Then, why do some people still read them," she asks, "if they're so dangerous?"

"Precisely because it is forbidden," the fireman says.

"Why is it forbidden?" she asks.

"Because, it makes people unhappy."

Sam studies on the chalkboard a sample outline for a five-paragraph essay.

"Are you happy?" asks the young woman on screen.

Sam looks at his notes, "Are you happy?" with an asterisk beside it, same with "Montag," "Clarisse," "A film by François Truffaut." Sam can't stop staring at these words, his leg still bouncing beneath his desk, dirt from his cowboy boots on the tile floor. The film's paused, and he's not sure how time's passed, how many scenes he's missed.

"Professor Brackett?" a young woman says from a desk beside Sam. "Why's Cassandra your favorite name?"

"Cassie, right?" Charlie says from the front of the class.

"Yes, sir," the young woman says, her pencil in hand. "When you took attendance, you said you'd tell us why, if you had a daughter, you'd name her Cassandra."

Sam looks at her floral dress, her dark Black skin, her braided bun, square-cut bangs. On her desk, a three-ring binder and notebook paper full of notes.

"Call me Charlie," Sam hears his professor saying. "And, for me, Cassandra's the most compelling character in western literature, certainly, one of our most tragic."

"Didn't she predict the Trojan War against the ancient Greeks?" Cassie asks. "The fall of Troy?"

"Yes, ma'am," Charlie says from a rolling chair in front of the paused film. "Daughter of the last king of Troy, present-day Turkey. So lovely, the Sun God, Apollo, fell madly in love with her. When she refused to sleep with him, he cursed her. Gave Cassandra the ability to see the future, then made it where no one would ever believe her."

"Homer's *Iliad* and *Odyssey*," Cassie says, searching for forgotten memories from her high school sophomore year. "She reminds me of Clarisse in *Fahrenheit*."

"How so?" Charlie asks.

From across the class, the smell of chalk dust. Behind Charlie in his rolling chair, the film still paused on an image of Montag and his wife in bed, Montag reading a comic book in blue pajamas, his wife beside him with long blonde hair in a butterscotch-yellow nightgown. She stares at nothing. The class sits silent, listening and not listening to Cassie's explanation. From across the room in the dark, Sam and Charlie see each other.

* * *

A zero on a gas station meter clicks to one, and Grady glares in the afternoon sun across fumes and a gas station pump at a frail older woman.

She stands in flat white sandals on asphalt soaked in motor oil and gasoline. Her wrinkled hand grips a plastic pump nozzle, no one else with her. She looks from Grady across a vast parking lot. Not a single automobile with them at another gas pump.

From the corner of his eye, blood stains the tailgate. "You should lock your door," Grady tells her, numbers on the machine click, click.

CHAPTER TWENTY

Sunlight bright behind him, Dylan opens a glass door into Sizzlin Stockade, makes his way through a crowded foyer in his blue sleeveless shirt and grease-stained jeans. He notices three young siblings playing on a bench beside a gumball machine. A sign next to an oak wood host stand, "Welcome. All You Can Eat, $5.99. Please wait to be seated."

"Sarah here?" he says to a young hostess. On her nametag, "trainee."

"Yeah, she's … "

Dylan furrows his brow, sees at the other end of the restaurant Sarah push open a gray metal door from the kitchen. Untying an apron, she speed-walks across the dining area to Dylan.

At the host stand, Sarah grabs Dylan's rough hand, hurries him from the foyer along hanging heat lamps warming vegetables and steak in a buffet bar. In his heavy work boots, Dylan smiles, nods to diners sitting at tables, Sarah rushing the two of them along another buffet bar full of fruits, salads, and desserts. They stop at a wall of windows.

"I was so hungover at work," Dylan says. "Why'd we stay so late at Cristine's party?"

Sitting in a booth across from each other, Dylan realizes Sarah's trembling.

"Sarah?" Dylan says. "Sarah, what's wrong?"

She folds her arms, looks from him.

"Sarah, you're scaring me, say something."

Her hand to her mouth, and she can't look at him, won't stop staring at families enjoying themselves in a restaurant where she's worked now for a year, where she applied for and got her first job. Silverware clatter on plates, muted music on the speakers. She looks to the foyer dividing the dining area in half, tables on either side of the divide, booths along restaurant walls. Without turning to Dylan, Sarah asks, "Has your dad said anything yet about the missing boy?"

"My father?" Dylan says. "What missing boy?"

"You don't know?"

"Know what?"

"How do you not know?" she says.

"Know what?" Dylan says again, agitated.

"They found the killer's station wagon," she says, turning to him. "Whoever it was killed a husband and wife on Interstate 35, down near Purcell. Stole their pickup truck and a bunch of guns. Dylan, when he was on his way back to Sulphur, Tate found their bodies. They've sedated him at home. All Oklahoma's law enforcement's out searching for their missing twelve-year-old son and dog. How have you not heard anything?"

Dumbfounded, Dylan doesn't know what to say. "Tate?" almost to himself. "I … I … drove all day across western Oklahoma. I … haven't talked to anyone, came direct here after work. Where's Sam?"

Sarah scoffs. "Where's Sam? He won't return my calls. I haven't seen your brother since Monday night. Dylan, I lied to Tate," she says. "I lied about Sulphur, told one of our closest friends everything's fine. For three days now, I only see Sulphur when I open my eyes. Holding open that door for that boy. Now, Tate." Dylan touches her hand. She shakes her head. "Dylan, there's something," she says. "I'm not … " She turns from him.

"Sarah, what?"

"This afternoon, I fell asleep before work, had a dream about you standing at the nave of an empty cathedral, waiting for me in a black suit. Only … only your eyes … ." She looks. "Dylan, your eyes were pitch black. And, you said, 'This is a requiem.' And, I asked 'why?' Then, you described three paths forward for me."

"Three paths?" Dylan says, notices Sarah staring at his tricep, his ink crucifix tattoo.

"First, that God spared me in Sulphur," Sarah says, "to do good." Her words calmer. "The second path was God's warning me, something's coming."

Dylan looks to Sarah studying his hands on the Formica table.

"The third, there's no God, everything's coincidence. I have no reason to be afraid. Then you reached out your hand from the nave."

Dylan almost laughs. "Sarah? That wasn't me. You … you know that, right?"

Sarah says nothing. She sees at the back of the dining area Andrés in his hairnet, Andrés carrying a plastic pan full of dishes through the metal door to the kitchen. She grabs napkins from a dispenser.

"Sarah?" Dylan says. "You know I would never do anything to hurt you, don't you?"

Sarah stares at him, struggles to find words. She sees his beautiful brown eyes, wants to disappear in them, drive alone in her red Jeep across an Oklahoma she hasn't seen. She wants to take photos of places and show them to him when she returns. "Dylan," she says to him. "I think I'm losing my faith."

CHAPTER TWENTY-ONE

Matthew's father holds his Bible. The Johnson Family Bible. A book Matthew's father has had since he was seven. His oldest possession, a gift from his dad. He stands alone at an oak wood pulpit, opens his Bible to the first page, a cursive inscription written with quill ink. He caresses words his father wrote. "Building a city upon a hill, create a home in our hearts. Do good, Thomas. Dad." From center aisle of an empty church, the best view of the pulpit. Pastor Thomas lit from a projector with purple light. Behind him, black velvet curtains.

In his thoughts, his two youngest sons play with toy trucks on patterned carpet, his wife, Alice, beside Matthew in a front pew, his family where they belong.

Thomas looks to his Holy Bible, wonders about words written many years before God stole his father's memories, before God reduced his father to a rambling dying man in a nursing home. Where did his family and city go wrong? Why this particular punishment?

"Can any Christian remain indifferent?" Thomas hears himself saying, then stares at empty church pews, imagines row after row full for Wednesday evening service in an hour. Thomas thinks about consoling a city, how to pray for the safe return of a missing child, how to comfort parishioners worried for their own children. Thomas quotes his favorite preacher and statesman. "Science is a magnificent material force," he says, "but science is not a teacher of morality." He pauses, studies his father's inscription. Crime-ridden streets, and Thomas imagines them worse. He rubs his hands across his young, troubled face, sees Sulphur across his state. "If civilization is to be saved from wreckage threatened by intelligence not consecrated by love," Thomas says, "it must be saved by the moral code of the meek and lowly Nazarene." He's suddenly serene.

Calm, Pastor Thomas stands in a purple glow. In his tailored navy suit, he glances to his pocket watch on its silver chain. He stares across Pastor Jacob's empty church pews with a cautious smile. High above him, a ceiling fan, its blades whooshing through air.

CHAPTER TWENTY-TWO

A young girl sits up sudden in bed. "Witches!" she screams. "Cousin Sarah!"

In the dark, her bedroom door swings open, Sarah breathless, flicking on a light.

"What?! What is it?"

"Witches!" The girl scrambles to her headboard in a nightgown. "Under my bed!"

"Nancy!" Sarah catches her breath, her hand to her heart. "Jesus, you can't do that. You nearly gave Cousin Sarah a heart attack."

"But, it's true!" Nancy says, too scared to move too close to either side of her small bed. "I heard them under there."

"Okay, kiddo," Sarah says. "Let's look for witches."

Barefoot in her work clothes, Sarah takes a step on plush brown carpet.

Nancy gasps. "No, Cousin Sarah! Too close!"

Sarah kneels, her hand on plush carpet. She points under the bed. "Nothing."

Nancy grabs a pillow. "Outside, too!" Beside Nancy, two double-hung windows where Nancy refuses to look.

Sarah stares at nothing under Nancy's bed. She pushes herself from carpet. She hears chirping crickets, sees darkness beyond double-hung windows. Beside the windows, posters on a lilac-colored wall of cartoons and the film *Grease*.

Standing in the middle of Nancy's bedroom, Sarah says, "Nothing there, either."

"But, at the park, boys from school said witches are coming to get me." Nancy clutches her pillow. "I heard them, under my bed and scratching the windows."

"Boys at the park?" Sarah starts toward Nancy's bed. She stops, glances at her bare feet on carpet, nods to Nancy. "May I?"

Nancy looks from her pillow to Sarah, waves Sarah to her bed.

Nancy's still sitting close to her headboard, and Sarah kneels beside her bed. "There're no witches," Sarah says. "You know that."

"But, boys from school said so."

"Nancy, boys say 'hello' hitting and punching each other. At your age, in particular, I'm not sure they're best at providing credible information."

Nancy loosens her grip on her pillow, imagines all the times at school she's seen boys with their wrestling becoming actual fistfights.

"You were practicing softball at the park?" Sarah asks.

"Yeah," Nancy says.

"How's your pitch?"

"Better," Nancy says, still afraid of her windows.

Sarah notices. "Hey, why don't we slide your feet under the covers, try to sleep?"

Walking in the dim hallway, Rachel's surprised to hear Sarah. She stops at the door to Nancy's room, remembers Sarah's babysitting til the end of Pastor Jacob's Wednesday evening service. Through the doorway, she sees Sarah kneeling beside Nancy's bed.

"Study today with your math tutor?" Sarah asks.

"Mhmm," Nancy says.

"What'd you work on with them?"

"Multiplication tables."

"Multiplication tables, you say?"

"Witches aren't real?"

"Where's your bat?" Sarah asks.

Nancy looks up to Sarah, questioning. "In the closet with my glove."

"Move it beside your bed," Sarah says. "Next time you see a witch, grab your bat. Show these witches some might."

From the hallway, a faint smile on Rachel's face. Beside her along the wall, framed photos of her father with his new wife and Nancy.

Nancy whispers to Sarah. "You're babysitting tomorrow night, too?"

"Of course," Sarah says.

Sarah's shutting Nancy's door, moonlight through the double-hung windows across Nancy in bed.

"You're good," Rachel says.

Sarah turns from the closed door, hugs Rachel immediately, intensely.

"Oh my God," Sarah says in their embrace. "Uncle Jacob told me you're staying here, but I didn't believe him. The killer, I am so sorry."

Rachel leans back from their hug. "Uncanny," she says, looking at Sarah. "Aunt Carla and you. How's such a resemblance even possible?"

Sarah blushes.

"I remember babysitting you—when you'd scream werewolves were in your closet, me failing to comfort you the way you did in there with her."

"You didn't fail," Sarah says, suddenly serious.

"Let the record show, then."

Staring at Rachel's maroon cardigan, blonde hair, blue eyes, Sarah hesitates, then says, "You look like your mother, too, you know? Please forgive me for saying. I recognize it's ten years since we saw each other last, since your mother's passing, but I remember precisely how she looked, the scent of oakmoss and jasmine when she'd hug me." Hand to her heart, she stops herself from saying anything about Sulphur.

Rachel smiles for a second time today. "What a lovely memory to have. Thank you."

Sarah's hands slide in her pant pockets. She walks down the hall to the stairs. "Night," she says over her shoulder.

"Night," Rachel says, realizes no photos of her or her mother exist along the walls. She sees in her mind the wall of sheriff photos, the bloody gift certificate from this morning, a crayon-drawn sign on the bedroom door beside her, Nancy's Room.

Downstairs in a candle-lit living room, the scent of honeysuckle. Sarah checks a locked deadbolt. Outside in the front yard on a large Magnolia tree, leaves rustle with a strong gust of wind, Pastor Jacob's house lit with a single porchlight beside a purple door.

CHAPTER TWENTY-THREE

Sam's rough hand sketches an evening sunset, clouds across open prairie, an endless expansive sky. Along the foreground, silhouettes of two men sitting on a bench, staring into the background at their distant darkened downtown. Beside his drawing, a whiskey tumbler, Sam sketching at a wood table where a red lamp glows gold in the dark.

"Streets are bad here," an old man says with a Minnesotan accent.

"I don't understand," another old man says with his strong Oklahoma drawl. "Streets are no worse here than anywhere."

At a table beside Sam's, the old man from Minnesota laughs. "They're worse, bud. Every second, bump, bump, bump. Barely a year living here, I'm replacing tires."

"Where ya from in Minnesota?"

"Don't change the subject. Minneapolis. My God. Your streets are awful. Where're sidewalks? Even if they exist, they're crumbling. A major city without sidewalks. Is it a joke? Don't people walk? Literally, this place forces a person to own a car, it's spread out, sprawling. Your interstates connect homes in suburbs to one-story strip malls with large parking lots in front of them, why? I'm travelled, retired navy, never seen anything like it. Moved here to take care of grandkids, and we're walking our third grader between neighborhoods across a six-lane expressway to our closest school and library, no crosswalks. Do you want people to read? Why don't your city buses don't run Sundays?"

Cigarette smoke drifts to the smell of liquor and beer, Sam's pencil shading the downtown skyline. Behind him in the dark, red lamps glowing on wood tables. He glances from his sketch, a muscular young man standing in a tank top at the metal door entrance, checking identifications. "No names," Sam remembers.

"Bridge collapsed few years back," the Okie says. "North of Tulsa, up around Osage Nation. No injuries, thankfully. This local woman, first woman elected county commissioner in our state, she argued maybe next time the bridge would collapse with school buses on it. School buses, she reminded 'em, always stopped on that bridge to let kids from the bus."

The old man from Minnesota drinks his vodka, shakes his head.

"So, Bennett, she gets herself a list of all her county's structurally unsafe bridges, learns our state legislature isn't interested in investing in rebuilding infrastructure. So, Bennett, all across her county, she places signs at bad bridges to convince folk to pass a local bond issue, repair their bridges themselves. 'This bridge is dangerous.' 'Don't drive here.'"

"Did it work?" asks Minnesotan.

"First bond to pass in state history for county bridges," says the man from Oklahoma. "Passed every precinct in her county. Repaired twenty county bridges on school bus routes."

"You're late," says the Minnesotan, Sam noticing an attractive middle-aged man standing in a slim-fit business suit beside him, slow jazz on the speakers. Sam glances from the man's short preppy haircut to Charlie Brackett in the distance, his professor busy making drinks for a crowd gathered at the bar counter.

"Couldn't be helped," the middle-aged man says with a deep voice. He unbuttons his suit coat, sits with the two older men. "She here?" He lights his cigarette, crosses his legs. Sam notices his shined black shoes.

"She left a message on my answering machine," says the Okie, clears his throat, coughs. "She's on her way."

"What do you think of this idea of hers, creating a newspaper for the community?" asks the man in his suit. He glances beside him to Sam sketching.

"Worked in New York and San Francisco," says the Minnesotan. "Keeps people informed. Your friend, she's doing her homework, smart."

"And, her idea from Dallas for a community center?" asks the man in the suit.

"Why a community center?" asks the Okie.

"Create a space for young people when their parents and grandparents kick 'em out," says the Minnesotan, "give 'em a place with warm beds at night, a basketball court, books, board games, access to mental health services, financial literacy. Keep 'em from heroin, homelessness, hustling on streets."

The middle-aged man smokes, ashes in an ashtray beside a red lamp. "We raise money from the private sector," he says. "Invest along this street in streetlights and sidewalks, prioritize safety, walking at night to these bars. During daytime, we need a coffee shop, community center, and bookstore focusing on our history and culture, maybe a restaurant with a patio on the sidewalk. Create a distinct district with our own neighborhood watch. Think small business loans. This road's Route 66, for Christ's sake. Either here or Classen, close to Free Spirit Club. They'll take us serious when we own property."

The old Oklahoman laughs. "Take us serious?" He lights his cigarette. "Your banking friends? You realize we're still illegal under state law, lawyer?" He smokes.

"Sorry, I'm late," Matthew says, sliding into the seat opposite Sam. "My father's sermon ran long."

Matthew notices his sketch, surprised. "You draw?"

"Since I was young."

"May I?" Matthew asks.

Sam turns his sketch to Matthew, the red lamp glowing between them, conversation between the three men beside them blending with jazz and a growing crowd.

"Talented," Matthew says, studying the sketch's sunset, its depth of field.

Sam looks from the red lamp to Matthew. First time he's seen Matthew all day, Matthew in a plain gray t-shirt, Matthew's hardened hands holding Sam's sketch. Sam looks past Matthew to the crowd gathered around the bar counter. He sees two men pointing, worried, to the bar's north wall.

Sam looks to the pool table behind him, sees laser beams from *Space Invaders*, the arcade game glowing beside the payphone on the north wall. Next to *Space Invaders*, an industrial-sized metal fan blowing warm air across Sam. A nineteen-inch television on a barstool beside the payphone. Sam's father on the television screen in his sheriff's uniform, ignoring reporters on the stairs of the County Courthouse, Sheriff Ford with DA Curtis talking in front of City Hall. Then a photo of young Enrique Ramirez above the words, "Missing: Age 12. Statewide Hunt for Sulphur Killer."

Pale as a ghost, Sam turns from the muted television. "Cristine's dad with my father?" he whispers.

"Why's one of 'em wearing a cowboy hat?" asks Matthew, studying Sam's sketch.

"Because, you rodeo," Sam says, his words fading, "and I like westerns." He looks toward the bar counter at the two young men pointing to the television.

Matthew looks from the sketch to Sam's shaggy brown hair, his distant blue eyes, his well-kept beard shaping his worried face. "What's wrong?" Matthew says.

Sam's lost in red lamps, stares at men sitting at small wood tables, at men talking, standing along the bar's walls. "Can a place be forgiven?" Sam asks.

Shattering glass across the room. A young man confused at the bar counter, yelling, "What the hell, man, my drink." A police baton across the young man's face, Sam's eyes widening in horror.

The metal door entrance swings open, a police baton across the forehead of the muscular man checking identifications, another baton hitting the young man in his gut.

Sam grabs Matthew's hand, pulls him from their table, dodging rocks smashing through all the bar's windows, beer bottles crashing to concrete floor. Sam covers his head, his other hand pulling Matthew's across the room toward two darkened glass doors. The crowd pushed to the ground, scrambling, hand-cuffed, officers swinging batons.

"Nobody move!" Sam hears. "To the ground, filthy faggots!" By the dozens, police rush into Circa Club. "Murderers!" police yell. "Child killers!" And, the metal door collapses. Officers pushing *Space Invaders* to the ground, yanking the payphone from the wall, kicking the metal fan from an electrical outlet. Police batons busting liquor bottles, bottles thrown against men's bodies.

The middle-aged man in his suit slips beside Sam, slams to concrete, breaks his neck.

Gripping Sam's hand, Matthew pushes open a glass door, running on gravel with Sam onto a patio past evergreen bushes and stone benches where they first met. They jump a wood fence, fall to their backs, slide down a steep dirt hill onto a concrete parking lot.

"Get in!" yells a woman's voice, taillights from her truck flashing red, Matthew's forearm to his eyes, and he climbs into the back of her pickup, Sam after him, tires squealing, her truck racing across the hotel parking lot.

Red and blue lights flash across the night sky, Matthew breathless. From the tailgate, he stares at men jumping the fence from Circa Club, falling down the steep hill.

His heart racing, dirt on his face, Matthew scoots against the speeding pickup truck's fixed side wall. Five other men beside him, beat-up, bruised, bloody. Shocked, Matthew looks to the plastic bedliner, can barely bring himself to look up from it. When he does, Sam's against the truck bed's other side wall.

His pearl-snap shirt ripped, Sam looks to his torn Wranglers, silent and shaking, bleeding from his forehead. He sees his scuffed cowboy boots, his sore clenched fist.

Her engine revving to a torrent of wind across her truck, her pickup swerving from the parking lot to a service road along hypnotic headlights from I-240.

Shuddering, Matthew turns to the rear window. On the truck's radio, a man swoons with an acoustic guitar and static, "Just what the truth is, I can't say anymore." Matthew looks to Sam, clenches his fist tighter. "Cause I love you," he hears over orchestra and guitars. "Yes, I love you. Oh, how I love you." And, the song gives way to distorted garbled wailing.

Staring across the pickup truck, Matthew sees a grimace on Sam he's never seen, then rage. Sam punches the metal tailgate, hits it harder, harder, harder, again and again.

CHAPTER TWENTY-FOUR

Dawn. Sarah's father stands alone on a quiet concrete bridge. He stares at a barren river, a ceramic coffee mug in his hands, sun rising behind him.

Behind an emerald green guardrail, he drinks coffee with the flavor of Brazilian nuts and butter, scents from coffee his father drank. Below the bridge, a dry riverbed with dirt and grass winding westward to another distant bridge. Alongside the brittle basin, remnants of a park.

Jesse looks from the river to Hubcap Alley, his heavy eyes following the emerald green guardrail and lit lamps til the bridge becomes the road where he's built his business, his auto repair shop just a block from his home.

A train horn blares, and Jesse looks behind him. A public bus passes the silhouette of a grain silo into Capitol Hill. At the end of the bridge, the train makes its way along the river that divides north from the south side of town. For reasons he can't explain, he's worried about his daughter.

Jesse remembers his father's rough hacking cough, 1934, a bloodstained handkerchief to his dad's mouth. Six-year-old Jesse hearing his father say, "No water." A wood table in a kitchen covered with dirt, dirt across windows and walls. He watches his mom sweep dirt out the open front door. From their front door, scorched great flat plains.

At age six, Jesse's a bigger kid, stocky. He lives in small-town Guymon at the far end of the Oklahoma panhandle. His parents promise he was born in a sea of green grass prairie. Jesse's twelve-year-old brother, Jacob, swears it rained once upon a time. But, Jesse sees only dark clouds across the plains, layers of topsoil scattered across the land.

At night by candlelight, Jacob tells Jesse about pastoral Ireland, immigrant grandparents, medieval legends about warriors fighting for cattle and land, Irish warriors so fierce they rode naked into battle armed only with swords. One night, Jacob tells Jesse about a privileged British boy whom these warriors captured in fifth century CE, describes how the boy becomes property of a warrior chief, works as a slave with sheep in the Irish hills for six years of hunger, cold, and rain. The boy escapes, returns to Britain, hears the Irish people in a dream, begging him to bring Christianity to their warrior nation. Jacob describes the way Irish druids became Christians, how Irish Christians became monks living in monasteries who, by hand, copied and preserved classical literature, the Bible, and works of antiquity for all of Europe.

From Jacob, Jesse learns a prayer the former slave preached. "I arise today through strength of Heaven," Jacob says. "Light of the sun, radiance of the moon, splendor of fire, speed of lightning, swiftness of wind, depth of sea, stability of earth, firmness of rock."

Their father refuses food for their family from FDR's government, coughs on his bloodstained handkerchief. "No handouts," he says, Jesse watching his mom stare at empty cabinets, soup bowls upside-down beside drinking glasses and coffee mugs in cupboards.

Their neighbors pack covered wagons. Behind them, sand dunes, abandoned plows. "We're staying," their father says, Jesse and Jacob staring across their farm at starving cattle. "Rain will come again," he promises, "so will crops. Rain follows the plow."

Jesse holds a flier, his father ripping it from him. "No," his father says. In the dirt, the torn flier promising money from the U.S. federal government for shooting their cattle.

Their mom cries herself to sleep. By candlelight, Jacob whispers, "Drought's starving 'em, Jesse. Government will pay six to eight bucks for calves, fifteen for steers. More than we'd get for 'em on the open market. Daddy's too sick to stop us." Tears fill Jesse's eyes. "Jesse, quit. We can't feed 'em anymore. Or, ourselves."

Behind a barbed wire fence, Jesse aims his rifle. He stares at scrawny cattle, many he's birthed as calves. "I can't," Jesse says. He drops his gun. Their mom stands at the front door, crying. Jacob grabs Jesse's rifle, walks with tears in his eyes along barbed wire, his adolescent face full of anger, aims the rifle proper, shoots. Few days later, their father dies—dust pneumonia.

At age fifty, Jesse's an army vet from a Korean War no one remembers, a former Guymon High School linebacker staring at a barren riverbed. He drinks his coffee.

He washes his ceramic mug with water and soap in his kitchen sink, places it in a cupboard beside other upside-down dishes. He dries his hands, puts a skillet on a stove.

Inside a neighboring house, Sarah's mother puts a washcloth full of ice on a woman's swollen eye, loud snoring behind the two women.

"Here," Sarah's mother says, the other woman with the cloth to her bruised face. "I'm gonna check your airways, make sure there's no obstruction in your nose. You good holding the cold compress?"

The woman nods, and Sarah's mom forces a smile. Sitting at a small dining table, Carla massages the woman's nose, maneuvers her cheekbones, checks for facial fractures, checks her mouth for cracked teeth, checks her arms and fingers for broken bones. The snoring louder.

Across the woman's cheeks, Carla studies bleeding cuts, reaches for a yellow bottle of Betadine, rubs the golden-brown antiseptic across the woman's wounds. She grabs Neosporin, rubs the anti-inflammatory across lacerations on the woman's eyelids. She holds the woman's free hand. She looks over her shoulder to a recliner, sees the woman's snoring husband. Empty beer bottles surround a muted television. Carla turns to the woman holding a washcloth full of ice to her beaten face. She squeezes the woman's hand.

Outside on the woman's front porch, fresh air. Carla's standing in nursing scrubs. She walks along her tree-lined street, houses lit amber orange from an early morning sun. Shotgun houses, she remembers they call them. *Such an odd name*, she thinks to herself. She studies other houses built close to the street— a living room up front, one or two bedrooms in a line, kitchen at the back, porches, vinyl siding, and small yards. Her family's house the only one with a gray roof and pointed turret.

Exhausted, Carla falls face-first in bed, hungry from her overnight shift. A box fan blows across her. In her mind, doctors' messy handwriting, prescription scripts, stethoscopes, and blood pressure measurements, her neighbor's bruises and swollen eye. Carla's left foot pushes her shoe from her other foot.

She wonders if Sarah brought home leftovers from Sizzlin Stockade, but she is too tired to check. She hears in her head water crashing against rocks, looks to a table beside her bed, stares at a book of poems from José Martí, her first crush. She sees herself arrive alone as an eighteen-year-old by ferryboat in Miami. She thinks about Martí and revolution, worries whether she made the right decision to leave Cuba, scared this morning at age thirty-six she'll never again see her parents. She sees Cuba's Communist government seize her grandmother's grocery store. Beside the book of poems, a framed oval-shaped photo of her wedding day, Jesse lifting her bridal veil to kiss her.

Jesse opens their bedroom door, holding a tray with a blue Iris in a mason jar. Beside the blue Iris, breakfast. He sets the tray beside the book of poems.

"Mind reader," Carla mumbles, still face-down on a pillow.

Jesse sits on his side of the bed, takes off his watch. "How was work?" he asks.

Carla rubs her eyes. "I can barely see I'm so tired." She yawns, sitting up, grabs a plate of sausage, biscuits, and gravy, smiles when she sees grape jelly.

After breakfast, Carla and Jesse make love, him on top of her, her hands through his curly hair, his coarse hands on her face, Carla worrying her body's become too big with age, his hazel eyes staring into hers. Her worry fades.

Carla rests after across his hairy chest. She traces her thumb across his clavicle, sees the woman's face from this morning, bruises she's mended over the years on many women outside the hospital, God-fearing women from church, neighbors and friends' neighbors. Carla thinks about Jesse's brother, Jacob's first wife and the violent way Rachel's mother died a decade ago. Carla cuddles closer to Jesse, her silk black hair across his chest, falls asleep in his arms, the box fan blowing across them in bed. She doesn't hear when he says, "I dreamed about Guymon last night."

Jesse holds her tighter, glances to Carla's empty glass of water beside her book of poems on the nightstand. He thinks about all the lakes across land-locked Oklahoma, how every single lake in the state is man-made, younger than him.

CHAPTER TWENTY-FIVE

Broken glass beneath Sheriff Ford's boots. Lights flash blue and red from his police car. "Purcell Pawn" across a shattered store window. "Gun's cursed," an old man in overalls says, his words wheezing. He coughs. "And that's the only thing gone."

Sheriff Ford kneels in front of a smashed glass display cabinet studying shelves with handguns and price tags, a vacant spot.

"Ain't the first time someone stole it," says the burly old man. "We was robbed last summer, someone stole it. Ain't seen it til we get a call from a detective few days ago down in Ardmore, saying he'd found our stolen gun. He drove up here Monday to return it before July 4th, Tuesday. Today's Thursday, and it's gone again."

"Gun was here yesterday?" Ryan asks.

"Couldn't tell ya, Sheriff. Drove Monday night to McCurtain County with my wife, spent July 4th and Wednesday with her and her parents. Saw our shop with broken windows on our way home. Called y'all. Told my wife I hope I never see that jinxed pistol again so long as I live. Good riddance."

Ryan notices a glass shard in the cabinet stained with blood. He stands from tile floor, familiar pain in his back and right knee. He thinks about all the missing guns from the Ramirez family's stolen truck. He turns a knob on his two-way radio. He asks the old man, ".38-caliber Taurus?"

"That's the one."

"McClain County," a woman's stern voice says through radio static.

"Ford," Ryan says. "Tell your sheriff we found where our killer got his weapon."

"Killer?" the old man says.

"Copy, Sheriff. Purcell Pawn?"

"Yes, ma'am."

"In all my eighty years ... " mutters the old man, covers his mouth, looks at the smashed glass cabinet.

"Tell forensics to run tests on bullets found in Mr. and Ms. Ramirez," Ryan says, "verify those bullets came from a gun with a rifled barrel."

"That last part again, Sheriff?" says the dispatcher.

"Rifled barrel," Ryan says, frustrated, imagines spiral grooves cut into a gun barrel, raised spaces between grooves, heat inside the barrel shaping a bullet according to a gun's make, model, and caliber.

"Copy, Sheriff," the dispatcher says. "We found the Ramirez boy this morning."

Silence. Ryan rubs his face. "He's dead?"

"Copy, Sheriff."

The old man lowers his head, his hands into his coverall pockets.

Glass crunches behind Ryan, Derek walking into the stuffy room.

Sheriff Ford's at his police car moments later. "No press!" he shouts at Derek.

"No cameras here, Sheriff." Derek shrugs beside the broken pawnshop window, points across a parking lot with only three cars. "Been listening to the police scanner. I just want to find him before something worse happens. That's why I followed you."

"Something worse," Ryan says under his breath, stares across his police car roof at blue and red lights. He hears traffic on the interstate, remembers John Bullock's hand tremble three days ago when they buried his son.

Derek stares an hour later from the police car's passenger window at flat farmland. An hour of silence, Sheriff Ford driving. Derek unbuttons a cuff on his white button-up, unbuttons another button on his forearm, flips his cuff inside out. He glances at Ryan, his gun in his holster.

"We'd debate whether we should roll up Marine uniform sleeves," Derek says. "Serious disagreements as eighteen and nineteen-year-olds with military leaders about professionalism and discipline. Whether it'd look proper on a combat uniform. How a man should present himself at his workplace, on a date." Instinctually, he folds back his sleeve, uses the cuff to determine the width, folds the band of rolled cloth just beneath his elbow. "First year I was drafted, I started a newsletter in Hanoi for Marines stationed with me, wrote about our great uniform debate of '68."

Ryan stares at yellow lines dividing a rural two-lane road through his windshield, a semi-truck in front of them.

"I say debate," Derek says, "but we gave two shits what leaders called professionalism. Summer's stifling heat in North Vietnam, hot and humid, relentless rain April to October, guerrilla warfare in jungles." Derek unbuttons his other shirt cuff, looks to barbed wire fence along the rural highway. "Practical necessity," Derek says. "We rolled up our sleeves til they made it official revised policy summer of '69. To prevent heat injury, military leadership said. Language I'd written originally to promote the idea in the newsletter."

Ryan glances at his police radio, at Derek thirty years younger than him, Derek's button-up shirt sleeves rolled precise, Derek's shirt collar undone, his dirty blonde hair across his angular face. Ryan looks to his rearview mirror at a steel mesh partition. No one following them on the rural road. Through his windshield, yellow dividing lines now dashes. He clicks his turn signal, passes the semi-truck.

"My parents moved from the city to the country after I finished school," Derek says. "Everything's so disconnected." A hollowed-out factory abandoned in a field. "My dad operated railroads across the state. He's retired, says good union manufacturing jobs are disappearing, says he misses when railroads connected Oklahoma's small towns. Suppose he's right, I don't know. I've always been more a city guy, especially since we moved back. Wouldn't know what to do with myself out here. Suppose it doesn't matter. Everyone wants to live in the suburbs now."

Ryan looks to his rearview mirror, sees the semi-truck fade in the distance, his sheriff's car the only vehicle on the sunlit highway.

A star-shaped badge on the Sheriff Ford's black uniform. Gray in Ryan's brown hair. Worried about Rachel, Derek looks to the console at a folded sheet of paper with an address written across it. Back to Ryan's badge, he asks, "Really think the original owner of that stolen pawn shop gun could lead us to the killer?"

Ryan glances at his dashboard, then his windshield to a speed limit sign, fifty-five mph. "Guess we're about to find out," Ryan says, seeing in his mind the Sulphur killer's bloodstained notes, the dead Ramirez family. Memories from southeast Oklahoma, sandstone cliffs overlooking a green forest shaded with autumn colors rolling into a distant blue lake, Robbers Cave, stories about mound builders in the area a thousand years ago, Caddo and Osage tribes in the 1600s, French hunters before the U.S. Civil War, and after the war, the fugitives. He's certain he made the right decision Sunday morning to keep Sarah and his sons' names out of any newspaper article Derek would write, off local news on channels four, five, and nine.

He drives his sheriff's car on the rural road toward sunrise.

CHAPTER TWENTY-SIX

"No," Sarah says, a tear falling from her eye, Dylan in front of her, kneeling, holding a silver wedding ring.

"What?" Dylan says, disoriented, staring up at her on bended knee, confused.

Sarah's at the doorway to her wooden tool shed, her makeshift darkroom, her teary eyes trying to focus on anything else in her backyard. Her cottage house on a corner lot, its gray roof and white vinyl siding, the pointed turret where she sleeps. Dylan, instead, kneeling on a small set of wood stairs.

Dylan catches his breath, his stomach heavy. He glances to the ground then to her. "I … I don't understand," he stutters. He looks away from her again, cheeks flushed, embarrassed. He stands up quick, pushes the ring into his pocket. "I … " and he starts across the yard.

"Dylan!" Sarah says, starting after him, stopping to close the tool shed door. "Dylan, wait." She follows him along a chain-link fence. "Dylan, be reasonable."

"Reasonable," Dylan scoffs, walking quick across her yard in his work boots and grease-stained jeans, his sleeveless blue shirt. "Reasonable."

"Yes, reasonable," Sarah says at a distance. "Dylan, we're too young."

He stops at a gate, staring at the sunrise, his hand on a latch. Across the fence, a flat open field, sunlit distant tall trees blowing with warm wind. "Do you love me?" Dylan asks.

"This is not about love, Dylan."

"But, do you love me, Sarah?"

"Dylan, of course I love you … "

And, he turns to her. "Then, let me love you," he says. "Let me protect you and keep you safe."

Sarah looks away to her red Jeep parked along the street beside her backyard, Dylan's black Roadrunner parked in front of it. She looks across the street to the field, imagines her father at his auto shop a block away behind the distant tall trees. She sighs.

"Dylan, do you remember when we first met?" She turns to him, folds her arms. "And, we sat across the river on the hill in front of my school? We told each other about our dreams? How you wanted to work as an engineer, maybe have your own auto shop? How I wanted to work as a photographer? You held my hand for the first time, said we can be anything we want. I told you how my mother married young, how I wanted to wait til I finished college to prove I could make my own money, take care of myself. Dylan, I still have those dreams. I know you do, too."

Warm wind blows across them, Dylan thinks of murders in the newspaper, the love of his life standing across from him in her sleeveless yellow floral blouse, radiant in the morning sun in a matching headscarf, denim bellbottoms. He's scared suddenly he'll never kiss her again, touch her soft skin, run his hands through her silky-smooth wavy hair. "Sarah," he says, "we can still do all those things, follow our dreams. Why does it matter, waiting?"

"Because, it matters to me," Sarah says. The wind warm again, silence between them, chirping crickets and birds across her small backyard.

Dylan glances to the ground, his work boots, back up to Sarah. "Nothing matters," he says, turns to the gate, unlocks the latch.

"Dylan," Sarah says.

"I … I'm gonna be late for work," he says, walking down a hill to his Roadrunner.

Sarah sighs, watching Dylan get into his car. She folds her arms, shakes her head, hears his engine rev. She turns from the chain-link fence, walks alone across her backyard barefoot in grass toward the tool shed. She starts up creaking stairs, reaches for the door to her darkroom.

CHAPTER TWENTY-SEVEN

"Here you go," a young man says to Cristine, handsome in his black jean jacket and black denim pants, his words blending in with the sounds of a busy shopping mall. He stands from a charcoal-colored square tile floor. Water sprays up behind him, then splashes down into a shallow fountain. "Hold out your hand," he says with a southern accent, his dimples distinct, his chiseled face scruffy.

In her palm, he places a gold-plated pearl earring.

Speechless, she beams, her other hand to her heart.

"I'm Grady," he says, smiles with his hazel green eyes.

"Cristine," she says. "Thank you so much. How did you … "

"I saw it fall," Grady says. "Thought you might miss something so elegant."

With a sigh of relief, Cristine clasps the pearl to her ear. "My father … it's a Christmas gift from last year," she says. "I'd never forgiven myself if I'd lost it. He gave me a matching necklace, too. I still haven't worn it."

"You should," Grady says. "Bet gold shines brighter on such a pretty neck."

Cristine blushes, checks her other ear.

"And, such fair hands, too," Grady says.

Cristine looks past him to the crowd in the food court, dozens of people sitting around the octagon-shaped water fountain—talking, eating, laughing.

Grady glances over his shoulder, then to Cristine. "Waiting on someone?"

Cristine looks at her watch. "My best friend's meeting me," she says. "But, I'm off work a half-hour early, so … "

"So, no great hurry, then?" Grady says.

Impressed with his confidence and scent of his earthy cologne, Cristine smiles. "What'd you have in mind?" she says.

After they leave the food court, Cristine and Grady stand at a display counter full of ice cream, a lone Chinese man working, waits for them to decide. Next to the young worker, a neon sign lit in the shape of an ice cream cone yellow, pink, and blue.

Grady points to pistachio. "May we try a sample, please?" Grady asks the man behind the counter, the smell of greasy burgers and fries drifting through the restaurant.

With their ice cream cones, Cristine and Grady walk along a railing, the food court below on the first floor, a row of stores beside them, sun shining through a skylight. Echoing across the mall, the sound of water splashing into the fountain.

Cristine glances to Grady's black hair slicked to the side, his thick bangs brushed into a small pompadour. "You really play harmonica?" Cristine asks him.

"Since I was ten," Grady says. He licks the top scoop from his ice cream cone.

"I was in ballet," Cristine says. "Took dance lessons first grade through high school. Always thought I'd be a ballerina, travel the world," she says. "Strange to know as a child what you want only to find yourself clueless as an adult." She looks to the skylight, then Grady. "Never could play an instrument, though. Who taught you?"

Outside in the shade, Sarah waits beside an entrance to the mall. She watches a family of four walk past her with shopping bags into a parking lot, the family's two kids running along a pumpjack rotating behind a tall white metal fence.

"Slow down!" the young mother yells to her laughing son and daughter, the only other sound the whirring pumpjack. Sarah looks to a clear blue sky, then her ring finger, thinks about Dylan, how they never have serious fights. She massages her hand.

"All apologies," Cristine says, grabbing Sarah's hand, guides her across a crosswalk into the parking lot. "I forgot we weren't meeting in the food court, and this totally Casanova guy showed up while I was waiting for you. Took me for ice cream at Braum's."

"Then, you got in his van?" Sarah says.

"Oh, stop," Cristine says, pretending to be pouty, locking arms with Sarah. "Actually, he's not much older than us, muscular like a Marine, but maybe only a bit taller than you. He's so cute."

Cristine puts on sunglasses, climbs in the passenger seat of Sarah's Jeep, its windows and top down. She watches Sarah turn a single key in the ignition. "You seem so dour," Cristine says, "and I don't like you dour. What is it? I was ten minutes late, fifteen minutes being unforgivable, and I really meant my apology."

"It's not you," Sarah says, driving along parked vehicles, glancing at the pumpjack.

"You're not going to tell me?" Cristine says. Sarah thinks of the murdered Ramirez boy, then Dylan kneeling with a silver wedding ring. At a stop sign, she sighs, feels numb.

"Can we talk about it after work tonight?" Sarah says, waiting on traffic.

"After work?" Cristine says. "But, I thought ... "

"Yeah, I know, but I'm not feeling particularly kid-friendly today," Sarah says. "Would you babysit Nancy for me? I called Stockade. I'm picking up Natalie's shift tonight."

"*You're* not feeling kid-friendly?" Cristine says, shocked. "Jesus Christ, girl scout, what hope's there for the rest of us, then?"

Sarah's Jeep turns onto a service road, passes vehicles in a long line exiting toward Crossroads Mall from I-240. Her red Jeep turns with the service road, drives along I-35 and grass fields. In her rearview mirror, Sarah doesn't notice a pickup truck with a camper, the only other vehicle behind her. She stops at an intersection, I-35 and Southwest 89th Street.

Bloodstained fingers tap a steering wheel, the tall man's eyes fixed on the red Jeep, Grady and Vera at his side in the truck cab.

Grady stares at dry blood on his brother's hand as it turns the steering wheel west. Warm, arid air rushes through where a passenger window once was, where Josefina Ramirez hid from shattering glass and bullets.

"You're a real lady's man," Vera says to Grady, leers at him. She twirls her finger through his thick black hair. "You do know that, don't ya, right? A real son of a bitch, too. No ice cream for the kids."

Grady looks from his brother's bloodstained hand to a dirt-covered wind-shield, the red Jeep braking at a four-way stop on rural Southwest 89th. Vera, reaching over her shoulder, slides open the rectangular window into the camper.

"You hear, kids?" Vera blares behind her. "Uncle Grady's a real son of a bitch." Their truck bumps to a stop, Vera still leering at Grady.

In the pickup's rearview mirror, Grady sees inside the camper, a small hand coloring with a crayon, drawing within the lines in a children's book. The cartoon coloring book on a beige blanket beside a sleeping two-year-old, a pink pacifier in her mouth. A smaller hand grabs for a crayon box, Grady staring at a reflection of his three-year-old niece plopping down on the blanket in only her diaper. She sits beside her five-year-old brother. Her brother on his stomach, drawing in his coloring book. She hands him her crayon. She looks at an unzipped duffle bag full of guns.

Grady looks to blood crusted on his brother's hand, scoots closer where the passenger window once was, watches grass fields along Southwest 89th. From the corner of his eye, he catches Vera whispering something into his brother's ear. Her hand over her mouth, her fingernails painted pink. Her other hand brushes her brittle black hair from her greasy face. His tall brother stares at the rural road, smirks.

Grady looks past Vera to a side profile of his tall brother, his brother's thick mustache, at where his brother parts his tangled dark shaggy hair, his brother's hair hiding where surgery removed a brain tumor when he was twelve, just like their dad.

Grady turns from his brother, bites his thumbnail. He glances at his jean jacket, looks from his passenger window to the grassland disappearing into a harvested wheat field. He looks through the windshield at the red Jeep braking at another four-way-stop.

The Jeep turns right from Southwest 89th onto a dirt road, Pennsylvania, then drives into a new subdivision down a street lined with pine trees.

In a rolling cloud of sunlit dust, their stolen pickup truck stops.

"This is the house," Grady's brother says, his words guttural.

At the intersection, the pickup idles. Grady looks from his passenger seat. His brother points past him to an old two-story farmhouse at the end of a long dirt driveway with no cars or trucks.

"We'll start here tonight," Grady hears his brother say. "Work our way through the neighborhood across the field, leave no witnesses."

CHAPTER TWENTY-EIGHT

Matthew's asleep, passed out only a couple hours in ripped clothes from the night before. He's on his back, his futon mattress beneath him on concrete floor, his bruised arm above his afro. Sunlight across him from the wall of windows. But, in his dreams, Sam steps from the darkness, Sam toned and tall in a fitted plaid pearl-snap shirt and Wranglers, Sam's icy blue eyes, Sam's swagger Matthew's memorized.

"Holy, Holy, Holy," Sam says to him. "I have seen the face of God."

"Tell me, then," Matthew says in the dark, staring at Sam's lips and light-peach skin, Sam's well-kept beard and casual way Sam's shaggy brown hair falls across his forehead. "Why does God hide His face? Tell me, what does He look like?"

Sam smiles.

Matthew's sitting suddenly in a pressed-metal rocking chair. On a porch, he sees through a brick archway framing his view of a golden prairie, grassy fields and hills rolling in the sun as far as he can see. He looks down, a yard with a garden, green grass and flowers from the porch to a short brick masonry fence topped with wrought iron rails. Tall pine and oak trees shading the yard, canopying a narrow street separating Matthew from prairie.

Matthew's confused. He realizes he's at a house he's rebuilt. But, he's not sure when, and he's not sure where. He leans forward in his metal rocking chair. To the west, he sees a red brick sidewalk along the masonry fence. Past the wrought iron rails, the narrow street rolls along prairie, then disappears at a train stopped on a bridge. Across the bridge, downtown. Matthew knows where he is. Staring at the prairie, Matthew sees the summer he was born, his grandfather standing shoulder-to-shoulder on stairs with parishioners outside of the Calvary Baptist Church. Beside the three-story maroon brick church, Walnut and Second above a stop sign. Matthew's grandfather glances up at stained-glass windows. Sixty-years-old in 1960, his memories intact. A crowd behind him, a thousand people in their Sunday best gathered across the sunlit green fields, waiting on a hill in the heat to hear Reverend Martin Luther King, Jr. preach.

Matthew turns quick, sees Sam tap a straight razor on a tumbler.

"Ready?" Sam says.

Matthew sighs. "Ready." He relaxes his head on his metal rocking chair. He hears water wrung from a cloth, closes his eyes, feels a hot towel on his face. He sees his grandfather, twenty-one-years-old in 1921, building Calvary with Deep Deuce's Black residents. Seventy-years-old in 1970, Matthew's grandfather is on a sidewalk downtown, describing to his ten-year-old grandson the Black architect who designed Calvary Baptist, about Black men who built the church in a week.

Matthew feels a soft brush on his face lathering cool, thick shaving cream. Scent of Eucalyptus and menthol. He remembers his grandfather showing him decaying storefronts, deserted Black-owned businesses, boarded windows on Calvary, abandoned Deep Deuce.

He hears Sam stir shaving cream with soap and water, the soft brush lathering shaving cream across his neck. Matthew worries he'll never see his grandfather again.

"No one really dies," Sam says, a tear falling from Matthew's eye.

"I'll finish the cabinets tonight," Sam says.

White wooden cabinets along a plank wood kitchen floor. Above cabinets, glass tiles Matthew's watched Sam restore to their original condition. A mosaic blend of blue and white squares along a wall surrounding a porcelain sink and across countertops. Above the sink and counters, cabinets Sam's rebuilt with glass doors, cupboards he's rebuilt to the ceiling. From a window above the sink, sunlight shining across wooden chairs and a rustic table Matthew's designed, sturdy chairs Matthew watched Sam build by hand.

Matthew feels a blade shave down the side of his face, hears metal tap the tumbler on a barstool beside him. Matthew turns, sees Sam twisting a cap on a flask in front of open porch windows.

His back against a headboard, Matthew sees their bedroom. He's sitting on a solid wood platform bed Sam's built. Matthew's sketchbook propped up on his knees, he sketches a house built in 1926. Beside him, Baldwin's *Fire Next Time* on a nightstand, a gas heater by the bedroom door, an air conditioner unit in a double hung window by a wood dresser. His attention turns to the full length of his body. He relaxes his eyes, face, and forehead. He ashes in an ashtray on the bed, thinks about their home on Third Street. He waits for Sam to finish work on the farm. He smokes a joint he's rolled.

"Look across the land," Matthew hears Sam saying. "Imagine a canvas. We can build anything we want." Matthew stares through the brick archway at the sunlit fields. He knows who he is.

On his futon mattress, he shakes awake. Half-asleep, sunlight bright in his eyes, his father standing over him in a tailored suit.

"And, God delivered his enemies into his hands," Matthew hears his father say.

He shields his face from the sun. He barely sees Sam's sketch at his father's side, a torn crumpled sunset with silhouettes of two men sitting on a bench, one of them wearing a cowboy hat.

"Stand up," Pastor Thomas says.

All sound in his bedroom disappears. From his futon, Matthew looks to concrete floor. He looks behind him at the brick wall of windows, to trees outside blowing with wind. He rubs his face, chuckles, stands up.

Silence. Thomas stares at his son, Matthew with the promise of a preacher, Matthew the bull rider, Matthew standing beside his drafting table in ripped clothes, Matthew a disappointment in jeans and a dirty gray t-shirt, Thomas humiliated, Matthew's soul at stake.

Thomas lunges, punches Matthew's jaw, slams his son on his back to concrete floor. Thomas punches Matthew's face again, again, and again, cracks his nose, Matthew's arms flailing to his face. He tastes blood in his mouth.

"Stop!" Matthew screams, pushes his father crashing into the drafting table. He feels his bloody face in pain. Can barely breathe. His arms sore, he pushes himself from the floor, vision blurred. Dazed, stumbling, Matthew sees his father on a pile of broken wood. Matthew growls, rushes at Thomas. "Do I scare you?" he yells, spitting blood, standing over Thomas. "Huh?"

Through swollen eyes, Matthew glares at his father hurt on the pile of wood. Thomas coughs blood again and again. Matthew's fist clenched at his side, his body aching, adrenaline racing. He gasps, hears himself struggle to breathe. Breathless, Matthew turns from his father, stands in the middle of a place he's rebuilt with his grandfather. He sees waves from the pool reflecting across his bookshelf, red brick walls, *Metropolis* movie poster.

Shaking, Matthew unclenches his fist, steadies his trembling hand. He walks past the pile of wood and his father to his open bedroom door, doesn't look back.

CHAPTER TWENTY-NINE

Dusk. Sam's at a payphone. His hands in his back pockets. He checks the payphone's coin return slot, nothing. He's at a corner of a tan brick gas station, 7-11. Worried, he looks at a pickup truck parked beside him, at brake lights on its flatbed trailer. He's holding a ten-dollar bill, his driver's license. He looks to the payphone on the wall, at windows along the gas station, to a liquor store next door.

"Can I get quarters, too?" he says minutes later at a cash register.

With wrinkled hands, an old Vietnamese woman puts his glass whiskey bottle in a brown paper bag. She counts his change back to him. "Thanks," Sam says. *The Oklahoman* on the counter, "Local Banker, Father of Three, Killed in District Attorney Vice Raid."

He's at the payphone again. He puts a quarter in the machine, the phone to his ear. Matthew's number he's memorized, but he slides a note from his back pocket, stares at it, dialing numbers. He waits to a hypnotic hum of a dial tone.

Sam's halfway across a crosswalk, cars idling around him. He stumbles, glances behind him at the gas station, drinks whiskey from the bottle. He turns, sees the truck with the flatbed trailer drive past him into a neighborhood on the west side of the street, the pickup's brake lights disappearing into a setting sun. Northwest 36th and Pennsylvania above a stop sign in a field.

He's in the field, walking along the west side of Pennsylvania. He wipes whiskey from his lips in the same ripped pearl-snap shirt and Wranglers from the night before, hasn't eaten all day, hasn't changed. He looks to his cowboy boots, following a worn winding path in the grass.

"Desire lines," Sam hears Matthew say. "When you see a worn path in grass along the side of a road, creating a line, you know people have a desire to walk there, even if no sidewalk exists but should. It's like reading the land." At the sound of Matthew, Sam smirks, branches cracking beneath his boots, steady hum of a dial tone.

A block away, on a broken sidewalk, Sam's drunk between automobiles parked diagonally along a row of red brick buildings with boarded storefronts.

He walks beside streetlamps with cast iron lanterns, shields his eyes from their golden glow. Disco thumps behind darkened windows on an abandoned pharmacy built in the 1920s.

Sam looks to a highway sign, Oklahoma US 66. He staggers under an awning, walks past a gas pump in front of a deserted filling station.

He's at his truck. On his door handle, his swollen hand crusted with dark blood and abrasions across his bruised knuckles from punching the metal tailgate last night. Sam's other hand in his pockets for his keys. He looks over his shoulder to Circa Club, windows shattered across the tan building, its metal door entrance on the ground. He sees a note on his windshield under a wiper blade.

His keys drop. The parking lot empty. The note flutters beneath the wiper blade with warm wind. His sore hand through his hair, he grabs the folded paper. "Dear Sam," it reads. "I couldn't. But, one day. Thank you. Love, Matthew."

Sam can't move. He looks to his pickup's green hood, thinks about metal, paint, primer. Blurry words across the page. He covers his mouth, pukes. He kicks his driver side mirror from his truck, punches the door.

"Whoa!" Charlie runs at Sam from Circa Club, Sam still kicking his truck.

Numb, Sam's slumped in his pickup's passenger seat. No idea how long he's been in his truck, his head against his window. His driver side door closes.

"Okay, kid." Charlie takes a deep breath. He wipes dirt from his plain white t-shirt. "I found your address on your driver's license. I'm gonna take you home."

Sam says nothing, stares at shattered glass and debris scattered across Circa Club's parking lot. His engine turns over.

No sense of time, Charlie driving south, Sam sees from his window silhouettes of trees and houses along a dark blue and purple sunset. Above a stop sign in a field, Northwest 36th and Pennsylvania.

Charlie glances at the speedometer, taps a pack of Camels on the steering wheel. "Care if I smoke?" Charlie asks.

With watery eyes, Sam can't move his heavy head from his passenger window, stares at Tudor and well-built houses in a neighborhood from the 1930s. No sidewalks.

Charlie shrugs, reaches in his corduroy pant pockets, looks across the dashboard, pushes the truck's cigarette lighter into its socket. Silence between the two men. Engine whirring to the sound of passing cars.

From his window, Charlie looks to a tall distant brick tower behind a grocery store in a neighborhood to the east. When he's twelve, his mother shoots herself. He's the same age when his father becomes despondent, kills himself, too. Charlie remembers sneaking from his parents' funeral, hiding for hours, climbing a narrow winding steel staircase til he's on a balcony at the top of the brick tower. Strong gust of wind. He stands alone behind railing overlooking a Methodist university where his mother taught dance, his father religion.

The lighter clicks from its socket.

Charlie lights his cigarette, grabs the crank on the door, rolls down his window. Warm wind rushing through his big curly blonde hair. "How long did it take you to rebuild your truck?" Charlie asks. Silence.

Charlie smokes, ashes in the wind. "Haven't drove anything in a decade, by the way, so be patient. One of my fosters had a shop behind his house," Charlie says. "Good guy, older man. Polish. He worked on old cars out there all the time, especially Sundays after church. Wasn't really my thing," Charlie says, "church or cars, but I'd watch. He'd put me to work. Taught me how to change a tire, change the oil, even watched him rebuild an engine once." Charlie clicks his turn signal, looks to his missing side mirror, changes lanes.

Sam stares at a darker purple sky, violet clouds above homes along the street.

"Strange," Charlie says. "Hadn't thought about that guy since I don't know when. Suppose I'd forgotten any fosters were worth remembering." He glances at his speedometer, eases from his accelerator.

Sam remembers rust across his pickup, removing fenders from each wheel, finding the old truck with Dylan and Sarah in a junkyard. His hand hurts in his lap, his head aching against his passenger window. Memories of his pickup truck without a hood, without a grill, with a cracked windshield, engine not working. Dylan taking off the pickup's damaged suspension last summer, Dylan welding a new frame with Sarah's father at his auto garage. Sam restoring the cloth bench seat, putting the truck cab back on a frame, adding seatbelts, installing new gauges in the dashboard, repairing the fuel tank. Scent of fresh paint and primer. Driving his rebuilt pickup for the first time, wind in his face on a country road. Coming home to hear his mother say she has cancer.

Charlie rolls up his window.

Silence in the truck cab.

Charlie clicks on headlights. No other cars on the road. At the next intersection, a sign for W&W Steel. Charlie thinks about iron as a chemical element, his foster parents when he's twelve teaching him Oklahoma was at the bottom of a sea two million years ago, learning the difference between the Stone, Bronze, and Iron Age, the birth of agriculture, learning art and human life began in Africa, another foster when he's thirteen locking him in a closet with a Bible.

Charlie drives Sam's pickup truck under I-40, drives across a bridge over the dry Oklahoma River.

At a railroad crossing, they wait for a passing train, Sam staring to the west at the Stockyards along a distant horizon, where Dylan and he take their cattle to slaughter.

Railroad signal lights stop flashing, and Charlie realizes he hasn't seen the south side since he left town a decade ago.

They drive in the dark along houses and churches Charlies's forgotten, car washes and strip malls he's refused to think about for a decade, before he's a Marine with Derek in Vietnam. For eight miles, working-and-middle-class homes along side-streets from Pennsylvania, no neighborhood names.

"Dear God," Charlie whispers, shocked. "When did they build … ?" And, he stares stoically at an elevated interstate he remembers newly under-construction when he's fifteen learning how to drive. His eyes follow chain restaurants lit in the night along I-240, car dealerships with oversized American flags on flagpoles.

Under an overpass, Charlie drives to the sound of automobiles above them. Charlie shakes his head. "Two close friends and I, when we were growing up, we'd take city buses from the north side where we lived, make Super 8 and 16-millimeter films over here when this place was all forests, farms, and fields." Through his windshield, a new neighborhood he's never seen along the east side of Pennsylvania, middle-class homes built since the 1960s, construction halted on houses in a field where, along creeks and trees, Charlie filmed westerns and war movies with Derek and Rachel.

Sam's face aching, he rubs his forehead.

In his rearview mirror, Charlie watches the receding interstate. "Which one's yours?" Charlie asks, not expecting an answer. He reaches in his corduroy pockets for Sam's license.

"Past all this," Sam says. "Last house on the left."

Charlie laughs. "What?"

In front of the old farmhouse, the porch swing creaks. In the cottonwood tree beside the barn, an owl hooting.

"Alright, kid," Charlie says to him, Sam's arm barely around Charlie's shoulders. "One at a time."

With each step, Sam's boots thud his porch's wooden stairs. He's dizzy, can't stand, turns, points to his pickup.

"No, no," Charlie says. "Stay with me. Tunnel vision on your front door."

Whiskey on his breath, Sam turns to Charlie. He looks to his scuffed boots, his ripped pearl-snap shirt. "He'll know," Sam says. "He knows." He looks to Charlie, whispers, " ... why did you laugh? You laughed ... "

"What?" Charlie says, fumbling keys in the lock.

Charlie holding him up, Sam falls unconscious.

A pendulum sways hypnotic in his grandfather clock, and Sam sees his mahogany staircase hazy, unconscious again, Charlie laying him on his sofa.

Charlie pulls a short chain beneath a lamp shade. Beside the lamp, a paper flier offering to buy the farmhouse. Charlie looks across the living room for another light switch. He hears the owl outside, sees the kitchen on the other side of the staircase. He glances to the open front door.

He's at the kitchen sink, filling a glass from the faucet. He stands in his striped Adidas on gray brick floor, a narrow dark hallway beside him to the laundry room and backyard. From the window above the sink, Charlie stares at Sam's horse asleep in front of the barn. Charlie looks to the wheat field, trees, and creek full of his childhood memories.

"Here, drink this," Charlie says.

Sam can't open his eyes, Charlie handing him a glass of water. "No ... "

"You're dehydrated," Charlie says, "probably nauseated. Whiskey does that to ya. You'll want water back in you, bud, or you're gonna have a helluva hangover."

Sam grabs the glass, spilling water. He sits up, woozy, hangs his head, holds his glass with his good hand. His other hand bruised, swollen, bloody across his chest. He drinks water til it's gone. "You laughed when I told you where I lived."

"Laughed?" Charlie says, confused.

"In my truck … " Sam can't lift his head, gives Charlie his empty glass. "You think you're better."

The sole sound in the living room the tick of the grandfather clock, the only light the lamp beside Sam. Charlie sits in front of the sofa on an area rug.

"*Last House on the Left*," Charlie says. "First film I saw when I returned from Vietnam. Tough film to watch. Literally, first day. Military drops us at port in San Francisco. I find a place in Mission District, near 16th and Mission. Mostly Chicano, Latino neighborhood. Of course, I don't speak Spanish, don't know the city, don't know a soul. So, I go on a walk, end up in a different neighborhood, The Castro. *Last House on the Left* is on a marquee at this old Spanish Colonial movie palace. Double feature with this Bergman film, *Virgin Spring*. So, when you said you lived at the last house on the left, I laughed. I brought you a couple cups of water, not just one. Thought you'd find 'em both useful."

Sam looks up, his head in his hands, two glasses in front of him on a coffee table, one full. "You were in the war?"

"Quảng Nam Province," Charlie says. "South central part of the country, about twenty miles southwest of Da Nang. Not too hard to find on a map. Fought, for instance, in a place named Happy Valley." Charlie grins. "Incidentally, it wasn't."

From the rug, Charlie watches Sam drink another glass of water, Charlie suddenly quite aware of their age difference, a decade separating them.

"What's it about?"

Charlie furrows his brow. "What's what about?"

"This film reminding you where I live."

"Revenge," Charlie says. "Between the two movies, I'm sitting in the mezzanine's front row, processing all the violence in *Last House*. This guy beside me introduces himself, same age as me, says his name's Ace, says *Last House's* based on this thirteenth-century Swedish ballad, *The Virgin Spring*, same story structure, characters. Two herdsmen rape and murder a sixteen-year-old girl on her way to church, steal her belongings. After her murder, her attackers and a young boy with them find themselves at the young maiden's home. Unknowingly, her parents give 'em shelter, discover their daughter's bloody clothes in their guests' bags. Christianity's new to the country," Charlie says, "fledgling, hardly any churches, many Swedish people still worshiping Norse gods. The girl's father, a Christian convert, enacts a brutal vengeance, murdering all three guests Old-Testament-style, including the innocent young boy." Charlie smiles faintly. "You seem more alert, sir. How ya feeling?"

"Like I'm in a Swedish ballad," Sam says, then rubs his forehead.

"Cuts on your hand don't seem too deep," Charlie says. "Snuck a look at 'em while you were slipping in and out of consciousness. Would've taken ya to the hospital, if I thought ya needed stitches."

Sam touches his wrist, winces.

"Should probably run water over it soon," Charlie says, "keep it from infection."

Groggy, Sam imagines Charlie closer to his own age, the living room spinning again. Sam sees Charlie at a movie palace with Ace. "Or, the modern Prometheus," Sam says.

"Prometheus?"

"*Frankenstein*'s subtitle," Sam says. "None of this is right," he whispers. "Suffering." Sam sees Matthew buying a bus ticket, Matthew standing in a subway train, Matthew walking in winter on the streets of New York, architecture school. Matthew gone from therapy sessions and sitting strapped in chairs, Matthew gone from his father, gone from Sam. Sam turns from Charlie with tears in his eyes.

"Why are the wicked allowed to live," Charlie says, "grow old and win prosperity? Yet, they had said to God, away from us, we do not want to know your ways. I rescued poor men when they cried," Charlie says with the cadence of a poet or priest, "orphans, people none would help. Desperate, ruined men would bless me. And, I brought song to the widow's heart." Sam shuts his eyes, remembers the rest as Charlie speaks the words. "Yet, horror has rolled over me, driven off my dignity like wind. My wealth has vanished like a cloud and, now, my life spilling out of me. I hoped for good, got only wrong, hoped for light, got only darkness. I go about in sunless gloom."

Sam shakes his head, turns to Charlie, his tears gone. "I know who I am," Sam says. "I don't understand why I can't be who I am with him."

Charlie sees himself at night in San Francisco on a waterfront pier with Ace, stares at Sam. "To suffer is to exist," Charlie says. "I am so sorry."

The lamp lit beside him, Sam lowers his head. "All the same, we endure," Charlie says. "We exist, find exceptions to pain. But, we're not alone in our suffering."

Silence again between the two men. The creak of the wood floor beneath Charlie, the tick of the grandfather clock.

"I hated Ace's friends," Charlie says, regrets the last six years of his life. "Selfish men, who cared only for consumerism and status, masculinity, making fun of people, dominance. Nothing else in common, except their attraction to similar-looking men, maybe small talk and sports, contempt for women, no solidarity with women. So many personal, historical, and community traumas they refused to say aloud. I wanted brotherhood."

Charlie shrugs, glances at a silver watch Ace gave him, nine forty-five p.m., his bartending gig across town at ten. "Always late," he says, looks behind him to white curtains in front of four bow windows, sees an outline outside of the porch swing. He sighs.

From his sofa, Sam stares at Charlie on the area rug in his white t-shirt and corduroys, the former Marine. "You loved Ace?" Sam says.

Charlie's unsure how to respond, lost in Sam's light blue eyes. He looks to patterns across the rug. "I think he loved me, too," Charlie says, "best he could. Took me too long to realize I couldn't fix him, that it wasn't my job. Maybe I needed Ace at the time, though." Charlie smirks. "I called a cab, shoulda been here by now, should be here any minute. You, sir, need to run water over your hand," Charlie says. "Wasn't kidding about infection."

Sam looks to his hand, his ripped pearl snap shirt. A knock at his front door.

"Finally," Charlie says. He stands from the rug, taller, more muscular than Sam realized. "You gonna be alright, kid?"

Sam's head hurting still, he looks from his aching hand to his college professor.

"Of course, you are," Charlie says, slides cigarettes from his corduroy pant pockets, packs the box against his hand. A knock again at the front door.

Sam looks from Charlie to white chipped shiplap paneling across the living room walls from when the farmhouse was built in the 1920s. Dizzy again, his head in his hands.

Charlie walks from the coffee table and area rug, slips a cigarette from the pack, unlocks, opens the front door.

A knife swipes swift Charlie's throat. Stinging, burning through skin and veins. Blood across white walls. His hands to his neck, Charlie struggles to breathe, the tall man rushing the living room, knocks Charlie to hardwood floor.

Sam leaps behind the sofa, the tall man running at him with a knife, slipping, sliding on the area rug, crashes into the coffee table. From behind his sofa, Sam staggers to the open front door, warm wind gusting from outside. From darkness on the porch, Grady. Sam spins around, boots thudding up the mahogany stairs til Grady grabs Sam's ankle, twists it, trips him face-first to the stairs, yanks Sam's shaggy hair. Sam turns, kicks Grady hard in the face.

Blood gushes from Grady's nose, Grady's hands to his face. Through wood railing, Sam sees the tall man below, pushing himself from the broken coffee table, Grady cursing in pain in front of the grandfather clock. Stumbling to his feet, Sam runs upstairs, sees at the west end of the long hallway the open door to his room. Dylan's bedroom door locked in front of him. Sam grabs short rope from the ceiling outside Dylan's door, an attic ladder unfolding, thuds to the floor. Behind him, Sam hears Charlie downstairs gurgling blood, Grady's muffled, "Upstairs! Fucker ran upstairs!"

With his swollen hand, Sam grabs a wood beam on the ladder, screams in agony, hears the tall man running past Grady in work boots up the wood staircase. With all he has, Sam pulls himself up the ladder, scrambles into the attic, pulls up the attic door.

Boxes and childhood toys around him. The knife stabs through the attic floor, the tall man grunting below him, furious, tall enough to stab again and again into the ceiling, stabs the blade through Sam's foot.

Sam's scream fills his house. He hears Grady cussing incoherent, smashing the grandfather clock to the ground, glass shattering. Sam pushes his foot from the blade, collapses to the ground, scoots past boxes into a corner, a trail of his blood behind him. The knife stabbing again and again through the attic floor. Sam's hands to his ears.

Downstairs, Charlie's on his back on plank wood floor. Warm wind across him from an open front door. He hears Grady breaking photos, punching walls, kicking the grandfather clock. His hands on his neck, Charlie stares up at the ceiling, waterfront pier, turns his head to white curtains across the living room's four bow windows, dies.

CHAPTER THIRTY

"Sarah here?" Dylan asks. "Is Sarah here?" trying not to stutter. He turns from a purple front door, looks to pillars on the porch. He's in work boots from the oil fields, waits in his blue sleeveless shirt, night wind warm across his arms. His hand in a pocket of his grease-stained jeans, holding his rejected wedding ring.

He hears a deadbolt unlock, turns, sees Cristine. "Cristine?" Dylan says, confused.

"Dylan?" Cristine remembers her vague conversation from earlier in Sarah's Jeep, sees Dylan's Roadrunner parked along the street.

Dylan looks to an address beside the front door. "Where's Sarah? Nancy?"

"Where're your keys?" Cristine says.

"What?"

"Your keys. Give me your keys."

"What, why?" Dylan scoffs. "I haven't been drinking."

Cristine holds out her hand.

"You're not serious."

Cristine says nothing, a laugh-track from a TV sitcom behind her in the living room. She tilts her head, glances at her hand.

Dylan hears the sitcom, rolls his eyes. "Fine," he says in a huff, his hands in his pockets for his keys. He gives them to Cristine.

"Thank you," Cristine says, looks to a candlelit living room behind her, Nancy in front of a wooden television set on the carpet, sitting cross-legged in her nightgown, her face lit with images from the TV.

"I'm walking you home," Cristine says. She looks to Dylan. "Sarah's at work. Whatever it is, if you respect her, and I know you do, give her time to get her head right. You do the same. Y'all can talk tomorrow. But, for now, friend, I'm walking you home. You're getting rest."

Dumbfounded, Dylan laughs. "What?"

Minutes later, Cristine knocks on a bedroom door, stares at framed family photos along a dark hallway. Behind her, a sign on another door, Nancy's Room drawn with colored markers. Above her, a ceiling vent blowing cold air, overlapping dialogue downstairs on the sitcom. Cristine's hands in the front pockets of her stone-washed jeans.

The door unlocks, opens to Rachel in her pajamas, yawning.

Cristine's speechless, admiring pink floral embroidery on Rachel's white pajamas. Cristine thinks about her abandoned knitting project downstairs. She struggles to say, "Would you mind watching Nancy for twenty minutes?"

Television broadcasts black-and-white reruns of *I Love Lucy*. Across from the TV, a sectional sofa along a wall of windows, a swimming pool outside with waves reflecting across the empty candlelit living room.

Nancy's in the kitchen, scoots a chair from a table, moonlight shining through a side glass door. She pushes the chair against cabinets, climbs in her socks on a granite countertop. She opens a cabinet door, grabs a plastic bag of potato chips. She climbs from the counter to the chair, reaches up to close the cabinet.

Her hair in pigtails, Nancy walks into the living room, shoving chips in her mouth. She listens to Lucy and Ethel talking, hears footsteps coming downstairs. Dylan in the foyer by the front door, waiting with his arms folded.

"Rachel, this is Dylan," Cristine says.

"How do you do?" Dylan says, his handshake firm. He realizes he's never met Sarah's cousin, remembers Pastor Jacob introducing Rachel to his church Sunday evening.

With her hands in her front pockets, Cristine walks to the sectional sofa. "Nancy, Rachel's gonna watch you for a moment, okay? I'm gonna walk Uncle Dylan home."

Nancy's staring at *I Love Lucy*. "He's my neighbor, Cristine, not my uncle."

Cristine sighs. "Prodigal child." From the sofa, she grabs silk yarn, a knitting needle, slips them in her cloth bag. She adjusts her baseball cap, her golden hair under it in a braid. She looks to Lucy on the television screen beside a reflection of her yellow t-shirt with "Okie" in the center. From candles in a brick fireplace, an aroma of honeysuckle.

Outside, a large Magnolia tree in the front yard, its leaves rustling with warm wind at thirty miles per hour, a number Dylan heard a weatherman predict on local news.

The warm wind stronger, Cristine closes the purple front door behind her, hears the deadbolt lock. She looks beside the door to a lit porch light.

They're in the middle of a cul-de-sac, Cristine staring at brick homes encircling them, Dylan walking with his arms folded. Behind them in Pastor Jacob's yard, the Magnolia tree blows with the wind. Cristine looks south to a series of unfinished, one-story houses, wooden frames with concrete foundations. Scent of drying cement.

"Did you know we were the first family to live in our neighborhood?" Cristine says. "Right when they built I-240." She stares at the only streetlamp in the cul-de-sac. "At a Sunday evening ribbon-cutting ceremony for the first houses on our block, Nolan pulled his first loose tooth. Wouldn't stop. He was six, and I'd just turned four. Both of us well-dressed along a long red ribbon, standing beside our parents. Dad serving his first year as district attorney, and Nolan keeps digging in his mouth, asking me to help, wiping blood on his suit."

Cristine looks above the streetlamp at powerlines, remembers her father at the ribbon-cutting ceremony naming their neighborhood, "Prairie Queen." She thinks about Nolan in Norman, ready to begin his third year at OU, preparing for law school.

Behind them in the distance, Dylan hears traffic on the interstate. He looks to his work boots. "You know, I coulda just walked to Sarah's work, right? I don't need my car."

Cristine shrugs. "I know." She walks with him past a fire hydrant, glances to a sign, Southwest 77th Street. "Glad you didn't, though."

Two blocks from Pastor Jacob's, they're on a sidewalk along a chain-link fence. Behind the fence, an elementary school where Dylan and Sam attended fifth and sixth grade. Dylan hears a swing set squeak. He looks past the fence to a basketball court where, playing one-on-one with Nolan, Dylan learned defense.

"Full moon," Cristine says. She points past trees canopying the street. "Sublime, shining across the field like that."

Dylan looks at stars scattered across the sky.

From the corner of her eye, Cristine watches Dylan. For a second, she imagines a parallel universe, a world where she's in love with Dylan, him with her. For the first time, Cristine sees in Dylan what Sarah's always seen in him, how he stares at stars with wonder, the same way he stares at Sarah.

A mile south, Cristine and Dylan walk along his family's farmhouse, an owl hooting in the cottonwood tree beside the barn, Dylan and Sam's childhood tire swing swaying at the end of rope.

Dylan looks across his moonlit yard to the picnic table Sam built, at chipped white paint along their brick house. He hears branches break beneath his boots, listens to leaves rustling above him on the cottonwood tree like waves in a sea.

At the front of his house, Sam's pickup truck in the driveway.

Cristine covers her ears. "What is that?" she says to a loud, repetitive thud. She looks to Dylan.

Dylan stops, his arm suddenly in front of her, the thudding rhythmic, louder, thumping. He raises his index finger to his lips.

Cristine nods.

Side by side, Cristine and Dylan walk from the corner of the farmhouse, the thuds louder from the front porch. Dylan walks toward Sam's truck, looks around it to the long dirt driveway, sees the pickup's dented driver side door, its missing mirror.

"Dylan." Cristine points to the porch, front door swaying, thumping its door frame.

"Sam wouldn't leave the place like that," Dylan says, starting up his porch stairs.

Their footsteps echoing, Cristine follows, her hands in her pockets. She looks to the creaking porch swing.

Dylan looks to Cristine, a worried look on his face. He turns, nudges open the door, darkness across his living room. Dylan's hand inside on the shiplap wall, flicks a light switch, nothing.

"Dylan?" Cristine says, sees the grandfather clock broken across the wood floor, shattered glass and torn photos across the mahogany staircase.

"Stay behind me," Dylan says, glass breaking beneath his boots. He stops at the bottom of the stairs. "Sam!" he yells, glances beside him to the kitchen.

Cristine gasps. "Oh! Dylan, oh, God, blood!" She points to the living room's floor, her other hand to her mouth.

Dylan sees the blood-stained plank wood floor, the broken coffee table, looks to the top of the stairs. "Sam!" he yells again. "Sam! Fuck." His mind races. "Cristine, the kitchen. Call the cops, hurry!"

Cristine can't move, stares in shock at blood across the sofa and white curtains.

"Cristine, the cops!" and, she snaps out of it, frantic, runs into the kitchen. She looks across gray brick wall for a phone.

Dylan looks past the sofa, sees the gray brick fireplace across the room with a poker. He looks again to the staircase. Sam could be up there hurt, their father's guns upstairs, locked in a safe. "Fuck."

Slowly, he walks across his living room, focused on the fireplace. With each step, glass breaking beneath his work boots. He cringes, wonders where his father is, why he hasn't seen Sam since Monday, whose blood is on the floor, the fire poker in reach.

"Dylan," he hears Cristine say from the other side of the room, breathless. "Dylan, the phone's dead."

Dylan turns from the fireplace, sees a bloody arm slump to the floor from behind the sofa. Horrified, Dylan looks up, sees Cristine across the room in the kitchen doorway, "Cristine!"

Cristine's pulled violently into the kitchen, someone else's hand over her mouth, a knife stabs into her side.

Dylan rushes across his living room, can't see Cristine.

She holds the knife at bay, can't see who's holding her. A muffled "no." Then, she's higher, thrown to her back on the kitchen table. Her head's pounding. She looks up, dazed, the young man from the mall standing over her, Grady. Dylan darting into the kitchen, knocking Grady to gray brick floor.

Cristine hears the two men wrestle, tackle each other into cabinets and chairs, Cristine's hands to her aching head.

Grady pins Dylan to the gray brick floor, Dylan grabbing Grady's wrist, stops the hunting knife from stabbing his eye. Trembling, Dylan grips Grady's wrist, the knife blade pointing down at his face.

"Cristine," she hears Dylan say from the floor. "Run!" She hears footsteps running across the ceiling. Her vision blurred, she tries to sit up from the table, sees knives in a rack on the kitchen counter.

Cristine falls from the table to the brick floor on her knees, screams. She sees Grady on Dylan, Grady's knife at Dylan's face, Grady shivering with rage. She hears thudding down the stairs, crawls to her feet, sees a dark narrow hallway to the laundry room and backyard.

The tall man at the kitchen doorway, looks down at his brother.

Dylan slams Grady's hunting knife into a cabinet, uppercuts Grady hard in the nose. The tall man lunges from shadows.

"Get out, run!" Dylan yells, and Cristine limps from the kitchen to the hallway, holding her hurt knee. She turns, sees the tall man hurl Dylan onto the kitchen counter, the tall man stabbing Dylan over and over in his face and eyes. Cristine screams, crying, runs past the washer and dryer, flings open the door to the backyard.

"Fucker, no witnesses!" The tall man kicks his brother on the brick floor, Grady holding his bloody nose, grabs his knife, runs after Cristine.

Through linens on clothing lines, Cristine runs. Her screams carried off with each gust of wind. She pushes rows of sheets out of her way, sees an outline of someone chasing her through linens til she's racing from the farmhouse across a flat open field.

In the front of the farmhouse at the intersection of Southwest 89th and Pennsylvania, a pickup truck parked along the dirt road. Vera in the passenger seat, biting her nails. She looks behind her at the rectangular window into the camper, stares at a duffle bag and coloring books on the blanket, thinks about her three kids back at a motel, scratches her brittle black hair.

Cristine runs along trees and a creek. Ahead of her, the unfinished neighborhood, hint of relief on her face. She grabs her hurt knee, hobbles toward a bulldozer and halted construction on a house. She stops on a slope, hears branches breaking nearby. The wind relentless, she runs down a dirt hill, limps past stacks of two-by-fours and bricks. She hears her footsteps on concrete foundation, looks around her at wood beams and plywood walls. She glances up at the night sky, someone else's footsteps running behind her into the unfinished house.

Cristine hides against a plywood wall, silent, slides slow along plywood toward the front yard. She stops at the sound of footsteps on the other side of the wall. She waits. Trying not to scream. The footsteps closer, closer, then gone. She limps from the house, runs down the street along construction site after construction site.

She stops, looks behind her, no one. She turns to the sound of wind ripping tarp. She sees in the distance the cul-de-sac. She runs, starts to cry, Dylan's Plymouth Roadrunner parked at the end of the street, the Magnolia tree in Pastor Jacob's front yard.

Inside the house, Nancy's walking to the kitchen in her nightgown. Tired, she rubs her eyes, *I Love Lucy*'s end credits muted on the television.

Rachel's in the candlelit living room, kneels in pajamas beside the wall of windows, flips through vinyl records arranged in a mid-century modern turntable console. Her father's albums alphabetized as always. The Beatles, Credence, Eagles, Fleetwood Mac.

She looks from vinyl records to an oval-shaped swimming pool in the backyard, stares at a diving board and shimmering water. Can't believe she's in her father's new house, babysitting for the first time in a decade. High school ten years ago. She looks to honeysuckle candles in the brick fireplace, a portrait of Nancy on the mantel, a rotary phone on a table beside the sofa. She worries why Derek hasn't called, wonders where he went this morning chasing after Sheriff Ford.

"Nancy, take your things upstairs, please," Rachel says. "All your sports stuff, like Cristine asked before she left." Rachel turns to the albums, Beethoven at the front.

She stands, puts a record on a turntable, the television screen still muted. All at once, she hears from console speakers the sound of woodwinds in an inverted A-minor chord, rhythmic strings, violas, cellos.

Limping, Cristine runs across the front yard, stumbles past pillars onto the porch. Her hands in her pockets for keys, nothing. "Shit." She turns, sees Grady running in the dark down the middle of the street, rushing toward her with his glistening knife. She spins around, sobbing, screams with gusting wind, bangs on the purple door. "Help me!"

Inside, walking up carpeted stairs, Rachel listens to violins accompany strings from Beethoven's Symphony Seven. She's unsure if she heard something else.

Lit under porch light, Cristine bangs on the front door. "Nancy!" she screams. "Nancy, please! Rachel, open the door!" She looks behind her, Grady closer, running past Dylan's car. She turns, pounds harder. "Oh, God, Rachel!"

Over symphony music, Rachel hears her name. Confused, she looks behind her down the carpeted staircase at the dim foyer.

Bawling, Cristine throws her entire body against the door, Grady in the front yard. The door unlocks, opens, Rachel in her pajamas. "Cristine?"

Cristine falls into the foyer, kicks the door closed behind her, can't stop crying. "Lock it, he's coming," she says from the floor. "He killed Dylan."

Rachel's eyes widen, eight-year-old Nancy's at her side, grips her hand. Rachel turns to lock the deadbolt.

The door bursts open, full orchestra soaring across the speakers. Knife in hand, Grady's stunned to see Rachel and the kid.

Nancy screams, and Rachel pushes her into the living room.

"Run!" Rachel yells.

Grady with his bloody nose, hears in his head his brother's warning, *No witnesses! Kill 'em all. Rob this place, too.*

Grady's knife swipes at Cristine, misses, Rachel yanks Cristine from the foyer, Grady losing his balance, chases after them.

Nancy unlocks, opens a glass backdoor, runs across the patio, screams into wind, Cristine and Rachel running hand-in-sweaty-hand in the living room.

Cristine behind her, Rachel runs out the open backdoor. Desperate, Grady kicks Cristine's legs. Her hand slips from Rachel, and she crashes to the sofa, Grady slamming shut the backdoor between the two women, locks it. Rachel stops, turns, sees Cristine through the wall of windows. "No," she whispers.

Grady looks to Cristine, and she leaps up, runs across the sectional sofa, Grady chasing after her, swipes his knife. She lunges to the flat top of the wooden television set, running across it. Grady yanks her hair braid, pulls her back to him.

Mortified, screaming, Rachel bangs against the wall of windows, watches Grady throw Cristine across the floor.

Face down on plush carpet, Cristine's disoriented, her knee in excruciating pain. Her baseball cap beside her, she can barely look up, reaches for the foyer. She feels a cold blade stab her lower back, unleashes a bloodcurdling scream.

Rachel grabs a chair from the patio, hurls it through shattering glass windows.

Like all the times before, Grady hears his brother in his head, punches his knife into Cristine's back, blood splattering on his maniacal face. Rachel swings Nancy's baseball bat into his shoulder, swings again, hitting his knife from his hand, knocks him from Cristine. He stops moving.

Her breathing heavy, Rachel grips the baseball bat, stares at Grady unconscious in his denim pants and black jean jacket. Rachel won't let go of her bat, can't slow her breathing. She glances from Grady to Cristine on her stomach, Cristine's blood across beige carpet.

Rachel kneels, turns a lifeless Cristine on her side. She grips her bat tighter, her other hand to her mouth. Beethoven's symphony calmer.

Rachel steps from Grady, glances to the turntable console in front of the wall of shattered windows, the swimming pool past the patio in the starlit backyard. She looks back to Grady and Cristine. Beside them, a large square window overlooking her father's front yard. Rachel's car in the driveway. Her keys on the foyer wall.

Behind her, glass breaks. Rachel turns, sees Nancy on the patio.

Nancy looks past Rachel, frightened, Cristine and Grady's bodies on the carpet.

"Nancy," Rachel whispers. "Please. Don't move. I'm coming for you."

Wind blows out candles in the fireplace.

Grady grabs Rachel's ankle, and she trips, falls on Cristine, Nancy screaming, the baseball bat slipping from Rachel's hands. Barely conscious, Grady's unsure where he is, Rachel kicks his hand til he lets go.

"My car, Nancy!" and, Nancy darts across the living room, Rachel right behind her. Disoriented, Grady sees his hunting knife beneath a window ledge. He grabs it, sees Nancy, Rachel, the purple front door.

The passenger door flings open, and Rachel pushes Nancy inside her car. She runs to the driver's side, unlocks it. Behind the steering wheel, she sees Grady on the front porch. "No."

Nancy slides from her passenger seat to the floorboard. She covers her head, and Rachel turns keys in the ignition, puts her car in reverse, sees Grady staggering past the Magnolia tree toward them.

Tires squeal down the driveway, Rachel speeding in reverse from her father's house, her car sideswiping Dylan's. Her foot slams on the accelerator, and she puts her car in drive, speeds from the cul-de-sac as fast she can.

Nancy's in the floorboard, crying. Terrified, breathless, Rachel looks down to her, Rachel's hands in a death grip on her steering wheel. She sees in her rearview mirror the unfinished neighborhood, disappearing into darkness.

CHAPTER THIRTY-ONE

"When did this all begin?" asks a young man with a Spanish accent.

"When did all what begin?" says a young man with a southern drawl.

"What we were just talking about."

"What do you mean?"

"What do you mean, 'what do I mean?'"

"Tipping?"

"*Monopoly*," says the young man with his Spanish accent. "You know? Board game from Parker Brothers?"

"Wait, what?" Jeremiah says with his drawl. He wipes a table with a washcloth. "What're you writing about again?"

"*Space Invaders*," Miguel says.

"What?" Jeremiah laughs. "Why?" He walks his dish bin to his next booth.

Miguel puts down his pencil, closes his spiral notebook. "Scholarship essay, remember?" Miguel says. He glances at a Spanish-to-English dictionary beside his notebook. "When were we talking about tipping?" he asks.

"When were we talking about *Monopoly*?" Jeremiah says.

"We were talking about a history of arcade games," Miguel says, "then board games, when they started."

"Oh, yeah," Jeremiah says, stacks dirty plates on a table in a booth behind Miguel. "You asked about Backgammon, Chess. And, I told you Backgammon's probably the oldest, Persia, I think, about 5,000 years ago, maybe Senet in ancient Egypt around 3,000 or so B.C. You really never played Dominoes?"

"Hand-to-God," Miguel says.

"Blowing my fucking mind for a living, Miguel," Jeremiah says. "Madness. Pure madness. I'll teach you sometime, easy." He stacks plates in his dish bin, grabs empty drinking glasses from the table. "Sundays after church, I play Dominoes with my dad. My Uncle Joe, though, on my dad's side, he's a real motherfucker, breaks Dominoes when he's losing. Smart guy, too. Couldn't tell it looking at him. Put himself through technical school for welding. Got a room full of history books and Encyclopedias. You got a ride, man?"

"Girlfriend's on her way," Miguel says, hears strong wind gusts outside, looks from his booth to tinted windows beside him, stares into the night across an emptying parking lot, sees headlights speeding across an elevated interstate.

Jeremiah sprays disinfectant on booth seats and a table behind Miguel. "So, why *Space Invaders*?" Jeremiah says.

"What?"

"Your scholarship essay, man. Why write about arcade and board games for something so important?"

"Because, they're art, and art's important," Miguel says.

Jeremiah chuckles.

"What?"

"What do you mean, 'what'?" Jeremiah says. "Arcade and board games are entertainment. People play 'em for fun."

"But, didn't you just say *Monopoly*'s a critique of landlords and income inequality in early 1900s America, that its creator intended it to reflect when it was made," Miguel says. "That's what art does, right? Hold a mirror to society?"

"*Monopoly*'s an exception," Jeremiah says, wipes his cloth across the booth seats. "Gonna prove real hard for ya to convince me and them scholarship folk *Killer Shark* or *Space Invaders* have something to say about anything. You're a senior this year?"

"This fall, yeah. You?"

"Same. And, after high school?"

"Computer science," Miguel says. "Try and build and design arcade games myself, we'll see. Gotta get money to go, first." He nods to his notebook, looks up as Sarah approaches with the coffee pot, smiles. "Thanks, Sarah."

"No problem," Sarah says, refills his cup of coffee, then looks to Jeremiah. "You're our new busser?"

"Jeremiah," he says, wipes his greasy palms across his apron, shakes her hand. "Pleased to meet you," he says. "Welcome to my kingdom." He gestures behind him as if he's Vanna White on *Wheel of Fortune*, and Sarah sees a dining room with no one else in it, tables and booths full of leftover food and dirty dishes.

"Impressive," Sarah says.

Jeremiah shrugs, looks over his shoulder. "Ain't it, though?"

Miguel drinks his coffee. "Still have tables?"

"Just the one," Sarah says, sighs. "A family finishing up, about to pay."

Jeremiah leans on Miguel's booth, looks across the dining room at the south wall, a clock above the buffet bar, 10:10 p.m. "So, Sarah," he says to her. "You believe in God?"

"What?" Sarah says, shocked.

Jeremiah grins. "Nah, just kidding." He folds his arms. "You think *Space Invaders* and *Killer Shark* are art?"

Holding the coffee pot by its handle, Sarah shakes her head. She tries to refocus. "*Space Invaders?*" she says. "Are you serious?"

"This guy is," Jeremiah says. "Writing a scholarship essay and everything about it."

Sarah looks to Miguel's notebook on the table. "*Killer Shark?*" she says, almost to herself. "Sure," she says, nonchalant.

"Sure?" Jeremiah's surprised.

"Sure," Sarah says. "I prefer *Pong*, but they're all visual storytelling, like an advertisement or a movie using images to tell a story. Or, the way photography works." Sarah pauses, sees herself at home in her makeshift darkroom. "Actually, makes total sense. *Space Invaders* sounds suspiciously like *Invasion of the Body Snatchers* or any sci-fi movie ever."

Miguel drinks his coffee. "Sounds like a story with a plot to me."

Jeremiah grabs his dish bin, walks to another table. "Sounds like I'm in school with a bunch of know-it-alls," he says. "Fuck." He tosses dirty silverware to his dish bin. He wipes macaroni from a toddler's high-chair. "Is it true, every year, the entire western half of Oklahoma catches fire? Just burns out of control?"

"Sorta," Sarah hears Miguel say, his words muffled in her head. She turns to the restaurant's west side, a family of four at a square-shaped table. Sarah suddenly thinking about Dylan, what she's avoided all night, their fight this morning. Hiking plans next weekend in the state's panhandle, how she's never been, rejecting his marriage proposal in her backyard, a broken look across Dylan's face she's never seen.

She hears something about wildfires and cross timbers, Miguel telling Jeremiah Oklahomans describe the panhandle's farthest northwest corner as "No Man's Land," shortgrass prairie and talus slopes surrounding "Devil's Tombstone" and "Old Maid Rock." Sarah looks above the buffet bar, clock on the south wall, 10:14 p.m., Jeremiah bussing tables. She walks to help him, feels as if she's sinking in quicksand, drowning in a wedding dress, time standing still, restaurant closed at ten. Her hand to her head.

"How it's always been here," Miguel says. "Nothing to stop it, not during drought or strong winds. Fire sweeps across everything," he says, "burns across the plains. All the natural oils from wild cedar trees fuel the flames til there's a river in its way."

Jeremiah wipes his washcloth across a table, doesn't know what to do next year after high school, stares at a five-dollar bill by salt and pepper shakers, wipes them, too. From the corner of his eyes, Sarah's at the table beside him, stacking dirty plates on a tray.

Miguel looks to the clock on the south wall, 10:15, then beside him to the window. "Have a good night," he hears Sarah say. He sees two children outside, the two brothers hitting each other, leaving the restaurant, laughing, their young parents waving back at Sarah from the foyer. The mother at a cigarette vending machine, pulls a lever for a pack of Newport's. The father puts on his cowboy hat at the door. "When did tipping begin?" Miguel hears Jeremiah say.

"Feudalism," Miguel says. "Rich Americans brought it here from Europe after our U.S. Civil War, after slavery. Europeans ended it, we kept it." He watches the family outside in front of the restaurant, wind strong enough to blow the father's cowboy hat from his head, his hat tumbling across the parking lot, him chasing after it.

"When's Diane coming?" Sarah says.

"Good question," he says, looks back out the window.

"I'm gonna lock up," Sarah says, unties her apron.

Their manager's voice calls out from the back of the restaurant. "That our last table?"

"Yes, sir!" Sarah says, pulls her hair into a messy ponytail.

"Don't forget to set the alarm!" their manager says.

Sarah puts her apron on a chair, nods to her tray full of dirty dishes on the table beside Jeremiah. "Be right back," she says to him, starts toward the foyer.

"What's *Invasion of the Body Snatchers*?" Jeremiah asks, wipes down another table.

Miguel scratches his chin. "Black-and-white fifties movie," he says. "Alien plant seeds end up on earth, these large pods." He looks over his shoulder, the dining room silent. Jeremiah's back to him, the lanky young busser carrying his dish bin to the next table. "You fall asleep near a pod, you die," Miguel says, turns, sees Sarah walking along the buffet bar. "Then, your double comes out of the pod. Emotionless, but with all your memories and physical appearance intact."

In front of Sarah as she walks, the west side of the restaurant, sepia-tinted chandeliers above every booth and table, booths along wood-paneled walls, everything clean except the one table where the young family just left, the dining area's concrete floor swept, scent of baked potato and steak. "Town's taken over one-by-one," Sarah hears Miguel say, "and you don't know who's a pod person, who's not."

Confused, Miguel scoots closer to the window. From his booth seat, he sees Diane's red Mustang parked across the parking lot beside Sarah's Jeep. "Finally," he whispers.

Sarah's in the foyer, grabs store keys from the host stand. She looks up, smiles, seventeen-year-old Diane outside in her mint green summer dress, standing at the glass double doors. Sarah waves, looks behind her, sees Miguel in his booth, gathering his notebook, apron. Jeremiah still bussing tables.

Sarah looks back to Diane staring at her from the other side of the glass doors. Diane's familiar feathered blonde hair, her fair skin slightly tanned. Diane expressionless, motionless, make-up perfect until Sarah's closer, sees tears in Diane's eyes, Diane's hands at her side, shaking. Sarah's eyes moving from Diane's hands and mint green dress.

Behind Diane, darkness, Sarah's eyes adjusting to an outline of a tall man. His face becoming clearer, Sarah gasps.

He moves swift in work boots past Diane, kicks the glass entrance, kicks harder, shatters the glass door to the ground.

Jeremiah grips his plastic dish bin, unsure what he's heard, looks to Miguel, Sarah turning to run.

"Don't run, we'll kill her," the tall man says, his drawl guttural, hollow.

Sarah stops at the host stand.

Outside in the wind, Diane's eyes squeeze shut. A gun at her back, warm tears down her face. Pistol pushes at her spine, someone shoving her into the foyer from her sandals, broken glass stabbing her feet.

Sarah hears screams.

"Cash register," says the tall man. "And, I'll make it stop. All three of you. Do the right thing." He turns, nods to his brother.

Grady spins Diane around to him. With his gun, punches her stomach.

"Diane!" Miguel yells, mid-run at the foyer, stops at the host stand, the tall man's gun at Sarah. Diane behind Sarah at the restaurant's shattered entrance, hunched over in pain breathless beside Grady.

His hands behind his head, Jeremiah's dumbfounded, slow to move into the dining area behind Miguel. Jeremiah's eyes on Sarah and a silver .357 revolver he recognizes straightaway from shooting ranges and gun shows with his uncle.

"Your manager in back, too," the tall man says.

Beside him, Sarah's rigid, sees the rage on Miguel's face. She looks past Jeremiah and buffet bars to metal kitchen doors swinging open at the back of the restaurant. A stout man in black pants and white short-sleeve button-up walks into the dining area.

Silence except his footsteps and the hum of heat lamps above buffet bars. The manager limps from his recent hip-replacement hurting, right hand near the keys on his belt.

"With purpose," shouts the tall man from across the dining area.

In the foyer, a metal coin release bangs closed on the plastic gumball machine, startles Sarah. The tall man turns over his shoulder.

"Won't be in a cash register," Vera says, slipping another quarter into the machine's coin slot. Gears turn and crank.

Sarah cringes, holds herself together, listens to a gumball knock against hard plastic and drop down the machine.

"They count money in the back office," Vera says, "keep it in their safe til morning."

Sarah stares at her store manager, the middle-aged man nervous in front of her, barely much taller than her, the tall man turning to him.

"Take us there," the tall man says, nods his revolver to the back of the restaurant. Grady pushes a barefoot Diane toward the front of the foyer, and she screams as she steps across shattered glass. Miguel grabs for her as she falls to the floor, and the tall man punches Miguel in the jaw to the ground.

"Miguel!" Sarah screams.

"Nobody moves," says the tall man, calm. He looks down to Miguel and Diane. "Nobody said move." His head hurts. He scratches his hair with his gun, turns to Sarah. "Nobody's gonna get hurt," he says.

"No witnesses," Grady hears in his head. Confused, he looks to his older brother.

His jaw sore, Miguel wipes blood from his lip. He's on his back, looks to Diane sobbing on her stomach. He looks from the concrete floor, the tall man towering over him.

"Tell y'all what," the tall man says. "Let's go to the manager's office together."

With her revolver, Vera joins him at his side. She turns, chewing grape gum, looks at Grady in disgust.

"Get!" she says to him, strident.

The tall man grins at the store manager. "Move." He nudges Sarah with his revolver, and she forces back tears. For a moment at the host stand, her eyes meet Jeremiah's, his hands still behind his head. "Behind her, son," the tall man says, pointing his gun at Jeremiah, Jeremiah watching Sarah walk from the foyer behind their manager.

From the corner of his eye, Jeremiah sees a glimpse of Grady's handgun, a gray .22 caliber automatic pistol. Behind Grady, the shattered glass entrance, wind strong across the dark, empty parking lot. Too far to run. Jeremiah sighs, follows behind Sarah.

Walking through the restaurant's dining area, Sarah hears a steady drone of electricity above every table and booth from sepia-tinted chandeliers. She stares ahead in a daze, booths along wood-paneled walls. She refuses to cry.

At the host stand, Grady grabs Diane's arm, yanks her crying from concrete floor. Vera points her revolver down at Miguel.

Sarah watches her manager disappear through metal kitchen doors. Behind her, Jeremiah and the tall man wait. Diane wimpers. Sarah looks to the stainless-steel industrial stove beside a stacked convection oven. Bright fluorescent lights beam down from the ceiling. Sarah's horrified when she hears rattling plates and distant spraying water, a conveyor belt.

The tall man's hand moves quick to Sarah's shoulder. His revolver to his lips. He listens to spraying water, moves past her, quiet. He turns to her manager, nods his gun to the hallway at a single metal door.

"Inside," he says. "Not a word."

Sarah's sick to her stomach. Without a sound, they walk past the stove. She listens to the distant dishwasher, worries about Andrés, imagines him in his hairnet holding a rack of dishes at the conveyor belt. Jeremiah walks into the steam-filled hall. His hand on a chrome latch, his boss beside him, Sarah and the tall man behind him. The metal door opens to a walk-in freezer, cold air rushing on Sarah and her store manager, Jeremiah staring at stacked brown boxes.

Sarah looks from the freezer door, Miguel and Diane slow into the kitchen, silent, side-by-side, Grady and Vera behind them with their guns. Sarah turns to see the tall man disappear down the hallway into steam.

Reluctant, Sarah finally steps into the cold, closed metal room—air acrid, bitter. She sees her breath. Cardboard boxes to the ceiling along all four walls, each brown box with silhouettes of two cows grazing, Sizzlin' Since '76 across each box.

At the back of the room, Sarah shivers, rubs her arms, sits on a freezer-burned box. Jeremiah on a box beside her, his hands clasped on his lap. He stares in front of him, Diane sitting beside the doorway on red tile floor, her arms wrapped around her legs. Miguel standing next to her at the door.

Miguel looks into the hall. No Grady or Vera, no tall man or store manager, no sound of spraying water, only whirring noises and steam from the dishwasher machine around the corner. Miguel looks from the hall to the freezer ceiling, a thermostat behind him on a metal wall, 37 degrees. He squats to the ground, holds Diane's trembling hand.

From the back of the freezer, Jeremiah stares at Diane's mint green dress. He glances at his greasy white apron. He counts time in his head, each breath, thinks about silence, how to endure it, something his uncle taught him. He looks to his apron and lanky legs, his clasped hands. A minute gone. Sarah sits calm beside him. The cardboard box he's sitting on icy through his work pants. He hears his own chattering teeth.

Sarah looks from her work shoes to the center of the ceiling, listens to the hum of a single light bulb.

A metal wall behind her, Diane feels tightness around her throat. She starts to gasp, can't. Her heart pounding. She's sweating, nauseous, feels like someone's strangling her. Miguel doesn't notice, still holding her hand, his other hand rubbing his sore jaw. Her stomach cramps. She squeezes Miguel's hand, her other hand to her chest, rips at her dress.

"Can't breathe." She wheezes, kicks at shelves.

Miguel turns to her, and she clutches his hand harder, Jeremiah and Sarah watching cans of food crash to the floor.

"Ain't it something?" From the freezer door, the tall man smirks at Diane.

Diane grips her throat. "Water."

"No water, ma'am," says the tall man. "Sorry to say. Did bring ya a dishwasher, though." He pulls Andrés from the hall, drops his limp body to the freezer floor.

"Andrés!" Sarah leaps to his side.

The tall man stands over them, scratches his hair with his revolver.

Sarah turns Andrés on his back, his face bloody, unrecognizable. She shakes him, desperate, realizes he's barely breathing, unconscious. His eyes swollen shut.

"Wasn't supposed to happen this way," the tall man says with his drawl. "House burglary gone wrong."

Diane, still gasping for air, collapses onto cold, tile floor. Miguel at her side.

"See, my brother here." The tall man grabs Grady by the arm from the hallway into the freezer. "Wrong all night. Got himself a broken nose from it. Swore no one was home. Then, we got here and told us three and a manager."

Sarah slaps Andrés. "Wake up!"

Diane thrashes, kicking boxes.

The tall man turns from his brother, winks at Vera behind him in the hall. He grins at the store manager beside her. He digs his fingernails into Grady's arm.

Grady cringes, falls to his knees.

The tall man turns to Diane, then Sarah. He lets go of his brother, kneels beside Andrés. He looks across from him at Sarah, rests his arms on his knees.

"Not much to do for him," the tall man says. He twists a knife already in Andrés' side, yanks it from below Andrés' rib cage, dark blood spilling to the floor.

Sarah screams in disbelief—didn't see the knife. She puts her hands on Andrés' side to stop his bleeding.

The tall man stands from the freezer floor, Andrés' blood gushing across red tile from his lifeless body.

"How much?" the tall man asks.

"Eleven hundred," Vera says from the door. From across the freezer, Jeremiah stares at her silver .38 caliber revolver.

"Never enough," says the tall man. He wipes his knife on his western shirt and jeans, Miguel behind him, panicked, scooting the flailing Diane from Andrés's blood.

Sarah's hand to her mouth, Andrés' body beside her, his blood on her face.

"Been wrong all night." The tall man sighs. He shakes his head. "Eleven hundred and an engagement ring."

Grady rubs his aching arm, no longer sure what his brother's thinking, too scared to look up at him.

The tall man reaches in his pockets.

Through her blurry eyes, Sarah sees a flash of silver fall to the freezer floor. In Andrés' blood, a small silver band with a pear-shaped diamond.

Pure horror on Sarah's face as she stares at the ring Dylan held in his hand when he proposed to her—his mother's.

Miguel turns from the tile floor, Diane's face bright red. "Water, you son of a bitch! She can't breathe!"

The tall man looks behind him to Miguel, kicks Grady. "Gonna be a coward, huh?" He kicks him again. "Be a coward."

The tall man stomps through blood past Grady to the door. He grabs Vera's hand, points her revolver to the back of the freezer.

Jeremiah jumps from his cardboard box. He stumbles to the back corner against stacks of boxes, shelves of food.

"We're family, or ain't we?" The tall man moves Vera's finger on the trigger.

Blood on her hands, Sarah looks up from Andrés.

"I'll help you, then," Grady says.

Sarah's eyes close, her makeshift darkroom. Developed color photos on clothespins. Her final months of senior year, blue lockers in high school halls, thrift store shopping on Saturday mornings across southside Oklahoma City, Sam hiking wooded hills in Sulphur, Dylan kneeling in front of her, his beautiful brown eyes. She rewinds the crank on top of her Pentax camera, the only noise in the room.

Shivering, Sarah stands from the floor. She turns to the freezer door, looks from Diane and Miguel to Grady and Vera, the tall man.

"Why are you here?" Sarah says to them.

The tall man smirks. "Our children," he says.

Vera shudders, her finger on the trigger, her husband's finger on hers.

Sarah hears Diane coughing on the floor, Miguel trying to comfort her, Jeremiah at the back corner of the freezer, scrambling over boxes. Sarah stares into the tall man's eyes. "No one will ever know your name," she says to him.

He grins. "But, they'll sure remember what I do." He points his revolver past Vera, shoots the store manager in his cheek, shoots him again in his throat.

Vera screams, Grady's gun firing twice into Miguel's forehead, Miguel's blood splattering across Diane, Diane dead. Grady shooting again and again into the freezer, his eyes closed, two of his bullets ripping into Sarah's stomach, another into Jeremiah's hand and eye, the tall man's finger on Vera's, squeezing the trigger.

In a daze, Vera drops her revolver to the freezer floor, runs through the narrow kitchen hallway into the parking lot. Warm wind across her. She stops at the pickup truck they stole, sobbing. Disoriented, snot dripping from her nose, she stares at stars.

In the truck, they swerve from a service road onto an on-ramp, the pickup roaring, rushing past a sign for I-240. Vera can't stop crying, her husband behind the steering wheel, Grady between them, Grady's face stained with blood. His tall brother grabs a crank on his door, rolls down his window, howls into the night.

 Epilogue

The child stands barefoot in dirt, gray clouds thickening to the south, his father tightening a saddle to a horse in front of him. Cold rain drizzles on the boy's arm.

"Go inside, son," his father commands from his horse, his words tight-lipped, stern.

The boy watches his father say something German in the beast's ear, and the two creatures take off, the horse stomping furiously south across farmland, kicking up dust toward a distant small town.

Rain falls sudden and heavy all around the boy, pings a metal roof on his house, batters the ground.

He's five, his eyes obsessed with his father riding, the horse galloping in rain through dirt and dust. He hears a train blare. He turns, sees his mother on the porch.

"Matthew." Sam sits up sudden, shakes awake in the attic corner, his face sore, bruised. Sunlight across him from an arched window, hurts to open his eyes, his leg in pain. He grabs his boot on his foot, tries not to scream. Boxes and childhood toys around him, cobwebs. He hears a helicopter above his house, a hovering sound he's never heard this far south in his city. A trail of his blood across the wood floor.

Wood beams above him, and he hears his brother in his head, yelling his name.

Sam's standing in his Wranglers, his blood-stained ripped plaid shirt, his mouth dry. The attic musty, stuffy. Sunlit dust particles around him. He grips a rusted handle on the arched window. With all his strength, he pulls, lifts the window half-way open, stops, and it falls shut. He hears his brother in his head, screaming. His eyes squeeze closed. Sweating, Sam lifts harder.

Outside in sunlight, Sam stands at the four-way stop, stares at the dirt road disappearing into blue southern sky. Dry blood across his face, warm wind through his hair. Behind him, police sirens and hovering helicopters to the north, ambulances. Sam turns to his family's farm, wheat fields and trees, cattle grazing east of his barn, his pickup truck in front of his house.

A year ago, his mother died.

With watery eyes, Sam turns to tall grassland to the south. A full moon still in a sapphire sky. He limps on the dirt road. With each step, stabbing pain in his boot. His forehead pounding. Beside him, an endless ocean of sunlit green grass fields. He stumbles. His mother hadn't spoken a word in months since her cancer, doctors can't tell him why.

He regains his balance, sees abstract colors, static.

Sweating, he starts to run, sits in a rocking chair beside his mom. He sees her in bed, wearing her nightgown, her body frail, her auburn hair nearly gone. He barely recognizes her. Her brown eyes staring into his. She takes his rough hand. "Spread my ashes in Sulphur. Look after Sarah and your brother." She blinks loose a tear. "I have a final story to tell you."

Sirens fade to the thud of his boots on dirt. "You rarely cried as a baby," she says. "I'd read you to sleep in an old rocking chair, sitting beside an upstairs bedroom window, staring at wooded green hills and prairie."

She struggles to breathe, caresses his hand. "Standing Bear," she says, "a great warrior chief, I've told you. When his son was sixteen and dying of sickness, his son begged his father to bury him in their sacred lands."

Sam's sprinting, shaggy hair dripping sweat, grasslands surrounding him, sunlit as if on fire. "The plains barren in 1878," she says, "the Poncas, forced from their homes on White Chalk Bluff in Nebraska, dumped here before statehood with no food or shelters on a makeshift reservation, July humidity, heat, and malaria killing them, one by one."

She stops, her words halting. "With his son's remains in a wagon, two horses, and twenty-nine members of his tribe, Standing Bear walks 600 miles barefoot across frozen winter prairie. Wind chill forty below. They see their blood in snow. Four months, and they arrive at a stockade, starving, frostbitten, skin falling off, arrested by U.S. Calvary for leaving a reservation, two days from their ancient burial grounds."

No more sirens, sound of cicadas around him through grasslands, chirping birds. Sam's breathing rhythmic. He's panting, pain piercing his foot. "Standing Bear stands trial," he hears his mother say, "first American Indian to ask a judge in a court of law, 'am I not a human being? Am I not a man? Do I not bleed? Can I not bury my son? Remember what I've said. You will grow old, Sam."

Alone in a distant field on the west side of the dirt road, South Tree, its sprawling, twisted branches, the old oak's green leaves canopying a road up ahead in a haze of heat. Sam stops running, turns, looks behind him.

BY James Cooper

ABOUT THE AUTHOR

To bring this story to life, Cooper dedicated years to researching Oklahoma history and the Stockade murders before completing a Creative Writing MFA at Oklahoma City University.

While pursuing an MA in English at Oklahoma State University, Cooper received an award from The Society of Professional Journalists for his column in OSU's O'Collegian concerning the need for federal hate crimes legislation. Cooper's essay on the 2013 tornado that devastated Moore, Oklahoma, "An Oklahoma Perspective on Tornado Alley," appeared in the Huffington Post. The Oklahoma Gazette published Cooper's 2011 two-part cover story on the history of OKC's LGBTQ community, "From Closet to Community." Advocate Magazine named Cooper one of its June 2020 "Champions of Pride." The New York Times profiled his 2019 campaign.

Cooper won re-election on Valentine's Day February 2023 to a second term with more votes during a traditional election than any OKC council candidate in, at least, 14 years. Currently, Cooper teaches English and Film Studies as the Artist in Residence at Oklahoma City University, where he's taught courses on writing and horror, focusing particularly the slasher and occult subgenres.

Photo by Nathan Poppe

Aaron Tackett, Aaron Wilder, Adam Cottrell,
Adam Cooper Kemp, Atlee, Austin, Bayley, Betty, Bo, Boyd, Britney,
Charity, Charles, Chloe, Chris, Christopher, Connor, Cristine,
David, Dennis, Griff, Jaclyn, Jason and Embark, JD, Jonny, Kim,
Kirsten, Kristina, Kori, Kristen, Krys, Lacey, Lauren, Liz,
Lou, Mark, Morgan, Neha, OCU Red Earth, Randy, Reid, Taylor ...

THANK YOU